It's Not Easy

Donald A. Dery

authorHOUSE®

AuthorHouse™
1663 Liberty Drive
Bloomington, IN 47403
www.authorhouse.com
Phone: 1 (800) 839-8640

Published by AuthorHouse 06/24/2016

ISBN: 978-1-5246-1495-9 (sc)
ISBN: 978-1-5246-1496-6 (hc)
ISBN: 978-1-5246-1494-2 (e)

Library of Congress Control Number: 2016909982

Print information available on the last page.

Also by Donald A. Dery

Fiction:

Smooth Talkin' Bastard

It's Not Easy

Non-fiction:

Plantations of Antigua: A Biography of the Sugar Industry
Volume I: St. John's Parish

In honor of the Fab Five: Jo-Ann, Bobby, David
Mike and Robin . . .
the generation they have given me: Eli, Sarah,
Sam, Kati, Jack, Hannah, Anna and Sophia . . .
and Rowena, whose advice and counsel
remain invaluable.

PART 1

Workaholic

1

The noise was gunshot loud. Roger Manning sat bolt upright in bed. It was his hotel wake-up call.

He had completed his work in Manhattan, arranged a late checkout, flopped onto the bed in his underwear to grab a couple hours of shuteye before his evening flight to Rome. It was already 6:30 PM. He dangled his feet over the side of the bed, rubbed his eyes, stretched, moved into the bathroom to shave and shower.

He was about to embark on a swing through Europe, an endless blur of meetings: breakfast meetings, lunch meetings, dinner meetings that always ran late, office meetings with customers and prospects in several countries.

It was his standard European trip. Cram as much as his system could endure into every day. Smile a lot, shake hands, stumble through his broken French or German; Dutch, Italian and Spanish were beyond him. Thank goodness most of his clients and prospects spoke passable English, a virtual requirement in the international aviation business.

Gawd, he was sick of this commute, had been doing it for ten years. Airplanes, hotels, cabs, meetings, lunches, dinners, it seemed endless. There were moments, like now, when he felt he should pull the ripcord and bail out of this crap. But he couldn't, loved his job, the challenges, the fun of making a score, the success for the company, of which he was part owner.

Roger was a tough, determined executive, not a buccaneer but a driven, take charge, "anything's possible/don't tell me No!", kind of guy, an attitude he had developed since childhood. His dad left when he was six, his mother struggling to house and feed her four children, two girls and another son, all younger than Roger.

He had had a hard-scrabble youth, toiling at rotten jobs in an area of Boston called Southie. Put himself through college slopping factory floors and cleaning restrooms, all of which taught him business was tough, demanding, but potentially rewarding if you busted your ass, took no prisoners. He was not gruff or harsh, far from it. He had a quick smile, great sense of humor, people liked him even before they really knew him. And he had a passion for work, his job, opportunity.

After graduation, Roger had been with a series of small marketing firms before landing with a company in Cleveland, where the CEO saw his leadership potential and "presto!" He became an international guru of sorts, one of four partners who owned the company. He had no social life to speak of, hadn't dated in months.

Roger knew his European negotiations would be hard, polite but firm, requiring pains-taking follow-up, detailed letters of agreement hammered out on his laptop, emailed to the customers or prospects before retiring for the night. Phone calls within a day or two to make sure they had read the emails, agreed with all of the terms, or it was back again to the negotiating table to start over. Enough to make a weaker guy gag.

Then he'd email the final approved versions to the home office, Aeronautic Supplies, Inc., in Cleveland: letters of agreement and detailed call reports summarizing every meeting to Dana McBride, his Administrative Assistant. She ran his life, controlled his calendar, served as his blocker, screening those who could enter his office or reach him on his private cell phone when traveling.

Dana was a decade older than Roger, had twenty-five years experience as an executive secretary and/or administrative assistant to senior executives at a large international company in Silicon Valley. Then signed on with Aeronautic and Roger. She was efficient, smart, dedicated, mature, knew how to handle the brass, how to prepare Roger for meetings, briefings, the background info to place at his side.

Dana also had Roger's authorization to proofread, edit and even rewrite portions of his letters of agreement and call reports mindful that he would be writing them in the evening, dog tired, blurry-eyed after a long day of negotiating. She had to be careful not to change the meaning of any sentence, just ready the documents, correct spelling and punctuation, then distribute them to Roger's three partners, the CEO, CFO, VP of Manufacturing.

Roger paused to scan his image in the mirror: still pretty good looking at 34, dark hair, dark eyes, slim physique but not skinny, same weight as when he played basketball at Boston University. Never a super-star; 6-4 couldn't compete against the opponents' seven footers, or even his taller teammates.

He was already packed, jammed his toilet kit into his roll-on suitcase, snapped it shut. Dressed in a navy blue suit and white shirt, open collar, no tie, he'd be stuck on an airplane all night. He checked out at the reception desk, walked through the air-controlled glass doors onto Park Avenue, his car and driver waiting at the curb.

The trip to JFK took longer than usual in Friday rush-hour traffic, arrived at the Alitalia terminal with ample time to battle the lines at check-in and security, then board his overnight flight to Rome.

Once on the aircraft, he stuffed his roll-on bag into the overhead compartment, settled into his first class aisle seat, his briefcase on the floor at his feet, his laptop resting on his knees so he could review his schedule for his days in Italy. He rose once to let his seat-mate, an elderly gentleman, slide over to the window.

He was engaged with his laptop, but not so immersed that he didn't notice the woman who entered first class, stowed her suitcase in the overhead compartment, settled into the aisle seat across from him. She was a stunning blond, younger than Roger by a few years if he had to guess, dressed in an exquisitely tailored, light grey Armani jacket and skirt, stiletto heels which she kicked off once seated, make-up looked professionally applied. She closed her eyes, leaned back against the headrest. Roger took that moment to give her a good look-over, liked what he saw. No engagement or wedding ring.

A flight attendant began serving a flute of champagne to every first class passenger with a smiling "Welcome aboard." Roger took his, the young woman opened her eyes, accepted hers, raised her glass in a silent toast to someone or something, smiled at Roger and he smiled back.

"Here's to an interesting flight," Roger said, raising his glass.

"I'll drink to that," she said with a smile. "And to a safe landing."

They each returned to their separate preoccupations, he to his laptop, she to her memories. The usual welcoming message, seat-belts fastened, no smoking announcements and related safety bulletins blared from overhead speakers. The plane backed away from the jetway, taxied for several minutes before swinging into position on a runway, accelerated for takeoff.

They reached cruising altitude and the captain snapped off the seatbelt sign. Roger kept working on his computer, reviewing and revising his business schedule, amending it to add phone calls for more appointments or callbacks to colleagues in Cleveland to update them on his progress, hear input, juggle opinions and suggestions to reflect positively on his strategy moving forward.

The fight attendant offered another flute of champagne, so Roger closed his computer, slid it into the seat back in front of him, leaned back and took a long swig. He glanced at the woman across the aisle; she also held a fresh glass of champagne, sat with her head back staring at the ceiling, obviously lost in thought.

He shifted in his seat, leaned into the aisle, addressed the young woman.

"I don't wish to be forward, but I'm going to be." He smiled. "The seat next to you appears to be empty, and this is going to be a very long and boring flight. Would you mind if I slid into that window seat so we could share some conversation . . . just to make the next couple of hours go by faster."

The woman hesitated, looked at Roger for several seconds.

"That would be fine, Sir."

"Marvelous. Don't get up. I think I can slide right past you, unless you'd prefer the window."

"No, I'm quite comfortable. Besides, it's a night flight so there's nothing to see."

"Right." With that, Roger laughed, moved across the aisle, slid in front of the woman, settled into the window seat next to her.

"Thank you, Miss. My name is Roger Manning." He offered his hand. She slipped her hand into his.

"Nice to meet you, Roger. My name is Cecily."

"That's a very pretty name. Does Cecily have a last name?"

("Oh, God. I better be careful how I answer this. Why? The flight

attendant will call me Ms. Sommers anyway!")

"Yes! It's Sommers. Cecily Sommers."

"Nice to meet you, Cecily Sommers. And thank you for agreeing to let me sit with you. These long overnight flights can be like getting a root canal. There's nothing to see out the window, as you said, and the movies are usually not worth the effort. So the only thing left is to work or drink, and I hate to drink alone. In fact, I really don't like to drink; two is my limit or I fall into a stupor!"

"Well, we wouldn't want that to happen!" She was laughing.

"Have you been to Rome before?"

"No, I haven't. I was supposed to be joined by a friend, but he didn't show at the airport. Something must have interfered with his plans."

"Well, your friend's loss is my gain!" Roger smiled and asked a passing flight attendant for a glass of ice water. Cecily did as well. Roger raised his glass: "Here's to absent friends."

Cecily laughed and returned the toast.

"Is this your first time to Rome, Roger?"

"No, I've been there many times. I sometimes feel like I live in Europe. I spend more time there than I do in the U.S., or at least it seems that way."

"What do you do?"

"I'm in charge of international sales for an aeronautics supply firm based in Cleveland. We do business with many of the regional airlines in Europe and the Far East, and we're also hoping to break into the major carriers. So I speak 'airliners' quite well, but I don't speak Italian!"

Cecily laughed again. *("This guy is interesting.")*

"We also work with regionals in the U.S., but that's not my worry. That's another guy's headache!" He sipped his ice water. "So, how about you Cecily. What keeps you busy?"

("Gotta be careful. Don't want to use the 'help guys relax' line because I think this guy would get up and go back to his seat. Don't know why I think that, but I do.")

"I'm assistant to an executive in the investment business," she lied. "Or, I was. I got laid off, and decided I'd cheer myself up by going to Italy for a week. I love Renaissance art and decided to check out churches and museums in Rome, and perhaps Florence. I'll have to see how my wallet holds out."

That part of her declaration was true. What she didn't say is she's a former pro, going to Rome with one of her "customers" who bought her a first class ticket, but the smooth talking bastard didn't show up at the airport.

"Well, Cecily, you certainly picked the right location. You can wear yourself out scouting Renaissance art in Rome, and in Florence. How long will you be in Rome?"

"Several days. I want to take my time, not rush myself."

"That's a very sound idea. There's an awful lot to see, some beautiful ancient architecture as well as the art that's primary on your 'to do' list."

"I won't believe I'm actually going to Rome until we land!"

"It's a beautiful city. Where are you staying?"

Cecily hesitated . . . the pause so long the silence grew embarrassing.

"Oh, I'm just asking out of curiosity, Cecily. I'm sorry if I alarmed you."

"No, that's not it. My honest answer is I don't know."

"You don't know?"

"Yes, I don't know. My absent friend made all of the air and local arrangements, and when he didn't show, I just got on this plane because I was holding a ticket. But I don't know what he arranged in the way of accommodations. I phoned him several times but there never was an answer, not even his voicemail."

Roger looked at her in surprise, sat up in his seat.

"Well, I hope that guy wasn't anyone special in your life."

"No, just a friend, sort of."

"So your 'friend, sort of' left you 'at the altar, sort of'. Lemme see if I understand this." Roger was smiling, but incredulous. "You got on this airplane because you had a ticket. But your 'friend, sort of' handled all of the travel arrangements, didn't tell you what they are, didn't show up at the airport. So you said 'the hell with it' and you're on your way to Rome, a city you've never been in, with no place to stay that you know of! Is that about right?"

"Yes! But I'm sure I'll find something."

"Find something!" Roger was shocked, but smiled. "You've never been to Rome, don't know the Vatican from a tin can, but you'll exit the airport and place your life in the hands of an Italian cab driver, and let him take you wherever he feels like dumping you! Correct?"

"I guess so, but you make it sound so . . . ."

"Nuts comes to mind." Roger sipped his water, turned to hold Cecily's gaze. "Look, Cecily, you're a very attractive woman, you're American, you're lost in a city about which you know nothing. Does that sound nifty to you?"

"No, Roger, it doesn't. But here I am. What can I do?"

"I'll tell you what you're going to do. This isn't a suggestion, consider an order." He smiled, shifted in his seat to face her. "I'm not for one minute planning to seduce you or cause you any more headaches than your so-called friend has created for you. I have a car and driver meeting me at Fiumicino/Leonardo di Vinci Airport, taking me into the city to a first class hotel, one of the finest hotels in Rome.

"Why don't you ride with me. I'll phone the hotel manager from the car . . . I know him and will secure you a room for at least one night. You'll be safe, you can rest and find yourself less expensive accommodations, if you wish . . . the concierge can help you.

"But, for god's sake, Cecily, I can't in good conscience allow you to walk out to the curb and turn yourself over to a strange cab driver in a strange city in Europe! I don't want to read about you in *Corriera Della Sera."* His voice was very firm, not scolding, but firm.

Cecily looked away, her eyes beginning to water. She dabbed them with the paper cocktail napkin. Sighed deeply, turned to face Roger.

"You're very kind, Roger. I hate to put you out, to be such an inconvenience. I know you must be very busy. But thank you, I really appreciate your assistance."

"My pleasure, Cecily." Flight attendants began to serve passengers dinner, so Roger returned to his own seat, knowing he and the young lady would want sleep after dinner during the long flight across the Atlantic and Western Europe.

Roger was outside the di Vinci Airport terminal first, standing next to a BMW, chatting with the uniformed driver when Cecily approached with a rolling bag and large shoulder satchel.

"Is the offer of a ride still good?" She smiled.

"Of course. This is Paolo; Paolo, Cecily. She's going to the same hotel." Cecily entered the car, Roger followed, Paolo put her luggage in the trunk, and they were off into traffic.

"Cecily, I always begin the drudgery of these epic trips with a weekend to get used to the time change and relax a little before I hit the road running."

"I see."

"Why don't you plan to rest after you check into the hotel because it was a long night and we landed at an ungodly hour, New York Time. You might wish to take a nap and a shower; that's what I intend to do. Then why don't we meet for a late lunch. I'll help you plot an art museum trip that'll keep you from ricocheting back and forth across the city. That'll save you a ton of cab fares."

"That would be very nice, but if you're really busy . . . ."

"I'm not. Let's consider it an appointment, not a date."

"You're very kind, Roger. Yes, an appointment!" She was smiling.

They met in the hotel lobby at 2:00. Cecily had changed into a cooler relaxing sun dress; still looked like a knockout, carried an Hermes pocketbook. Roger had shed his jacket, wore a short-sleeve sports shirt and the same grey trousers he had worn on the flight.

"Well, you look refreshed and ready to begin dazzling Rome!"

"Thank you, Roger. Did you rest this morning, or work?"

"A little of both, Cecily. I phoned our CFO, who was thrilled to have his phone ring at six on a Saturday morning, but that's why he makes the big bucks."

"Yeah, I'll bet he was. I slept like a log for almost two hours, and I'm sure I'll be hitting the sack again early this evening. The time change is a killer."

"Actually, I suggest you stay up until eight or nine, Cecily, then get a good night's sleep. By tomorrow morning, you'll feel human again because the time change will be behind you for the rest of your stay in Italy."

"Okay, if you say so."

They began walking toward the hotel's front door.

"There is a very convenient outdoor cafe just around the corner where we can relax, grab a light lunch and people watch."

"Oh, that sounds wonderful, Roger."

"But first, Cecily, stand here on this patio and look across the large piazza. It is called Piazza della Repubblica, and across the way are two magnificent churches you'll want to visit later on. I believe one has a spectacular Caravaggio."

"Well I'll definitely stick my nose in there! Thank you."

"Over lunch I'll help you select some art museums to visit, together with a few more churches, although churches aren't my specialty!" He was smiling, Cecily was laughing.

"Dare I ask what your specialty is?"

"Later. I don't know you well enough!" They both laughed heartily as they walked to the cafe and settled into chairs at a small outdoor table. A waiter appeared almost instantly.

"Per favore, Signore. San Pellegrino e vino rosso. Grazie." The waiter made no notes, just turned, disappeared into the tiny cafe.

"I thought you said you don't speak Italian!'

"I really don't. But I was trying to impress you with my menu Italian. I also know how to ask for the bill!"

Cecily laughed. "Well, I really *am* impressed."

The bottle of San Pellegrino, chilled in a Thermos-like clear plastic container, arrived quickly along with a carafe of red wine, two wine glasses and two glasses of ice for the sparkling water. The waiter poured both before retiring again into the cafe.

Roger raised his wine glass.

"Welcome to Roma, Cecily."

"I can't believe I'm actually here. It's like magic. I've read so much about this city . . . I never thought I'd really be here."

"Well, you haven't seen anything yet. Take your time over the next few days, enjoy Rome to the fullest."

"I intend to do just that."

Their conversation was somewhat limited for five minutes or so as Cecily looked around at the people and the architecture; buildings that really were very old, or constructed to look like Pretorian guards of Ancient Rome might have walked through them. When she had ingested enough atmosphere, she turned back to Roger.

"How often do you come here?"

"I'm here several times a year, Cecily. This is part of my normal swing through Europe. I travel a lot, either Europe or the Far East. Airplanes are my domicile, so to speak, as well as my business."

"What about your home life, family, kids, time to relax?"

"I was married in my early twenties, and have two children: Jen is eleven, going on fourteen, and Tommy is eight." He took a swallow of wine. "My wife, Janice, was killed by a drunk driver five years ago."

"Oh my god, Roger! I'm so sorry!"

"Thank you." He took another sip, hesitated before continuing. She sensed he was struggling to retain his composure.

"I'm devoted to my children, Cecily. Fortunately, they both were very young when their mother died, but as they're getting older it's tough for them to grow up without a mother. I try to fulfill both roles, to be a full-time Mom as well as a full-time Dad, but I'm neither." He looked down at his glass, twirled it slowly, raised his eyes and looked into Cecily's.

"Jen vaguely remembers her mother. She's a little girl one day and a borderline young woman the next. If we go to a seafood restaurant for dinner, she'll stand at the lobster tank and name them all, so then I can't eat one." He smiled, Cecily laughed. "How could I possibly eat Charlie!" He again looked down at his glass.

"The next morning she'll grab me before I leave for work . . . ask me about her hair, can she have pierced ears, use makeup, why is her body changing so much . . . questions to which a mother would be far more sensitive, far better at answering than me. But I'm all she's got." He remained staring at his glass, lost in thought.

"Tommy . . . he's all boy . . . PeeWee League, Cub Scouts and dirt . . . lots of dirt!" He gave a short laugh, paused. Straightened and looked at Cecily.

"I travel a tremendous amount, all of it international . . . I love my job, the challenges, the opportunities . . . But I intend to hire three area managers to do the heavy traveling so I can spend more time with my kids." His gaze again dropped to his glass. He talked to it.

"I do food shop with them . . . cook a little . . . haven't poisoned them yet." He smiled, then continued. "I'm a whiz at homework . . .but I'm just not home enough and I know that's tough on them, very tough . . . not to have any parent home on a regular basis . . . ."

He raised his face to look at Cecily. She could see he was struggling to maintain his composure, placed a hand on his forearm.

"I have a marvelous housekeeper who stays with them when I travel. She's really terrific, but she's not Mom, no one who lives with us as a family unit. I'm lucky to have her, I know that, but she's a poor substitute, if you know what I mean."

"I think I can understand."

"I phone my kids every night, or every other night, when I travel, just to hear their voices . . . to hear their excitement about successes at school . . . and to let them know I love them." He sipped his wine, placed his glass on the table. "I spend every second I can with them, but it's tough on all of us."

He paused again. Cecily withdrew her hand, said: "I'm sure some day you will meet someone special and think of marrying again."

He straightened in his chair, turned to look at her, his face taught, eyes hard, no sign of tenderness.

"I'm married to my job, Cecily. I'm one of four partners who own our company. We threw dice and I won the international travel. I love my work, and it keeps me from dwelling on the loss of my wife. I've never thought about dating, wouldn't know how or where to begin."

He paused again, his eyes focused on a distant memory. He sipped his wine, then continued.

"We four partners have been scrambling non-stop for over ten years to build our company to the point where we have a very solid worldwide reputation for quality, value, and on-time delivery. I really haven't permitted myself to relax. My kids keep me busy when I'm home, which I love . . . I love being with them. The travel is tough on all of us, but I'm determined to find a way to end it."

"My gosh, Roger! Do you mind my asking how old you are?"

He laughed. "No, not at all. I'm thirty-four, probably getting close to the age where no woman is going to consider me anyway. After all, I come with two growing kids."

"Well, I believe there's no age limit on love."

"I'll try to remember that in my dotage." He laughed and she joined him. He lifted his ice water, took a long swallow. "So how about you? Give me a little of your background."

("OMG, I've got to be very careful. I don't want this guy to know what I've been doing on and off for the past two years.")

"Well, I'm a native of New Jersey, living in Manhattan. I've bounced around a few different jobs. This last one was with an investment company *("lie").* It was a good job, but the company was very small and when the economy took a hit, I was declared surplus."

"Oh! That's too bad."

"Yes, but it's given me the opportunity to come here to Rome." She sipped her wine. "I love Renaissance art, have several coffee table books on the art of the Italian Masters, so I hope to visit a lot of museums and churches to see the real thing. Then I'll have to go back to New York and see what I can do about earning a living."

She looked at Roger, quickly looked away, embarrassed that she had to lie to discuss her "career."

"Well, you're good looking and you must be smart if you held that investment job, so I'm sure you'll find something fairly quickly. I wish you luck."

"Thank you, Roger." She was still looking at her wine glass.

"What about your friend . . . the guy who didn't show at JFK? He's not someone special in your life?"

"No, not at all. I have no one special in my life. I've had some offers, but never from the right guy. So, I'm twenty-eight, approaching the magic thirty when it becomes a lot harder for a woman to strike gold!" She smiled, coyly.

"I don't think you have to worry about that, Cecily. The right guy is out there, and he's searching for you as hard as you're searching for him. One day you'll collide, and bingo! It'll be solid gold!"

She gave a short laugh; Roger was smiling.

"Let's order lunch, and then plot that museum tour for you."

He signaled for a cameriere, gave him their orders. They enjoyed a leisurely lunch, talking about the world in general, nothing in particular, an easy, relaxing conversation, much laughter, with a second ice cold bottle of San Pellegrino. Cecily enjoyed two glasses of the vino rosso; after one Roger had switched to the ice water. Planning her museum itinerary consumed another half hour of light talk, most of it about art, about which Roger had little to contribute.

He glanced at his watch, almost 4:00, flagged the cameriere for their bill.

"Cecily, as we walk back to the hotel I promise to steer you safely across the street so you don't get picked off by an aggressive driver."

"That'd be nice, and I actually could use the walk."

The bill paid, they stood, locked arms, and began a leisurely stroll toward the hotel. They stopped at several outdoor book stalls jammed with hundreds of titles, all in Italian. They also took a slow walk around the Piazza, but did not enter either church.

They passed through the hotel's revolving glass doors, walked through the large lobby with its array of love seats between small tables, and headed for the elevator bank.

"Cecily, may I make a suggestion?"

"Of course."

"Let's each relax for a couple of hours, freshen up, then I'd be up for a light dinner, probably in the hotel's Cafe. I'd enjoy your company if that appeals to you. After that, I intend to crash so I get a good night's sleep. I have to spend a lot of tomorrow planning for a schedule of meetings on Monday and Tuesday."

"The sounds marvelous, Roger. I mean the light dinner part. How about eight o'clock in the Cafe?"

"I'll be there; look forward to it."

Cecily was waiting for him at the entrance to the Cafe. She was gorgeous in a flowered sun dress, her hair and make-up just so. She smiled as he approached. Roger was wearing an open-neck sport shirt, had changed into white linen slacks, reminiscent of a fraternity stud, which he had been at Boston University. He greeted her warmly with a quick peck on each cheek, the European greeting among friends.

The Cafe was overflowing with a typical Saturday evening crowd. For a five euro tip the maitre'd found them a comfortable outdoor table on the hotel patio adjacent to several flowering plants, a decorative barricade separating the restaurant from passersby.

Roger again ordered a chilled bottle of San Pellegrino for them both and a small carafe of red wine for Cecily. She raised her glass in a toast.

"To new friends." She smiled.

"Yes, or at least to *a* new friend." He also smiled.

They enjoyed easy conversation and each other's company throughout dinner, rehashing all they had seen in their walk back to the hotel, and all she was excited to see in her travels around Rome during her stay. She planned to take a train from Rome to Florence on Wednesday or Thursday, fly home to New York on Saturday to begin job hunting the following week.

Just after 9:30 PM, Roger asked for the bill, and when it arrived Cecily insisted on paying.

"Nope. My invite, my bill. Besides, I'm working and you're not!"

"Roger, you're too kind. But someday I'm going to catch up with you and it's going to be my treat."

"Okay, I'll make you a deal." Roger exhibited a wide grin. "When I get upstairs, I'm going to phone Paolo, the driver who brought us in from the airport, and tell him to pick you up here around ten or ten-thirty tomorrow morning, your choice. I don't need him until Monday.

"His instructions from me will be to drive you around Rome -- he knows the city like the back of his hand -- to show you many of the highlights, even stop at the Sistine Chapel or a church or two if you'd like to see the art. The museums are likely to be closed on Sunday, although some may be open.

"He'll bring you back here -- are you going to stay in this hotel, or move on to somewhere less expensive?" She didn't answer.

"Whatever, he'll drop you off before six so you can change and freshen up, then he'll be back at eight to collect us both so we can enjoy dinner at a really first class restaurant -- my invite, my treat!"

"Oh, Roger! Really, you're spoiling me."

"I'll take that as a Yes, correct? Please don't say No!"

"Yes, Roger, Yes!" She was beaming.

"Excellent." He drained his water glass. "Ten or 10:30 pickup in the morning. Which do you prefer?"

"Ten-thirty would be wonderful. I intend to sleep late."

"So do I, but I guarantee you Paolo will be out front by 10:30. I'm paying him, so you don't have to. Don't even tip him; that's all built into my contract with him. Buy him lunch, if you'd like."

"I don't know how to thank you. Roger."

"Just have dinner with me tomorrow night. You'll put me in a great mood to do combat on Monday and Tuesday." They both laughed; but for Cecily, it was an unhappy reminder of her "career" sitting at the bar of a fancy New York hotel, telling some guy she would "help him relax before he had to get back into the lion's cage on Monday morning."

This fella Roger was different, somehow. She didn't want him to know about her background; felt it was very important to prevent him from learning about it for fear that would jeopardize their blossoming friendship.

They entered an elevator in the lobby and rode to Cecily's floor. The doors opened, Roger stood to prevent them from closing as Cecily stepped out. She turned and faced him.

"Roger, I really don't know how to thank you. You've been so helpful, so sweet and gracious . . . My accommodations here, lunch and dinner today, and your giving me Paolo and his car tomorrow." She reached out and touched his hand. "I very much appreciate all you've done to make my visit to Rome so special."

"Cecily, it's been a pleasure. I can't describe what a marvelous beginning this has been to what I had anticipated was going to be dull, boring prep time." He squeezed her hand. "Sleep tight, and I'll see you tomorrow evening."

"I look forward to it. Good night, Roger." She turned, walked down the hall toward her room. Roger watched her go, stepped back into the elevator, rode to his floor anticipating a phone call to his kids, eager to hear their excited voices, then crash for a good night's sleep.

2

Roger awoke shortly before 9:00 Sunday morning, rolled out of bed did some stretching exercises for about twenty minutes, headed into the bathroom to shave and shower. He dressed in his shorts and a terrycloth robe hanging on the bathroom door, phoned room service to order breakfast, settled into an upholstered chair with the *International Herald Tribune* he found lying outside his door.

He phoned Paolo about 10:45 to see if he had collected Cecily.

"Yes, Sir. Do you wish to speak with her?"

"No, not necessary, Paolo. You're going to pick us up at 8:00 tonight, correct?"

"Absolutely, Sir."

"Terrific. Have a great day, and make sure she enjoys herself."

He finished the newspaper before 11:30, opened his briefcase and laptop, spread a collection of papers and folders on the desk in his suite. He first reviewed his entire schedule of meetings on Monday and Tuesday. They were all with executives at the same company, Aviana Air, a successful regional airline serving a substantial number of airports on the Italian mainland and the island of Sicily with a fleet of forty-five twin-engine, moderate-sized jets.

Aviana was eager to upgrade the interior of its aging fleet with more sophisticated cockpit electronics, compact seats, new carpeting, improved lighting, re-designed flight attendant uniforms. It would be a lucrative multi-million-dollar contract for Aeronautic Supplies, a deal Roger had been nursing for more than eight months.

His company designed and assembled advanced proprietary cockpit electronics. They also had an "amenities" division which would handle the design and assembly of compact passenger seats developed specifically for regional and discount airlines eager to cram as many people as possible into their cabins.

Roger's firm had agreed to use Italian designed and sourced fabrics if that would help close the deal, also agreed that cabin attendant uniforms could come from an Italian fashion house using Italian made fabrics, or fabric purchased off-shore by the Italian fashion designer.

He had four meetings: two on Monday with the airline's Vice President of Equipment, and Vice President of Electronics; and two on Tuesday, with the Chief of Maintenance, and the Chief Financial Officer and the Chief Executive/President. The CFO would attend every session. Roger's meeting with the CEO would be last, and would only happen if the CFO was a happy camper.

He knew his discussions would be long, technical, intensive, with each tiny aspect, every "t" and "i" examined six ways to Sunday, then re-examined and compared with the details of competitive proposals submitted by other aircraft supply vendors.

By the end of each business day, every participant would be emotionally drained, eager to retire to home or hotel, but duty bound to hang in for drinks, dinner and more conversation; then would come less rest than required to prepare for the circus to begin again the following morning.

Roger suddenly realized he had been staring at his computer screen for several minutes, but not seeing anything. His mind had drifted away from the press of business; focused, instead, on that young woman, Cecily Sommers. She had sparkling eyes, a nice personality, good looks and a figure sufficient to stop a train. It was the first time in several years he had paused to think about a woman, and thinking about her was enjoyable.

He was already three hours into his prep work, decided to take a break, called room service for another pot of coffee. It was more fun to think about Cecily than a discussion of the performance certifications of his firm's esoteric cockpit electronics or maintenance schedules and whether training should be done in the U.S. or Italy. So he stretched, relaxed with a cup of coffee and thought about what it might be like to lock lips with that blond.

He placed the empty cup on a table, "slapped" himself conscious, and arranged a conference call with Aeronautic's CEO/President and CFO, both undoubtedly preparing to enjoy a quiet Sunday with their families in Cleveland. He wanted to review the details of the convoluted Aeronautic's proposal so he'd be ready to address every imaginable question Aviana Air's executives were likely to ask; every objection they might raise.

And, he required guidance on the critical decisions he would have to make on the spot, decisions which would impact the financial return for his company; not just costs associated with design and assembly, but penalty clauses if delivery fell behind stipulated timetables. He expected the meetings to be tough, but if he was sharp (and stopped dreaming about Cecily) he was confident that meeting could be a contract signing.

The conference call with Aeronautic's CEO Bill Enright and CFO Brad Lewis began at 3:30 Rome time and lasted well over an hour. When they finally were getting ready to hang up, Enright and Lewis made Roger promise to conference call them "any time of the day or night" to give them the results of his Tuesday meeting, "good news or bad."

Roger went into the bathroom, took another shower to relax and cool off, then stretched out on the bed to re-play the entire conference call in his mind. He knew how critically important this contract would be to the financial success of his company and its worldwide reputation for providing extraordinary service to one of Europe's largest regional airlines.

He knew he should get up and pull other files dealing with his 4:00 PM meeting Monday with Ariana's Chief of Maintenance, but he lacked both energy and focus. He wasn't particularly worried about that discussion; the one with the CEO on Tuesday *did* concern him, but that was two days away . . . and the blond was his dinner date in only a few hours!

So, in a fit of confidence he drifted off to sleep.

While Roger had been punching his keyboard, swilling coffee and thinking about her, Cecily had been walking through two museums admiring an assortment of art from Renaissance Masters. Later, Paolo had stopped for lunch at an outdoor cafe, where she was mesmerized by the surrounding architecture, enjoyed watching people scurrying about their daily rituals, and relished her time alone with Paolo to discreetly learn more about the man who was beginning to seriously attract her interest.

They both were enjoying a delicious pasta dish recommended by

Paolo, sharing a small carafe of Italian red table wine.

"Paolo, I want to thank you for driving me around Rome, taking me to those two museums, and waiting for me while I admired the art. It was a fabulous morning."

"My pleasure, Miss. And I'm not the one you should thank."

"Yes! I understand that. Tell me. Have you known Roger, Mr. Manning, long?"

"Almost two years. Roger is a gentleman, a terrific guy, very thoughtful, generous to a fault, and apparently an extremely smart businessman. And he worships his children."

She was surprised to hear Paolo call Roger by his first name, had always heard him say "Sir"!

"Yes, I gathered that, and I agree he's a very interesting man. Do you ever hear him refer to a woman he's dating here or in the U.S.?" She displayed a sly smile.

Paolo looked at her and smiled.

"I was wondering when you might get to that question!" He laughed as she blushed. "No! I never have. He talks about his children a lot, and occasionally about his job, especially his meetings here with the Aviana Airline people. I chauffeur some of those executives, and Roger will occasionally pick my brain . . . like you're doing about him!" He roared with laughter as she blushed a deeper red. "The Aviana executives think the world of him."

"I'm sorry, Paolo! I'm so embarrassed, please forgive me."

"Not to worry, Miss. I understand where you're coming from, and I assure you this conversation is strictly between us. He will never hear a word from me."

"Thank you!"

"In fact, in all the times I've been with him, you're the first woman who's ever been in my car. So, if I were you, I'd consider that a check mark in your diary, or whatever." Again, he was smiling broadly. "However, you should understand that Roger is devoted to his job and his children, so you'll undoubtedly have to give him some time to think about something else, or someone else."

"Yes! He's made that quite clear."

"Well, if you're truly interested in him, my advice is you should not give up. But then I'm not a beautiful young woman!"

"Thank you, Paolo. I'll have to see how things move along."

"I'd say he's interested in you or you wouldn't be his dinner companion this evening. He'd be preparing for his meetings tomorrow."

"That's encouraging, thank you."

"Now I suggest we resume thinking of Renaissance art, and visit our next museum followed by a magnificent church."

"Paolo, your English is amazing! Where did you learn to it?"

"New York. I'm from New York. I met my wife there when she was touring. We fell in love, married here in Rome, her home town, thirty years ago, and we've never left. I love it here."

"I live in New York! West seventy-seven, across from the Museum of Natural History."

"Ahhhh! Beautiful part of the city. I was brought up in Little Italy, home of the 'West Side Story' musical, an Italian ghetto to those of us brought up there. I was very glad to flee with the woman I love!"

They both laughed, stood, she paid the bill, and they found his car.

The ringing telephone snapped Roger awake like an explosion. He rolled over, grabbed the receiver.

"Hello!"

"Hi, Roger. It's Cecily!" She sounded bright and cheery.

He rubbed his eyes, tried to focus on the voice, soft, soothing.

"Hi! How was your day?"

"Oh, gosh! It was awesome!" She sounded almost breathless. "Paolo showed me so much of Rome, and I got into three museums and a church, and got to admire original Caravaggio's and a Michelangelo! I can't believe it!"

"That's terrific, Cecily. I'm really happy for you." He yawned.

"You sound drowsy. Did I wake you up?"

"Yeah! But that's okay. I had a blistering day getting myself ready for tomorrow. Had a long conference call with the States, too."

"I'll bet they were glad you called to interrupt their Sunday."

He laughed, yawned. "What's the time?"

"It's 6:15, Roger. Are you still up for dinner? I really hope so . . . I have so much to tell you!"

"You bet I am. Paolo's picking us up at 8:00, and I want to phone my kids. How about meeting in the hotel bar in an hour?"

"I'd love that. See you downstairs."

She was seated alone at the bar, looking toward the entrance when Roger stepped through. She rose as he walked toward her, magnificent in a black silk shoulderless cocktail dress which complimented her ivory skin, long blond hair, deep blue eyes. He gave her a hug and a peck on both cheeks, stepped back to admire her appearance.

"Man, you look awesome, Cecily!"

"Why thank you, Roger. It's really good to see you, too."

Cecily had already ordered a cocktail, Roger ordered the same, sat next to her on an upholstered bar stool. They both were smiling.

"How are your children, Roger? Eager to talk with Daddy?"

"Oh, you bet. Jen, the older one, always asks me if I'm assembling airplanes because she knows I work for an aeronautic supply company. And Tommy just wants to knew what I'm flying! He thinks I'm a pilot! Kids are amazing!"

"I think it's wonderful that you speak with them so often."

"So do I!" He sipped his drink. "So, tell me about your day. I gather it turned out to be pretty special."

"It was, Roger. Let me say it was so gracious of you to treat me to Paolo's services for the day. He's fantastic, showed me so much of Rome, and stood by while I visited the museums and a church where I saw some fantastic art by Italian Renaissance Masters."

She went on enthusiastically, extolling the art with a series of descriptors -- composition, brilliance, color, saturation, light patterns, shadowing, depth perception -- and a dozen other expressions Roger didn't begin to comprehend viz-a-viz art in any form. He kept saying "Wow!" or "No kidding!", asked lots of dumb questions to keep her bubbling, enjoyed every moment of her girlish excitement until he could no longer restrain himself, burst out laughing.

Cecily looked confused. "What are you laughing at?"

"You, Cecily! You! You're like a schoolgirl who just got asked to the senior prom by the high school quarterback! I'm enjoying every moment of your excitement." He continued to laugh.

"Oh, you men!" She began smiling; placed her hand on his forearm. "You're impossible! You need a good shot of culture, that's what you need, to pull you away from all the mental gymnastics associated with your love of business! You've got to learn to love something else!"

"Well, maybe you can show me how."

She was caught short . . . paused before replying.

"I gladly accept that challenge, Roger."

"Good, that's a deal; simplest agreement I've concluded in a long time. Sure beats what I'm going to go through over the next couple of days, and probably more fun because art won't ask me a ton of questions!"

Cecily paused, realized she had misinterpreted what Roger had meant by teaching him something to love besides business.

"Tell me . . . I've done all the talking." She sipped her drink.

"First, let's find Paolo outside and go to our restaurant. I'll bore you over dinner with my day. It was nothing like yours."

He signed the bar bill onto his room, offered Cecily his arm. Paolo closed the car door behind them, slipped into the driver's seat.

"Paolo, we have reservations at that cozy restaurant partway up the hill on Via Francesco Crispi."

"Very well, Sir." The car moved into traffic on the Piazza roundabout and Roger and Cecily settled into the back seat to enjoy the ride. Paolo eventually stopped mid-way up a steep hill on a narrow street, parked cars and motor scooters jamming both sides. They left little room for the car doors to open, but Cecily and Roger squeezed out. Roger dismissed Paolo for the evening, would order a taxi back to the hotel.

The restaurant was located in an ancient stone building. It was intimately small, seating for about ten on the ground floor and an equal number in a lower level dining room. They were seated at the last table available, just inside the entrance, white starched linens, each place setting showcasing crystal wine and water glasses, fine Italian china, gleaming sterling silver flatware. A small cut glass vase of flowers and a short flaming candle graced each table.

A waiter appeared immediately and Roger ordered: "Uno Proseco e uno San Pellegrino, per favore."

"Well, I got the San Pellegrino, but what else did you order?"

"Proseco! It's a wonderful Italian sparkling white wine, very much like French champagne. I think you'll love it."

"Will *you* love it? That could be something you'll love other than business!" She smiled coyly.

"I'll join you in one glass, Cecily. But this doesn't let you off the hook to help me find something else to love!"

She blushed. He smiled, then laughed at her blushing.

She had been looking at her wine glass, raised her head to look directly into his eyes. She held his gaze for several seconds.

"As I said, Roger, I gladly accept that challenge!"

It was his turn to blush; her turn to smile.

"Well, I think you're off to a magnificent start."

The meal was outstanding, beyond delicious, delicate, served very elegantly in a variety of small portions; dishes gracefully placed and retrieved empty by the friendly waiter, who kept her wine and their water glasses full. After his one drink at the hotel and a small taste of Proseco, Roger stuck with the San Pellegrino.

Cecily feigned interest in the details of Roger's day, but was fascinated by his discussion of the depth of planning and strategy he and his colleagues had been using for the past eight months to get as far as they had in pursuit of a contract with Aviana Air. The ball was now in Roger's court; he had complete responsibility for successfully concluding the negotiations, which he hoped would happen Tuesday when he met the Airline's CEO. If that occurred, he assured her, there would be some massive celebrations in Rome and Cleveland.

They had lingered over dinner, desert, coffee and conversation for more than two hours. The restaurant ordered them a taxi, they rode the hotel elevator together. Roger got off at Cecily's floor to escort her to her room. She placed the key card into her door, turned to face him.

"Roger," her voice was very soft. "Roger . . . thank you, again, for a very special day and a lovely dinner." She suddenly put one arm around his neck, pulled herself up to his height, brushed his lips briefly with hers.

When she backed away, Roger held her hand.

"Cecily." He also spoke in a whisper. "I can't begin to describe how much I've enjoyed your company. I want to see you again while we're both in Rome, but my next two days will be brutal. Please save me some time on your dance card before you head to Florence. Perhaps you can help me celebrate my success in signing a contract, or console me in my sorrow if I don't!" They both laughed.

"Yes, Roger, I want to see you, again, and either celebration would be wonderful . . . well not wonderful if you don't get the contract . . . well Yes! It will be wonderful to console you."

They both laughed, she turned to enter her room.

It would be forty-eight hours before they saw each other again.

3

Roger was up and eager to charge at 6:30 Monday morning. He did his twenty minutes of stretching exercises, shaved and showered, ordered room service breakfast, sat down for a last-minute review of his notes for this morning's meeting at 10:00 through lunch, and the afternoon meeting at four until who knew when!

Paolo was promptly in front of the hotel by 9:00, allowing ample time for the morning traffic drive to Aviana Air's headquarters building not far from the airport. The day was sunny and hot, the BMW's air conditioning working overtime, at Roger's request, so he didn't show up for the meeting dripping perspiration

Upon arrival, Roger stepped out of an elevator into a third floor carpeted reception area brightly lit by an array of beautiful ceiling and wall light fixtures, modern Italian-designed modular furniture. He was five minutes early, but the receptionist did not have an opportunity to announce his arrival before Giancarlo Melli, VP of Equipment, and Guiseppi Valenti, VP of Electronics, came through a glass door into the reception area to greet him.

"Roger! Wonderful to see you! How was your trip?" This was Giancarlo, tall, trim, mid-forties, very outgoing, a personality which could sell rice to China He shook hands aggressively, smiling broadly.

"Hi, Roger. Welcome to our palace, again." Guiseppi was less gregarious, but still pleasant. Maybe five-five, his shirt buttons losing a battle with his belly, dark hair and mustache, cordial handshake and smile.

"Thank you, gentlemen. It's wonderful to be here, and I certainly appreciate your interest in all that we have discussed to date. I'm hoping we can conclude everything favorably."

"I think we're very close, Roger. Very close." This, again, was Giancarlo. "Let's move into our conference room and get down to business, as you Yanks say!"

They passed through the glass door the Ariana executives had entered, walked into a large open area crowded with low-walled cubicles, each housing an employee hammering a keyboard or talking on the phone. Some cubicles held two or three people, men and women, one seated, others standing against a low cubicle wall, engaged in animated conversations. Large windows on the room's long side walls streamed sunshine, assisted by overhead fluorescent lighting to magnify the brightness. There was a pervasive hum of business.

The three execs walked through double glass doors at the other end of the area, turned left down a hallway, entered a well appointed conference room: twenty-foot polished table, leather chairs surrounding it, large glass windows. Giancarlo grabbed a chair at the head of the table; Roger and Guiseppi sat to his right and left. They were just opening files when the conference room door opened and Carlo Meola, Ariana's Chief Financial Officer, entered, shook hands with Roger, waved to his colleagues, sat next to Guiseppi.

"My role here, Roger, is to make certain the three of you behave yourselves!" Everyone laughed heartily. Carlo was pleasant looking, very friendly, not at all what one would expect of such a highly-placed bean counter. But he was far more than that, Roger knew; he was the CEO's right arm; nothing would be confirmed if Carlo said it couldn't be done or didn't like the terms.

Roger would be conversing with Giancarlo and Guiseppi, but he would be *talking* to Carlo, and everyone in the room knew it.

Their conversation ranged across a broad spectrum of issues involving certification and installation of Aeronautics electronics, the training of the airline's cockpit and maintenance crews in Rome and the cockpit simulator at Aeronautic's Cleveland headquarters, delivery and installation schedules, associated costs. The meeting rolled on for over two hours, broke for lunch in the Airline's employee cafeteria, where the dialog continued. The CFO excused himself for lunch, told Roger he'd see him at 1600 for the meeting with the maintenance chief, Millo Salicini.

That meeting, too, rambled for two hours, delving more deeply into a variety of maintenance issues involving warranties, repair costs and facilities, training schedules, and the possibility of accomplishing maintenance training in both Rome and Cleveland.

By the conclusion of the meeting at 1830, Roger's head was spinning, he was talked out. Millo graciously offered to treat Roger to dinner, but he just as graciously declined, stating that he had to phone the U.S. to brief his partners on the day's discussions. That was partially true; it was also true that Roger would pay anything to get out of that building and that conference room for the evening. He knew he'd be back in it again tomorrow.

He shed his jacket as he entered Paolo's car, lay his head on the seat back and closed his eyes as Paolo navigated the evening commuter traffic back toward the hotel. They didn't speak: Paolo sensed that Roger needed peace and quiet.

Upon arrival, he thanked Paolo for his services . . . No, he would not require a pickup this evening . . . flung his jacket over his shoulder with one hand, carried his briefcase with the other, and headed for the elevators. Once in his room he tossed his jacket and briefcase on one queen bed, kicked off his shoes, got rid of his tie, flopped onto the other queen bed. He lay immobile for a half hour, eyes closed, re-living as much of the day and the two meetings as he could.

About 7:30 he picked up the hotel phone and called Cecily's room, no answer. "Damn it!" He'd try again later.

He stripped, stood under a hot, then cold, shower, felt somewhat invigorated as he slipped into slacks and collared polo jersey. He sat at the desk, began drafting a lengthy summary of the day's discussions, closing with an optimistic outlook for a satisfactory conclusion to all of the negotiations over the past eight months.

He was particularly impressed that CFO, Carlo Meola, had very little to say, almost no questions to ask. Roger took that as a positive indication that Carlo was a satisfied cookie.

By the time Roger hit his "Send" button it was pushing 10:00. He called Cecily's room again, couldn't believe his luck when he heard a soft "Hello!"

"Ms. Cecily, this is the Pope calling to see if you enjoyed your day in our beautiful city!"

"Oh, your Holiness!" She sounded animated, jovial. "Yes, I had a marvelous day. Would you like to join me to hear all about it?" She was hoping beyond hope.

"Well . . . No can do, Cecily. I have two important meetings tomorrow, including lunch with the airline's CEO and I don't want to do a face plant in my soup. I had an exhausting day today, and I've been working all evening in my hotel room. I want to phone my kids and then crash."

"I understand! Your lucky kids!"

"I'm sorry, Cecily, but I really want to be rested and sharp when I meet with my potential customers tomorrow. I went through the gauntlet today and I think tomorrow will be more of the same, especially my afternoon meeting with the CEO and his Financial Director. My decision has nothing to do with you, Cecily. You're a terrific companion and when I'm not under such GD pressure I would very much like to relax with you."

"'Companion'? 'Relax'? Well, that's a start, I guess."

"Please, Cecily. Don't make fun of me."

"I'm sorry, Roger. I enjoy your company, that's all."

"I understand, I really do. Let me get through my business commitments in Italy, and I'll be much better company."

"Okay. I'm going to hold you to that."

"Good night, Cecily. Try not to steal any artwork."

"Roger, Roger!" They both were laughing as they hung up.

He immediately dialed another number.

"Hello!"

"Hi, Jen. This is Daddy!"

"DADDY! Where are you? I miss you so much."

"I miss you, too, Honey. I'm still in Italy, but I'll be home next weekend. How are you doing?"

"Okay. I got an 'A' on a spelling test today, and tomorrow we're going to have a math test. Phooey!"

"Well, I wish you luck. Is your homework done?"

"Yep, I finished it awhile ago, and we're gonna have dinner in a few minutes. What are you doing in Italy? Does everyone really speak Italian?"

"I have a bunch of meetings, trying to get some airline people here to do business with my company. And, Yes! They all speak Italian!"

"Well, you don't, so how do you get anything done?"

"I speak some Italian. Like 'Buon Giorno'! That means 'Hello!'"

Jen giggled. "Daddy, can I get my ears pierced? Please?"

"I still think you're a little too young, Jen. But let's talk about it when I'm home this weekend."

"Okay. But just so you know, Hannah and Sara and Kati have pierced ears, and they're the same age as me!"

"Sara's older, so we'll see, Jen . . . I love you, Kiddo. Now let me say 'Hi' to Tommy."

"Okay! I'll get him. I love you, Daddy. Come home soon."

"I'm working on it, Jen. You be good. Let me say Hi to Tommy."

"Okay! Here's Tommy."

"Hi, Daddy! I love you, too!"

"Well, I also love you, Tommy, and think you're very special."

"Thanks, Daddy. Are you flying anything yet?"

"Not yet, Buddy, but I'll be flying home next weekend."

"Okay. Can we get ice cream when you're home?"

"You bet! Pizza and ice cream. That's a promise."

"Great! I can't wait, Daddy. Can we go to the aquarium?"

"Let's count on it. Tommy. I'll see you in a few days."

"Goodnight, Daddy."

"Goodnight, Buddy."

Roger hung up, sat staring at the phone for over a minute, wished he was home to tuck his kids into bed.

Roger's Tuesday morning duplicated Monday: up at 6:30, stretching exercises, shaved and showered, ordered room service breakfast, settled down to review the files for his Tuesday meetings.

The first session, with Vice President of Passenger Services, Gabriele Pozzi, would be focused on the fabric and color selections for aircraft cabin carpeting, the new passenger seats, bulkhead decor, and flight attendant uniforms.

Roger was not sure why he was even involved in this meeting. Aeronautic Supplies was providing upgraded, high-tech seats with electronic controls for seat-back adjustment, overhead lighting, A/C, attendant call controls, and passenger TV controls.

But it was not providing the material for the upholstery nor carpeting, would not be involved in the work to finish the seats or install the carpeting (local Italian firms would handle those chores), and Aeronautics had nothing to do with the design, color or fabric for flight attendant uniforms. That contract would be issued to a well-known Italian fashion house and a local fabricator.

The meeting was held in Gabriele's second floor office, a large den-like room cluttered with fabric cuttings, rolls of cloth, piles of loose thread, pattern books, a stack of fashion magazines.

Gabriele and Carlo were both seated at a conference table, rose to greet Roger as he entered.

"Roger! Good morning. It is good to see you."

"Thank you, Gabriele."

"Welcome for our second day of conversation, Roger."

"Thank you, Carlo. I feel a little like I've never left this building!"

All three laughed, settled into chairs around the table.

"Well, you're almost through the ringer, Roger, and so far I'd say you are doing quite well," said Carlo. "This conversation should be fun, as well as instructional, because I don't recall you claiming to be a fashionista and lord knows I'm not!"

"I think we're in the same Idiot Club, Carlo!" All three were laughing.

"I realize your limitations regarding fashion, both of you." This was Gabriele. "But, Roger, you have so much invested in the structure of what we're hoping to achieve, I thought it would be nice to show you how we plan to dress that structure, and I'd like to make sure you at least agree with our choices. I'm not looking to you for design guidance . . . far from it!"

"Well, thank god for that, Gabriele!"

("I can relax! This is just a courtesy meeting, not a negotiating session. And I heard Carlo say 'so far you are doing quite well!' Man, I can taste the contract! All I really have to do is not screw up this afternoon's lunch with Fabio Mazzetti!")

He settled back in his chair, opened his leather pad folder, but intended to take very few notes. He was really amazed the CFO chose to participate in this meeting, but so be it.

Gabriele began describing fabrics, colors and materials. After thirty minutes of this, Carlo held up his hand, stood, pleaded both ignorance and the pressure of another meeting, and left. Roger was jealous!

However, when Gabriele began to address flight attendant uniforms, his office door opened and four gorgeous women entered, each wearing different versions of the uniform: jacket and skirt on one, jacket and slacks on another, the third with no jacket but a beautiful blouse and colorful scarf, the fourth wearing a tailored apron for serving food.

Roger's mind immediately swung to Cecily, imagined her in the cute jacket and skirt on the first model. He could vaguely hear Gabriele in the background rambling on about fashions, but could not get Cecily out of his mind.

When the meeting finally ended, Roger was thrilled to shake Gabriele's hand, tell him how fantastic everything looked, thank him for his time, and race for an Aviana urinal to drain his bladder!

Roger's second meeting of the day was extremely important, the one o'clock lunch date with Aviana Air's Chief Executive Officer, Fabio Mazzetti, the ultimate decision-maker, and Mazzetti's righthand man, CFO Carlo Meola. Roger had geared himself for a potential grilling, mostly about the financial details of the contract he prayed would result from his eight months of effort.

He settled into an easy chair in the lobby to await Carlo and move on to wherever they were joining Signore Mazzetti.

Carlo drove them in his navy blue, two-door Maserati, a magnificent machine: Roger couldn't help marveling at the leather upholstery after having just spent over two hours getting a lesson in fabrics and stitching. The car was fast, Meola handled it like a professional race car driver

They pulled into a parking lot adjacent to a fifteenth century stone building. They were granted entry by a uniformed doorman who saluted Carlo, opened a massive oak door inlaid with gold trim and highly-polished brass fittings. The lobby was immense, two stories high, dressed in mahogany, statues on pedestals, magnificent paintings on the walls, a wood tiled floor, huge floral arrangements. It was church quiet.

They turned left into a cocktail lounge featuring more dark woodwork, statues and art, and settled into two leather chairs at a small round table. A tuxedoed waiter appeared quickly, took their drink orders and disappeared behind a long, highly-polished bar over which hung a row of cut-glass chandeliers.

"This place is beautiful, Carlo. I assume it's a private club."

"Yes, Roger, but more than private. It is also very exclusive. We have a corporate membership here because of Signore Mazzetti's personal relationship with the Prime Minister and several members of Parliament."

"Well, I'm honored to be your guest here."

"Not mine, Roger. Signore Mazzetti's."

He began to rise as a gentleman in his late fifties, maybe early sixties, approached their table. The man appeared very dignified, dressed in an expensively tailored navy suit, custom shirt and red tie, and red tie, well-groomed salt-and-pepper hair. Roger judged his eyeglass frames to be more expensive than Roger's car; noted the man wore a gold Rolex on his left wrist and a diamond ring on his right ring finger.

"You must be Signore Manning. I've heard much about you from Carlo and several other colleagues within our company." They shook hands.

"Yes, Sir. Please call me Roger, and I want to thank you for taking the time to host me in such a marvelous private club. Carlo was just giving me some of the background."

"It is my pleasure, Roger. Please call me Fabio; I don't like too much formality. Why don't we go into the dining-room. Leave your drink here, Roger, the waiter will find us inside."

"Thank you, Sir."

"Please, Roger, Fabio! If you say 'Sir' to anyone in Rome they will expect you to kiss their ring or genuflect!" All three laughed.

He led the way into the dining-room; the decor was again breathtakingly beautiful: carpeting so thick Roger's feet sank into it, statuary, art, wall sconces, chandeliers, more flowers, whispered conversations with no evidence whatsoever of a briefcase, notepad or file. Not allowed!

They were comfortably seated at an intimate table covered with bright white linen and dressed with crystal stemware, sterling flatware, and a modest center bouquet. Fabio ordered a drink and Roger's and Carlo's arrived from the cocktail lounge. The CEO initiated the conversation.

"Roger, despite the pressure of business, I hope my colleagues have left you a little time to enjoy our beautiful city."

"Not on this trip, Fabio, but that is truly my fault. My associates and I are extremely excited about the possibility of working with you and your colleagues, for whom I have enormous respect. So my focus has been entirely on business.

"However, I did arrive here Saturday morning and spent the weekend in a little play and a lot of preparation. And, as you know, this is not my first visit to Rome. On previous occasions I've taken ample time to enjoy your city. It's truly beautiful, and marvelously historic."

"Ahhh, that is well, Roger. But do not permit Carlo and the others to deny you some pleasure during their grilling." He smiled, as did Roger and Carlo.

"Have no concern, Fabio. We are spoiling Roger every time he comes to Rome!" More smiles.

"That is very good." Fabio paused. "So tell me, Roger. Despite all your travel, do you have a family that misses you when you are gone?"

"Yes, I do. I have two children, a girl eleven and a boy eight. I am a widower, Fabio. My wife was killed accidentally five years ago."

"Oh, I'm terribly sorry, Roger."

"I am as well, Roger. I had no idea."

"Thank you, both of you. I have a marvelous housekeeper who stays with my children when I'm gone, and I'm making plans to hire some regional managers so I can cut down on my travel. It's not easy on my children nor me."

"That is understandable, Roger. But I am certain I speak for Carlo and his colleagues, as well as myself, when I say we hope we continue to see you on occasion. We do not wish for you to disappear from involvement in our business."

("My god, did he just hint that I'm about to get a contract?")

"That won't happen, Fabio, I assure you. I have thoroughly enjoyed my association with Carlo and your other management people."

"Very good. Well let's order lunch, and then we can get down to business." They did. The waiter poured a superb wine ordered by Fabio, who proposed a toast "to our distinguished Yankee visitor!" All three sipped, then Fabio straightened, turned to Roger.

"Let's cut to the chase, because I assume you are as anxious as we are to understand where things stand."

Roger's heart stopped for a fraction of a second. *("Oh, god!")*

"I know you and your associates in Cleveland have spent many months developing strategic recommendations for us, and you have compiled a very detailed contract which appears to spell out everything except how we drink our coffee in the morning. I know you, especially, have been very involved, spending a lot of time away from home, from your children, working closely with my people here.

"Carlo and I, and a fleet of legal counsel, have reviewed every single element of the your proposal," he continued. "We have given it the same attention to detail we also have given to proposals from two other companies, one Italian and one French. It has been a very interesting and worthwhile experience for us."

"Yes, I'm glad to hear that . . . ."

"Don't interrupt, please." Roger froze. Fabio raised his glass.

"Pick up your glass, Roger." He did as he was instructed.

"Carlo, you will join us, please." Carlo raised his glass.

"Roger, Carlo and I wish to congratulate you and Aeronautic Supplies for entering into a very exciting partnership with Aviana Air for the improvement of our aircraft fleet, and the continued success of both our companies!"

"Oh! My god, Fabio. And Carlo! That is such exciting news! I mean, really exciting news!" Roger grin was infectious, he stood and shook hands with both executives. "My partners will be thrilled, as am I. Thank you so much for having such great faith in us." He sat back down.

"The pleasure is ours, Roger. As Carlo will tell you, he and our people have been extremely impressed by you, by your determination to deliver to us the best products possible at reasonable cost, and your willingness to go overboard in providing our cockpit crews and maintenance personnel with extensive training here and in the U.S."

"Thank you very much, Fabio."

"This contract is not a gift, Roger. You have earned it, and I mean that sincerely. Do you agree, Carlo?"

"Absolutely, Fabio." Carlo shook Roger's hand again. "It's been a wonderful pleasure working with you, Roger, and we look forward to a strong, continuing relationship between our two companies."

"I signed the contractual agreement just before I came here, Roger, so when Carlo brings you back to the office, you can pick up copies. You proposed twenty-five-million dollars spread over three years. We have settled on twenty-three-five over the same three-year period. I assume that is agreeable to you."

"Yes! I'm certain we can work within that framework and deliver all that we have promised." Roger was smiling, shaking his head. "This is so wonderful. I can't wait to call my colleagues in the States this afternoon and give them the good news!"

"Please extend our congratulations to them, as well, Roger."

"Yes! You may be sure I will."

"And please understand, we value your participation, so if you do hire talent to ease your travel schedule, we will still want you involved in our business and we want to see you here as often as it is convenient for you."

"I *do* understand that Fabio, and I promise I will not walk away from my commitment to Aviana Airlines. I'm in your corner, and will remain so. You have my word."

Lunch proceeded with light conversation, none of it related to business, and lots of laughter at the expense of Roger and Carlo as Fabio loved to tease. Roger shared a few off-color jokes, which also produced loud laughter. It was a pleasant couple of hours enjoyed by all three executives.

4

It was 4:30 when Roger got back to his hotel, late morning in Ohio. He shed his jacket and tie, retrieved the signed contract from his briefcase, placed a call to Bill Enright, Aeronautic's CEO. Bill was quick to pick up the phone when his secretary told him Roger was calling from Rome.

"Roger! What's the news?"

"Well, Bill, I'm holding in my hand a contract signed by Fabio Mazzetti, your counter part at Aviana Airlines, authorizing us to proceed with implementation of the proposal we submitted to them. Work to begin immediately!"

"Oh, good Lord! What great news! Hang on while I get Brad on the line!" Enright buzzed his secretary and instructed her to get Brad Lewis in his office ASAP. He bounded into Bill's office.

"Brad, Roger has a signed contract with Aviana Airlines. Signed just this afternoon, Rome time, by their CEO, Fabio Mazzetti!" Brad picked up an extension phone on Enright's conference table, screamed into the receiver"

"Roger! What great news! Congratulations!"

"We all deserve congrats, Brad. This has been very much a joint effort by a lot of our people."

"Yeah, but you were the lead dog, my man! When are you coming back so we can celebrate together? What are the dollars?"

"Well, we bid twenty-five million, as you know. The contract I'm holding is for twenty-three-five over the same three-year period, plus an option to extend for another three years!"

"WOW! That's fantastic!"

"I'm very excited and happy, as you might imagine. I'm meeting with several of the key Aviana executives for dinner this evening, which I suspect will evolve into a party. They're as excited as we are!"

"Awesome, Roger. Fantastic! So when are you back here?"

"Well, I'm scheduled to spend some time in London later this week, and will be in Cleveland on Saturday. I'm eager to meet with all of the people who need to get moving on various assignments. This deal is too important for any delays."

"I agree, Roger. This is Bill. Never mind the bottom fishing in London, get your ass back here so we can get everybody started. If you spend a couple of weeks here, you can resume scouting your other European potentials at a more leisurely pace."

"Got it, Bill. I'll do some administrative follow-up with Aviana over the next day or two, but I do intend to stop in London for a meeting Friday afternoon. That's also too lucrative to let slide. I'll fly home Saturday and veg-out on Sunday with my kids. See you early Monday."

"That's great! Again, congratulations, Roger."

"That comes from me, too, Roger." This was Brad, the CFO.

Roger began to dictate a series of orders to his two partners, determined not to permit anything to slide as the company prepared to launch their work on behalf of Aviana Airlines. He wanted the firm's cockpit simulator updated with the newest Aeronatic electronics; an engineering and maintenance crew selected to fly to Rome; Bill was to call Signore Mazzetti to express appreciation for the business; and Brad Lewis was to get his people crushing numbers to be sure the upfront costs would not jeopardize the company's projected earnings from the contract.

Finally, he said he would hang onto the original contact and Fed-X three copies to Bill and Brad.

"So, are we all on board?"

"Yes, Roger, as usual you're five steps ahead of us in the planning. Brad has made notes as you've been talking and we'll jump on everything as soon as we hang up."

"Okay. Dana has my drafts of all the call reports from yesterday. She's most likely proofing that stuff and will get you copies ASAP. I've got nothing else, so let's hang up."

"Good-bye, and congratulations again, from everyone here."

Roger pushed the red button on his iPhone and the line went dead. He smiled, then laughed, and literally danced around his hotel room, pumping air with a closed fist. His grin was a mile wide.

He sat on the edge of his bed, pulled the contract close, sat staring at Fabio's signature on the last page, accompanied by those of two witnesses, most likely corporate attorneys. He kept shaking his head, yelling "Yes!" Laughing out loud. Proud! Thrilled!

He was tempted to strip and climb into a relaxing shower to cool himself off before changing into more comfortable clothes. He glanced at his watch: after 6:00. He picked up the phone and dialed Cecily's room.

"Hello! Is that you?"

"Me who?"

"Yeah, that's you. How did your day go? Are we celebrating, or am I consoling?"

"Celebrating! Twenty-three-point-five-million-dollars worth of celebrating. It's a three-year deal with an option to renew for another three years. They signed the contract today, and I'm holding a copy in my hot little hands!"

"Oh, Roger, I'm so happy for you!"

"Thank you. I've already called my partners in the States and they've insisted I return immediately after my business in London on Friday. I intend to fly home Saturday and relax on Sunday. I need to get back so we can get all of the right people started on their responsibilities.

"I'm going to spend tomorrow and Thursday doing some follow up and administrative stuff for Aviana before I have to fly out of here Friday morning. I need to be in London for an afternoon meeting."

"Can we get together this evening to celebrate your success?"

"I'm afraid not, Cecily. Several of the Aviana guys want to have dinner and celebrate. They seem to be as excited as I am!"

"Well, pooh!"

"Look, let's have breakfast tomorrow at nine, and we can make some plans before you head for Florence."

"Okay." She sounded less than happy. "Actually, I'm probably not going to attempt Florence on this trip -- there's so much to see in Rome -- so if you're not completely preoccupied with work, can we play a little tomorrow? Pretty please!"

"We'll talk about that tomorrow."

"You're a beast! Work, work, work."

"I warned you."

"Yes, and I told you I'd help you think about something other than work, but you won't give me the chance."

"Let's talk about that over breakfast."

"Blah! But okay. I'll see you in the dining room at nine."

"No, let's meet here at nine. I'll call room service."

"Ah, I like the sound of that."

"Sleep tight."

"Good night, Roger."

Cecily was disappointed as she hung up. She was hoping beyond hope that Roger would be in a mood to celebrate his victory with her, an evening which might possibly lead to at least a kiss, or two.

But, No! Business first, as he had told her.

She ordered a room service dinner, did not relish sitting in a restaurant alone, even the hotel cafe. She watched a little CNN on TV, curled up with a book, but could not get her mind off Roger and how excited he must be to have successfully concluded a contract he had been pursuing for nearly a year.

She realized she had turned several pages of her book but had no idea what she read. She pushed the book aside, stripped and crawled into bed, determined to sleep or at least enjoy thinking about that handsome, personal, smart and fun guy who was growing on her like French champagne!

Paolo had advised her to be patient if she had an interest in Roger because "he's devoted to his job and his children." *(No shit!")* Paolo had also said she was "a beautiful young woman," so how long was it likely to take for Roger to recognize that, and understand she was interested in more than friendship?

("I've only known the guy for four days, for gawd's sake! Cool it, enjoy your time with him, and either wait him out or write him off and move on! No! I can't do that! I'll give him time; will try my best not not push him; don't want to lose him! Wait, wait, wait! I can do this! I'm sure he's worth it, and I'm positive he's developing an interest in me. So wait! Wait! Wait!")

She fell asleep imaging him holding her in his arms.

Roger rose at 7:30 Wednesday, an hour later than his usual up-and-at-em time. Dinner with the key Aviana players -- Carlo Meola, Giancarlo Melli, Guiseppi Valenti, Millo Salicini and Gabriele Pozzi --had been an extremely pleasant affair: marvelous food, plentiful wine (Roger managed to stick within his limits), numerous toasts, raucous laughter, great comradeship . . . all in a comfortable outdoor setting under a blanket of brilliant stars.

He hit the sheets about 1:30 and immediately fell asleep. He felt pretty rested, prepared for a tiring day drafting followup call reports of his Tuesday meetings to email to the client and his U.S. colleagues, plus action reports to the people in Cleveland who could expect to be meeting with him on Monday.

He shaved, showered, dressed in casual brown slacks with a white short-sleeve polo shirt, opened his laptop and organized his files on the desk in his room, placed a call to room service for an immediate pot of black coffee and two full breakfasts for delayed delivery at 9:15.

He was swilling coffee and hammering his keyboard, totally unaware of time, when there was a soft knock on his door. His watch said 8:50, he rose, walked barefoot to the door, swung it open.

"Good morning!"

It was Cecily, looking like a million dollars, long blond hair dangling behind a black silk blouse, black and white patterned skirt, makeup just so, comfortable walking shoes. She was gorgeous.

"Wow! You look delicious! Come on in!"

She walked into his room, glanced at the open computer and paper-strewn desk, settled into an upholstered chair.

"I see you've already been doing your favorite thing," she nodded toward the desk.

"Yeah, I got a head start on all I have to do today." He smiled, settled into another chair close to her. "You're a little early, but that's fine. Breakfast will be here about 9:15; eggs, bacon, juice, coffee, muffins, and fruit. Hope you're hungry."

"I could eat a horse. How was your evening?"

"It was very entertaining, Cecily. Lot's of celebrating, too many toasts, but really nice people. I think they'll be great to work with."

She shifted slightly in her chair.

"Well, I have an idea, Roger, and I won't take 'No' as your answer."

"Oh, boy! I can't wait."

"We'll have a leisurely breakfast here, then go for a walk to cherish some of the sights of Rome, at least those in this area. We'll grab a quick lunch somewhere, then I'll let you come back here and slave while I take in another museum or two."

"Sounds good!"

"It's not how I'd like to spend the day, but I know I'll lose if I try to peel you away from that computer for too long!"

Roger hung his head and starred at the floor for several seconds, straightened, looked directly at her, smiling.

"I'm very sorry, Cecily. I know I'm probably a pain in the ass, but I can't help it. This contract . . . It's the largest we've ever signed, and I can't afford . . . ."

"I understand, Roger, I really do. Perhaps one day we'll meet in New York. I'd like that!"

"I would, too, Cecily! I would, too, and I'll make it happen!"

"Let's dine and walk before we run out of time to do even that!" She was smiling.

They found an outdoor cafe not far from the hotel, enjoyed an hour of casual conversation and a light lunch. He gave her some suggestions of two or three museums she might wish to visit.

Back at the hotel, Roger settled her into a taxi, she blew him a kiss, and was off. He took the elevator to his room, fired up his laptop, organized his files and thoughts, began hammering his keyboard.

He launched an array of emails to the key players at Aviana Air, Monday and Tuesday, detailing the Cleveland activities he would be directing to make certain there were no lapses in the promised delivery of specific products or services. He also described Aviana's respective responsibilities in providing Aeronautic Supplies with the proper information required to help his company fulfill its contractual obligations.

He drafted call reports to the senior executives, engineers and maintenance people at Aeronautic Supplies specifying and prioritizing the various initiatives which had to be put in motion to properly fulfill the company's obligations to its newest and largest client. He emailed the reports to Dana for proofing and distribution to the appropriate department heads, with copies to CEO Bill Enright and CFO Brad Lewis.

By the end of the afternoon, Roger's back was sore from bending over his laptop, eyes were nearly blurry from staring at the screen, fingers ached from typing. He desperately needed a break, secured the computer in his briefcase, took the elevator to the lobby and walked outside.

He strolled two or three streets in the neighborhood of the hotel, lingered before several jewelry store windows, an exclusive men's clothing store, stopped to sit at a small cafe's sidewalk table, ordered an ice cold glass of Sorrel. He was suddenly hungry, downed a hot pastrami sandwich with French mustard, drank another cold Sorrel.

After his modest dinner, he glanced at his watch, slow-walked back toward the hotel on the opposite sides of the streets. A women's accessory store caught his attention, he went inside, looked around, bought Cecily a gorgeous Hermes scarf "for the hell of it!"

He returned to the hotel, went straight up to his room, phoned Jennifer and Tommy to hear their voices, answer their questions, re-affirm that he would be home on Saturday, and Yes! they would enjoy pizza, ice cream and the local aquarium. That was a promise.

"Daddy, don't forget you said we could talk about maybe getting my ears pierced!" Jen! Lord how he loved her! She was so eager to grow up before he was ready for her to do so.

He retrieved his laptop, devoted the balance of his evening to more paperwork, determined not to miss the slightest detail in assuring that everything required to fulfill the Aviana contract would be handled promptly and efficiently. He did not phone Cecily; too tired.

He awoke early Thursday morning, was about to shower when his telephone rang.

"Pronto!"

"'Pronto' yourself. What's happening?" It was Cecily.

"I am about to shower and begin another fascinating day."

"Really? What's going to be so fascinating?"

"Nothing, unfortunately. I have to do more follow-up work with Aviana. And I've got to send two Fed-X packages to the U.S. with copies of the contract. I'm also going to conference call my office, then do some preliminary planning for my next stopover in London tomorrow."

"Well, that sucks! I thought we were going to visit a couple of museums."

"I'm sorry, Cecily, but not today. I want to get this work out of the way. But let's plan to have dinner this evening."

"You're mean! I wanna play today, too."

"Can't do it, Girl."

"Well, go in peace then. I'll see you this evening, but you don't know what you're missing because I have reservations to tour the Sistine Chapel."

"That's great! You'll find it fascinating; I know, because I've been there, done that. You can tell me all about it and Rome's beautiful museums when we meet this evening. Okay?"

"Okay! But you're still mean."

"Comes with the job."

"Pooh!" They both hung up.

Roger immediately placed a call to his office in Cleveland, eager to discuss the reports he had emailed to Dana yesterday. Enright was out, but he was connected to CFO Brad Lewis.

"Did you receive all of my Call Reports, Brad?"

"Yes, I did, Roger, but I honestly have not had time to read them carefully."

"How about copies of the confirmation emails I sent to Aviana's executives?"

"Yes, I have those, as well. You've been very busy, Roger. Why don't you get out of the hotel, enjoy Rome, and give us a little peace."

He was laughing; Roger wasn't.

"Jeez, Brad, this isn't a frigging game. We've gotta keep these people happy."

"I know that, Roger, I'm just teasing you. Give us all time to digest the volumes of material you have in the emails. I know Bill will want to get us all in a room and go over this stuff line-by-line so everybody understands their marching orders.

"That's unlikely to happen until tomorrow morning, Roger. People need time to absorb everything you're suggesting, and Bill is out of the office today, on the road. Why don't we call you about seven your time tomorrow night; that'll be two our time."

"Make it eight my time, Brad. I'll be in London. I have an afternoon meeting with the people at Majestic Airlines, and I don't know how late that meeting is likely to run."

"Okay, three our time, eight yours."

"Thanks, Brad." They both hung up.

Roger replaced the files in his briefcase and pulled a folder labeled "Majestic Airlines", the large regional prospect with whom he would be meeting Friday afternoon in London. The folder contained a detailed dossier on the company, the scope of its business, its flight coverage areas and schedules, an inventory of its fleet by type and age of aircraft, the names and titles of its principal officers and those on its Board of Directors.

He began outlining his comments to the principals at Majestic; not a script, just a series of organized notes he could study on his flight from Rome to London. He skipped lunch to focus his attention on all that he was determined to accomplish on Friday. Equally as important were his meetings next week in Cleveland with his managers to prioritize and coordinate all of their efforts in addressing the Aviana contract

By late afternoon, he collared the concierge and gave him two Fed-X envelopes addressed to CEO Bill Enright and CFO Brad Lewis, containing copies of the Aviana contract.

It was pushing five o'clock when he elected to quit for the day. He showered, changed clothes, went down to the lobby bar and ordered a glass of wine, nibbled on a bowl of peanuts: lunch, sort of.

He looked forward to seeing Cecily, who was due to join him momentarily. The cocktail lounge was beginning to fill with early evening customers, the atmosphere subdued, calm, voices muted, three musicians (piano, guitar and bass) playing soft background music from the 1940s and 50s.

Cecily arrived looking ravishing. Roger slipped an arm around her waist, pulled her close, stared into her deep blue eyes for several seconds, struggled to resist kissing her hungrily, warm, long. They smiled at each other coyly, continued to gaze into each other's eyes for several more seconds. She placed her hands on his shoulders, slowly pulled away, sat on the upholstered swivel chair next to him. Roger ordered her a glass of chardonnay.

"How was your day today, Cecily? What did you do?"

"I saw the most amazing art . . . wish you had been with me to enjoy it." He didn't fall for the bait.

"What museums did you visit?"

"I didn't. I went to several churches, where you have to deposit a euro or two to turn on some lights that illuminate an old masterpiece owned by the Church. The lights only stay on about a minute. Then you have to feed the cash box another euro if you want the lights to come on again. Otherwise the painting hangs in the dark. That should be against the law, for god's sake!" She was annoyed.

"Well, the Church owns the art, so I guess they can do whatever they please."

"Yeah, well it stinks." She sipped of her wine, clearly upset.

"Do you plan to visit any more museums here in Rome?"

"Yes!" She stared into his eyes. "I was hoping maybe you and I could go together tomorrow, but I know you're flying to London for a meeting, more work."

"Yes, that's true."

"Always your job."

"Yes, Cecily, my job." He sipped his drink, placed his glass on the bar, his demeanor serious. "Please understand I did not come to Europe to play . . . I came to Rome with the intention of signing a very lucrative contract, which I've done. And I'm going to London because I have a prospect who's interested in what my company has to offer, and that may lead to another lucrative contract.

"I had no idea I would meet someone as lovely and fun as you. I welcome the opportunity to spend some time with you, Cecily. I *like* spending time with you because you *do* make me forget about work. I hope I've just kind of, sort of, demonstrated that!" He smiled again. "But play, serious play, has to come *after* I have fulfilled my obligation to myself, my partners and our employees."

"Gawd, you're a real workaholic."

"Yes, I suppose I am. I enjoy it, in fact I have a passion for work, for reasons I explained to you earlier." He sipped his wine. "Please understand that for the past half-dozen years all I've had in my life are my children and my job. And I'm passionate about both."

"I do understand, Roger, I really do. It's just that I wish you had a passion for passion! Frankly, *that* is what I'm determined to teach you!" She stared into his eyes until they dropped to his drink.

"Actually, Cecily, that sounds fantastic. I'd like to think the lessons could begin tonight!" He turned to her and smiled, winked. "But they can't. I need to get up early to catch my flight to London for another brain-twister. I admit I have missed companionship in my life.

"And I love that you're rekindling that emotion in me, I really do." He paused.

"I know my obsession with work is consuming. It's just that I have a hard time letting go because my partners and I are on the cusp of achieving our long-term goals. I'm sure that's not what you want to hear."

"Roger, please." She took his free hand. "I certainly under-stand your focus on your job, and your children. Please don't misunderstand me. But I've never met anyone like you before . . . you're different, and fun, and good looking, and kind . . . and I just want to be with you, that's all. I want to find a way to accomplish that without interfering with your devotion to your children or your career."

"Thank you for understanding, Cecily. And for continuing to press me to spend time with you. I want to be with you, too. Keep pulling my eyes toward you and away from my computer, and my heart and brain are sure to follow, Cecily. It's just going to take time."

"Yes. Yes. I understand."

"So, tell me, what did you do today other than lose your temper in churches?" He was laughing.

"I went shopping, a real touristy shopping spree. I couldn't resist the call of some of the specialty shops here in Rome. They're wonderful. I couldn't walk past them without going in, and temptation ruled the day." She was laughing at herself. "I spent more than I should have, but hey! Who knows if I'll ever get to Rome again!"

"Well, I, too, gave into temptation, and I have a little surprise for you." He reached onto the bar and slid a wrapped package in front of her. Cecily knew immediately what it was, the orange-colored flat, square box, sealed with brown ribbon, on which the name "Hermes" was printed repeatedly.

"What have you done? Why . . . What is this for?" She was beaming as she gently opened the box and removed the colorful scarf with a uniquely

Hermes design.

"This is because you've started me thinking . . . I mean about something other than my job. I find myself spending a lot of time thinking about you!"

"Oh, Roger! You are special." She clutched the scarf to her breast and smiled, put an arm around his neck, pulled him close, gave him a warm, loving kiss. He circled her body with both arms, kept his lips locked onto hers, wouldn't release her, slight tongue touch. When their lips parted their faces remained close, glistening eye contact, both smiling.

"I liked that a lot, Roger." She whispered.

"No more than I did! Lesson number one!" He whispered, also.

"I can't wait for lesson number two!"

Cecily looked down, admired the scarf in her lap.

"I can't thank you enough, Roger. This is precious. Thank you, thank you, thank you!"

"You're very welcome. And thank *you* for helping me realize that when I'm *not* completely engaged in work, there is more to life than business."

"Oh, Roger! I'm glad I'm making an impression!

"You certainly are." He drained his wine glass. "Now, let's move into the restaurant and have dinner. I'm starving."

Roger slid out of bed at 6:30 Friday morning, stepped into the bathroom to shave and shower, dressed, packed his suitcase when his phone rang.

"Good morning, you stuffed shirt!" Cecily was laughing.

"Hi! Good morning. Why are you up so early?"

"I wanted to say goodbye before you fly away and leave me all by myself in this big strange city."

"Ahhh, I'm sure you'll be fine."

"Yeah, but I want *you* to take care of me!" He laughed.

"Listen, I'll call you from Cleveland Saturday evening. Have a very interesting day today and a safe flight tomorrow. Maybe our planes will come close together. I'll be going to Chicago while you're heading for New York."

"Chicago, and then Cleveland? New York is more vibrant!"

"Maybe, but my paychecks and my kids are in Cleveland." He laughed. "Stay well, and I'll talk to you tomorrow night."

"Okay. You stay safe, too. I miss you already."

"Ahhhh, you're just a tease!"

5

Roger checked into a hotel in Knightsbridge about mid-day, showered, changed, grabbed a quick lunch in the hotel dining room, then left for his two o'clock meeting with executives at Majestic Airlines in their Newgate Street offices.

His appointment was with Geoffrey Butler, the airline's Chief Financial Officer, and Ian Pedrick, Director of Aviation Technology Innovation. It would be his first person-to-person contact with both executives, a follow-up to trans-Atlantic phone calls and emails.

The reception room was surprisingly plush, expensive wall-to-wall carpeting, polished mahogany reception desk staffed by a personable young woman, brown leather upholstered visitors' chairs, fresh flowers on the desk, a live tree in a decorator pot in one corner.

The receptionist rose from behind her desk, tall and slim in a Majestic Airlines uniform, welcomed Roger and led him toward two darkly tinted glass doors, which she opened to reveal a magnificent conference room. The table was surrounded by a dozen or more upholstered chairs, two of which were occupied by executives who stood to greet Roger as he entered.

"Good morning, Roger. I'm Geoffrey Butler, Majestic's money mogul. It's a pleasure to meet you in person at last." Butler stood a good six-four, slim build housed in a British tailored navy blue suit, hair neatly coiffed, very pleasant smile.

"Good morning, Sir. I'm delighted to make your acquaintance."

"Roger, I'm Ian Pedrick, the Airline's chief technology officer, and I, too, am very pleased to finally meet you." Pedrick also was tall and slim, well dressed, partly balding, sparkling dark eyes and ready smile.

"Good afternoon. I appreciate your time this afternoon. I've been eager to meet you both since we began our trans-Atlantic communications over a month ago."

"Yes! Personal meetings surely beat emails and long distance phone calls." Geoffrey pointed Roger to a chair, ready to begin negotiating.

"Did you just arrive in London, Roger?"

"Yes, Geoffrey, I did, about two hours ago. I've been in Rome for the past week working with Aviana Airlines."

"Really, Roger!" This was Ian. "May I ask what you're doing for them."

"Well, nothing yet; we start next week. They just signed a contract with us. We'll be upgrading all of their cockpit electronics with some state-of-the-art equipment developed by our engineers. We'll also be providing new compact automated seating for their entire fleet, which enables them to fit a greater number of people in the same square footage. And, we'll be counseling them on the color coordination of interior fabrics and upholstery, including flight attendant uniforms."

Roger was smiling, knew Ian and Geoffrey were bowled over at the extent of Aeronautic's agreement with Aviana.

"Crikey, Roger! That's quite a package! How long will all of that take?" This was Geoffrey.

"I want to know how and where you'll handle the training of both cockpit crews and maintenance personnel." This was Ian.

Roger spent a half hour describing his firm's assignments for the next three years, with an option to renew for another three years to continue updating Aviana's avionics, especially as they contract for new aIrcraft, which they wanted equipped with Aeronautic's technology.

He explained that training would occur in cockpit simulators in Cleveland and Rome, with electronic, maintenance and cockpit crews rotating through both facilities..

"We had no idea your firm was capable of all of that training and servicing in addition to product innovation and assembly."

"We like to think of ourselves as a turn-key supplier, Ian" Roger was smiling. "We don't do the upholstery work, that will be done by a local Italian firm. And we don't make uniforms, nor do we specify fabrics. That will be handled by an Italian fashion design house."

Roger laughed inwardly as he thought back to the meeting in Rome devoted to the fabric and colors of cabin attendant uniforms, a meeting where he kept his eyes wide open, his mouth shut, and his mind on how good the uniform would look on Cecily!

Geoffrey and Ian exchanged glances, obviously impressed with the scope of the product innovation and services Aeronautic Supplies had offered to Aviana and, presumably, would provide to Majestic should they come to agreement on finances and terms.

"Well, look, Roger." This was Geoffrey, leaning forward on the table as he addressed Roger across from him. "We've carefully reviewed all of the technical materials and specs you've provided to us, and we've studied all of the links on your corporate website. We're obviously impressed or you wouldn't be sitting here today."

"Thank you, Geoffrey."

"I must say, though, that what you've shared with us this afternoon is awesome. I think I speak for both Ian and myself when I say we would like to pursue the possibility of an agreement with your firm to help us achieve our goals in upgrading our aircraft fleet without investing in new aircraft. That's something we're not in a position to do just yet.

"We've spoken with several other companies, as you might imagine, but none of them have come across so prepared as you seem to be, to provide both unique product improvements as well as aggressive installation and training service on both sides of the pond, as you Yanks like to say."

"Well, thank you, Geoffrey. We like to think that's what sets us apart from the other guys."

"Roger, I'm sure Geoffrey would agree that we'd like to visit your company, see your facilities, get exposed to the new equipment you have designed, and then have a real sit-down with you and your management to see if we can agree on terms."

"That would be terrific, gentlemen. We'd certainly welcome an opportunity to show off our stuff, and work with you to detail how we can help you achieve your objectives. I'm not hesitant to say we're damned good at what we do!"

"It sounds like you are! So, let's plan it then," said Geoffrey. "I'll confirm with our people this afternoon. I assume you'll be back in your office Monday morning. Why don't we give you a day to throw away your mail and brief your management." All three laughed. "Let's talk by phone

Tuesday morning, ten o'clock your time." Geoffrey rose to shake hands, a sure sign the meeting was coming to a close.

"I look forward to it, Geoffrey. Thank you, and you, Ian, for your time today, your interest in our company and the scope of the innovations and services we're capable of providing to Majestic."

"We certainly look forward to visiting with you at your company headquarters."

Roger smiled broadly as he crossed Majestic's reception room, entered a lift for the ground floor, hailed a taxi to the Berkeley Hotel. He glanced at his watch -- just after four o'clock, 11:10 AM in Ohio — decided to hide in a corner of the hotel's bar and use his cell phone to call Bill Enright and Brad Lewis.

"Hello, Roger. This is Bill."

"Bingo!" Roger kept his voice low to avoid annoying other patrons in the bar, but it was loud enough for Bill to get the message.

"'Bingo!' What does that mean? I thought we were phoning you at eight o'clock tonight, your time."

"Well, my meeting at Majestic ended early, and I thought I'd try to catch you before you leave for lunch. We're on track for a deal, Bill." There was excitement in Roger's voice. He explained that the Majestic executives were impressed with the scope of Aeronautic's product and service capabilities, would phone him Tuesday to set a date for them to visit Cleveland and commence discussions on a possible contract.

"How many will be coming?"

"At least two, perhaps a third, which would be their chief pilot."

"Wonderful! When are you back in this area?"

"I fly home tomorrow, Chicago connecting to Cleveland. I arrive late tomorrow afternoon. I intend to spend time with my kids on Sunday, will see you first thing Monday."

"Sounds good."

CFO Brad Lewis and VP/Engineering Josh Steinberg had walked into Bill's office and Roger began peppering them with questions to make certain they were on top of the priorities related to the Aviana Airlines contract. He also advised them the Majestic Airlines executives would be arriving in Cleveland later next week to begin a contract dialog.

"Wow! That's terrific, Roger!"

"Thank you, Brad."

"Look, Roger, we're busting asses here to get the ball rolling," this was Bill, the CEO. "So get yourself back here and take command of this project from your office, not from a god-damned hotel room half a world away."

"Okay, Bill, sorry. Let's ring off and resume this discussion on Monday. I'm beat, need a shower and a stiff drink. Have a good weekend and I'll see you all Monday morning."

"Roger, Roger! Have a safe flight home." The line went dead.

Roger stood and stretched his back and arms. He was very tired, toyed with the thought of stopping at the bar for a libation, decided instead to retreat to his room, perhaps sneak a short nap.

He woke at seven, surprised he had slept for more than two hours. He felt somewhat rested, refreshed after a long hot and then cold shower. He dressed in slacks and an open-collared white shirt, relaxed in a comfortable chair in the cocktail lounge and gave the smiling waitress his order for a glass of chardonnay, snapped open the day's edition of *The Daily Telegraph,* lost himself in the headlines.

Minutes passed. He was suddenly aware of someone standing in front of him. It was a young woman, tall, impeccably dressed, curly brown hair framed her face and tumbled down her back, her eye and face make-up just so.

"Do you have a light, sir?" She held a cigarette between two fingers tipped with bright red polish.

"Yes, certainly." He opened a book of hotel matches lying on the low table beside his chair, lit her cigarette.

"May I ask, are you alone, sir?"

"Yes."

"May I join you for a drink?"

"Yes, but I should tell you I'm exhausted, and plan to retire early -- alone -- to catch a flight to the States tomorrow morning."

"No problem, Sir. I'd just like to share a drink and some small talk, if that's okay."

"Very well. Have a seat. She lowered herself into the comfortable seat on the opposite side of the small table between them. When the waitress arrived, the woman also order a glass of chardonnay.

"My name is Alison." She blew smoke away from him.

"Alison, my name is Roger. I judge from your accent that you're either Dutch or German, correct?"

"German, Roger. Stuttgart to be precise."

"And are you staying in London or moving on?"

"I'm moving on. I've been here for several days, on business. I'm in the cosmetics business, and my next stop is New York."

"Ah, I see. Well, I'm heading to Chicago."

"Have you been in London long?"

"No. I just arrived this morning, had a meeting this afternoon, and am leaving in the morning. I've been doing business in Rome for the past week."

"Rome! That's a beautiful city."

Roger couldn't figure her angle. She was quite beautiful, very friendly, didn't drop any of the lines one would expect from a gal eager to connect. Maybe she was, truly, just looking to share a drink and conversation. She made no move to touch his arm, no obvious flirtatious looks, winks, or tongue laps across her lips, just sat, sipped her wine, shared almost boring small talk.

"How long have you been in the cosmetic business, Alison?"

"Just a year."

"Really! What did you do before that?"

"I was a bouncer at a nightclub in Stuttgart."

"A bouncer! Man, that's hard to believe. Bouncers are usually muscle men with limited language skills."

"Yes, well I was different. I studied karate when my name was Siegfried; changed to Alison when I came out of the closet."

Roger choked on his wine, coughed several times, turned to look at Siegfried/Alison, laughed. "Fer Christ's sake! You're also one hell of an actor, or actress. And quite attractive. I never would have guessed you are . . . ."

"The word is transgender."

"Yeah! Right! Transgender!"

"And I'm not acting, Roger. I'm a woman, just like your wife."

"Well, not exactly like her, Alison." He was embarrassed, but they both laughed. "I'm not trying to put you down, really I'm not. But you're the first transgender person I think I've ever met, and you're a beautiful woman, so it struck me sorta . . . .

"Sort of 'Wow'! I get that a lot."

"Well, please excuse my rudeness. I didn't mean it."

"No problem, Roger. You have a safe flight tomorrow."

"You as well, Alison. Knock 'em dead in New York."

"I intend to!" She was laughing, as was Roger.

He dropped money on the table, enough to pay for her drink as well as his, left the bar, laughed out loud as he rode the elevator to his floor.

It was well after five Saturday afternoon before Roger retrieved his BMW 650 convertible from the garage at Cleveland's Hopkins International Airport, pushing six by the time he pulled into the underground garage below his condo building in the downtown area known as the Flats. This was a newly renovated section of the city previously dominated by austere shipping terminals; now sprouting fine restaurants, new office buildings, an aquarium and a number of modern condo and apartment buildings, some still under construction.

Roger rode the elevator to his fourth floor unit, a three bedroom condo with three-and-one-half baths, large living room with a view of the city and Cuyahoga River, formal dining room, modern kitchen.

As soon as he opened the door, he was swallowed by Jen and her brother, Tommy. They were beyond excited to have their Daddy home, hugged and kissed him repeatedly, made it difficult to juggle his suitcase and briefcase, not that he cared. Marina, the housekeeper, joined the children in welcoming him home, departed quickly for her car and her own residence.

Once free of hugs and able to move inside, Roger dropped his luggage and briefcase on the floor of the entry, headed straight for the bar in his kitchen to pour a short drink. He was exhausted from traveling all day, his body still on European time where it was just after 11:00 PM in London.

He played, wrestled and talked with Jen and Tommy for well over an hour, thoroughly enjoyed their excitement at his home coming, their numerous "guess what", stories from school, sports, books being read or not yet started.

They ultimately swung to the television set, so Roger rose, shed his travel clothes, slipped on comfortable workout slacks and a T-shirt, checked his mail, tossed most of it, pushed the balance onto his kitchen counter, retreated to his bedroom to shower and unpack while the children watched cartoons on TV. He got them bedded down by 9:30, then hit the sheets himself. Too tired to phone Cecily.

Just as he promised himself, Roger rose late Sunday morning, made himself a modest breakfast, sat in his living room with a fresh pot of coffee and read his way through the Sunday newspaper, the weekend edition of *The Wall Street Journal* and two issues of THE ECONOMIST, the most interesting items in his mail.

Jen and Tommy finally awoke, busied themselves with cereal, juice and laughter. Roger joined them while they ate, answered a gazillion questions about his trip, Rome, London; asked them a gazillion questions about school and their athletic and social activities while he was gone. And, Yes! As promised, they would get pizza and ice cream for lunch, followed by a visit to the aquarium. Giggles, cheers and excitement!

He parked on the couch in the living room after breakfast, prepared to open his briefcase and review some files. Before he could, Jen slipped into his lap, one arm around his neck, kissed him on the cheek. He smiled, knowing he was being set up for "the question!"

"Daddy, about piercing my ears . . . ."

He cut her off.

"Hang on a sec!" He reached into his briefcase and extracted a small package. "Open this first, and then we'll talk about your ears!"

Jen carefully unwrapped the package, opened the small box, exclaimed when she saw the shining pair of gold studs.

"DADDY! They're beautiful! And they're for pierced ears! Oh, Daddy, this means I can get my ears pierced, doesn't it!"

"Well, I hope so, Jen. Otherwise I'll have to return earrings, and I bought them in London. That's a long way to go to return a pair of earrings!"

"Daddy! I love you so much! When can I get my ears pierced?"

"Tomorrow, after school. I have a bunch of meetings, but Marina will take you to the doctor, and when I come home tomorrow evening I expect you to be wearing them."

"Oh, I will be, I promise! This is so great! Wait 'til I tell my friends at school! Thank you, Daddy!" She hugged him tightly, gave him a long kiss on the cheek, leaped to her feet to telephone a girl friend.

"Tommy!"

"Yeah, Daddy."

"I owe you one, Buddy. So think of a surprise I can get you . . . but no pierced earrings, okay!" He laughed, Tommy joined in.

"Lego!"

"You got it, Kid. I think they sell some Lego sets at the aquarium. If not, we'll stop somewhere on the way home this afternoon."

"Awesome! Thanks, Daddy!"

His afternoon with the kids was fantastic, full of laughter, teasing, holding hands, skipping, running, ooohing and awwing, happy faces and bright sparkling eyes.

They returned home about 5:30. Jen and Tommy busied themselves with books, Transformers, a new Lego set and TV, so Roger dialed New York.

"Hello?"

"Hi, Cecily. 'Tis I! How was your trip home?"

"Oh, Roger!" She was yelling. "It is so great to hear from you! How was your trip home?"

"I got home about six last night and crashed soon after I put the kids to bed. I was exhausted; sorry I didn't phone you. I slept late this morning, and my kids and I had pizza and ice cream for lunch, then went to the local aquarium. I pretty sure I'm going to survive." He was sipping a glass of ice water.

"Well that's good news. I'll bet the children were anxious to see their Daddy!"

"You have no idea!" He was laughing. "And I had a blast with them this afternoon. It was a lot of fun for all of us. I bought some gold stud earrings in London for Jen, and she's beside herself about them. She's growing up too fast on me!"

"Well, she must be thrilled. How was London?"

"I didn't see much of it, Cecily, just enough to cab it from my hotel to the offices of Majestic Airlines and back to my hotel. But the meeting went very well. They're interested in meeting with us here to see our facilities, check out our new electronic instrumentation in the flesh, and then have what they call 'a sit-down' to discuss a possible contract."

"Wow! You must be very happy!"

"I am, actually."

"Wish I could be with you to celebrate."

"It's really too early to think of celebrating, Cecily. If we sign a deal with them, then we celebrate."

"I miss you like crazy, Roger. When will I see you again?"

"That's hard to say right now. This coming week will be hectic as we get ready for the first team from Rome to show up, and we also need to prepare for the London group. I'll be speaking with them on Tuesday to set a date for their arrival. I don't know what the following week will bring, but it may be more of the same. So my guess is it will be ten days, perhaps two weeks, before I make it to New York on my way to Europe again, Cecily. And I miss you, too."

"Two weeks! You'll be so absorbed in your job you won't even remember me."

"Yes, I will. And I promise to call you every day until I see you. Besides, you've got to start pounding the pavement."

"What? What do you mean?"

"You've got to find yourself a job to replace the one you lost before going to Italy."

There was hesitation on her end of the line, then she recalled telling Roger she had been laid off by a small financial company.

"Oh, right! I'm going to get on that tomorrow, first thing." *("OMG! I forgot about that lie. Gotta keep my head on straight!")*

"I'm going to ring off, Cecily, but I'll call you again tomorrow evening. Maybe you'll have some good news on the job front."

"Okay, Roger. I really miss you terribly. Please stay in touch with me. I promise not to call you at the office if you promise to call me in the evening."

"You got it. I miss you, too, Honey. Italy was great, and I'm very eager to see you again. Sleep tight."

("He called me 'Honey'! He called me 'Honey'!!)

"Yes, you, too! I'll wait for your call tomorrow night."

Cecily paced her apartment, upset, flustered, not sure what she should do. She picked up the phone and dialed a local number.

"Margi, it's Cecily."

"Cecily!" Margi was surprised to hear from her, and her voice reflected it. "How was Rome?"

"It was magical, Margi."

"Lots of terrific art, I'll bet!"

"Yes! But that was the least of it."

"Good lord. Don't tell me you've fallen for some handsome Italian prince, or something!"

"He's not Italian, he's American, and he's fantastic! We met on the flight to Rome."

"Wow!" There was a slight hesitation. "Come on, girl, tell me all about him."

"How about we have dinner and I'll share all the gossip."

"Now there's an offer I can't possibly refuse!"

"Tonight, eight o'clock, at that French restaurant on Columbus midway between 77th and 78th?"

"You bet! I'll see you there.

They met shortly after eight. Margi was a good friend from college. Shorter than Cecily, maybe five-four, short dark hair, horn-rimmed glasses, a bubbling personality with a cute smile and a quick laugh. She was a copywriter at an ad agency; still single but hunting, had not yet found her Mister Right. They settled at an outdoor table, oblivious to the traffic noise on Columbus. Margi got right to the point.

"Okay, Babes, tell me what you've been up to, and forget the art stuff! I want gossip, even sin!"

Cecily laughed, began to describe in detail how she and Roger had met on the flight to Rome; how she had come to have a ticket but no known accommodations; how Roger had gracefully saved her butt by getting her a separate room in the same hotel; their dinners; her use of Paolo and his car at Roger's expense.

She also described Roger physically, his good looks and personality, his single status and commitment to his job above all else; his rapture at having concluded a multi-million dollar contract he had been negotiating with an Italian airline for over eight months; his lengthy conference calls to Cleveland; his preoccupation with work. And his two young children.

"Holy smokes, Cecily. It all sounds too good to be true! The two kids . . . is there a wife involved?"

"No, Margi, he said she was killed by a drunk driver several years ago. His kids are eleven and eight, so they've been growing up without a mother, and he has a killer travel schedule. I don't know how he does it."

"Well, he's not without his problems, but I'm happy for you! But no love-making yet . . . no sex!"

"Well, I was hoping . . . but No! He's awesome! I've made it clear I'm interested in a relationship, but he's backed away, always focused on his client meetings. He phoned me just before I phoned you, and he called me 'Honey' so I think . . . I hope we're getting close. I know he misses me like I miss him."

"How about the sticky part? Does he know about that?"

Cecily paused, sipped her wine.

"No! I lied to him, Margi."

"You *lied* to him! That's not a very smart way to begin a relationship, Cecily."

"I know, but I couldn't bring myself to admit I was occasionally hustling men in a hotel bar, and having sex with some of them for money."

"What did you say?"

"I told him on the airplane that I had been an assistant to an executive at a small financial firm and got laid off. Then when we were talking on the phone this evening he reminded me that I'm supposed to begin looking for a job tomorrow. At first I didn't understand what he was talking about . . . he had to remind me of what I told him on the airplane. I had forgotten my lie about losing my job at a financial company."

"So this guy has no idea . . . ."

"No, none!"

"I take it you're falling in love with him."

"Yes, Margi, I think I am. It's very early in our relationship, but I can't imagine meeting anyone better for me."

"How does he feel about you?"

"He's clearly interested in me, and I'm wild about him! He's very cautious, and married to his job. And he's very protective of his children. He said he has never taken the time to think about anything else but work and kids since he lost his wife. He's challenged me to change that, to sort of help him start over. I think I'm having some success, but it's not easy and I lied to do it."

"So he's in Cleveland as we speak?"

"Yes, but he expects to be back in a week or ten days, on his way to Europe again. And I think, I hope, he'll stay with me for a day or two before he leaves."

"Well, look." Margi reached across the table and clasped Cecily's hand. "That gives you almost two weeks before you see him again to think of a way to break the news. If he's truly interested in you, he'll find a way to forgive you. He's obviously no virgin, may have had a number of different women before he got married, and others since his wife died."

"Maybe the former, but not the latter. And I'll bet he didn't do it for cash."

"Leave that part out."

"Well, how . . . I don't want to lie to him again. I think I've got to tell him everything, and hope he'll forgive me, but I'm terrified he won't, Margi, and then what do I do?"

"You'd have to start over! That would be disappointing, Yes! Shattering, Yes! But don't even think like that now."

"He's promised to call me every night while he's in Cleveland."

"Don't break the news on the phone. Do that and you'll lose him for sure. You've got to tell him in person, look him in the eye, pout, cry. Do *not* allow him to find out from anybody except you. And from you, in person."

"Nobody but you knows, Margi. Who's going to tell him?"

"You never know, Kid. So do it the next time you two are together, before this relationship goes any further. And apologize profusely for lying to him on the airplane. You didn't even know him then, so that's a good reason to have shaded the truth. But now, Cecily, *now* you have to tell him the truth. Emphasize the lie, and your sorrow over having told it. That's all you have to do. I'm willing to bet he'll understand . . . but if he hears it from someone else, I'm willing to bet he won't be very understanding."

"God, Margi, I'm so scared. I don't want to lose him."

"Play your cards right, and you won't. But play them right!"

They ordered dinner, switched their conversation to subjects less distressing, including Margi's success at the ad agency. She had been promoted to Senior Copywriter, with a significant bump in pay, now assigned to one of the agency's hot clients. She was bursting with pride and joy, prompting Cecily to forget her problem as she became absorbed in Margi's enthusiasm.

They parted about 10 with a final caution from Margi that Cecily better level with her "dreamboat before he becomes a nightmare!"

6

Roger arrived at work at eight-thirty Monday morning after dropping his children at school. He went immediately to the office of CEO Bill Enright who, with CFO Brad Lewis and VP/Engineering and Maintenance Josh Steinberg, were already sitting around a small conference table, coffee cups in hand, awaiting Roger's arrival.

Once they got through the hello's, how are you's and a few digs at Roger's lousy Italian, they turned to the deluge of emails and call reports he had sent following his Aviana meetings, plus the actual contract itself, which had arrived Friday morning by Fed-X from Rome. They also were impatient to hear the details of his London meeting with executives from Majestic Airlines.

At Bill's recommendation, they focused on their priorities, identifying who was going to command which parts of the massive effort that lay ahead of them. Financials were at the top of Bill's list. He also was concerned the firm might need to hire one or two additional electronics gurus if Josh was going to raid the company's staffing and send two or three guys to Rome for several weeks.

After an hour of this, Roger brought up the subject of geographic coverage. He was responsible for international sales worldwide -- everywhere but the U.S. and Canada -- and could not be in six places at once. Most importantly, he was adamant that he cut back his travel to spend more time with his children. He wanted to find and hire a sales manager for the Far East and Australia, and another for Central and South America; his own time, for the foreseeable future, would be dominated by opportunities in Europe.

He also recommended that Brad, Gordon and he be promoted to Executive Vice Presidents, so the new hires could be given titles: VP/Area Manager - Far East/Australia, VP/Area Manager - South & Central America. Gordon White would be EVP/North America, and Brad would be elevated to EVP/Finance.

Bill signed off on both the promotions and the personnel hires, with compensation packages to be discussed within the week, giving Bill time to consult members of the Board's Compensation Committee.

Roger and Brad left Bill's office, each hurrying to their own "cage" to commence what was sure to be a hectic week. Roger vowed to work however many hours it took to get everything moving in the right direction with Aviana Airlines.

He also could not afford to neglect his other clients in Europe, especially the London opportunity, and things he had brewing in Argentina and Jakarta. And he was hoping to establish initial contacts with prospects he had yet to approach in Scandinavia and The Netherlands. His plate was full to overflowing.

He first called Dan Winslow, the firm's Director of Corporate Communications. Dan was a former newspaper and wire service reporter, gave up the Fourth Estate to move to the other side of the desk as a corporate executive; the hours and pay were vastly superior. He was tall, slim, good looking and well-spoken, knew every important business editor in New York, Cleveland and Chicago.

Roger briefed him on the Aviana Airlines contract, the promotion of Brad, Gordon and himself, his authorization to hire two area managers, and the potential for a contract with Majestic Airlines in London.

"Gawd, Roger, you guys are flying — pardon the pun!"

"I want maximum media exposure on each of these opportunities, Dan, and I don't want them lumped. Stagger them out over a period of days or weeks for maximum impact."

"No problem, Roger. My strategy will be to announce the Aviana contract first, because it gives us a legitimate opportunity to discuss the expansion of our business. Second, let's announce the promotion of the three of you, again citing our growing business in the U.S. and abroad. And third, we'll announce your plan to hire two area managers, again citing our expanding international business."

"Sounds good, Dan. Please let me see each announcement before you go public."

"I'm not going to touch the Majestic thing until we actually have a contract. And I suggest we coordinate with Bill. He's been meeting with underwriters prior to taking the company public. There's a rumor already on the street in New York; I'm surprised we haven't read about ourselves in the *Times* or *Wall Street Journal.* My phone's not ringing yet, but I expect it to, and this string of announcements is bound to cause some activity."

"Yeah, so what's wrong with that?"

"Let's check with Bill to see how soon he thinks we may make that announcement. If it's soon, we should delay so the SEC will not accuse us of trying to hype the IPO. We have to enter what they call 'a quiet period' for a month or so when we go public; we can't make any announcements of any kind."

"Hang on a minute!" Roger lifted his phone, punched a single button, was immediately connected to CEO Bill Enright.

"Bill, can Dan and I see you right now, for two minutes? . . . Okay, we're on our way." He replaced the phone, turned to Dan: "Let's go!" They entered Bill's office, sat on opposite sides of his desk.

"What's up?"

"You tell him, Dan." And Dan did, not leaving out any details of his announcement strategy to gain maximum media exposure. He also expressed caution about running afoul of the SEC if the company's initial public offering was anywhere near ready to be announced.

"Good thought, Dan. Thank you." Bill swung back and forth in his revolving chair, deep in thought about how much to discuss, mindful that Dan was not yet 'management.'

"Dan, let me ask Roger a question."

"Sure! Want me to leave?"

"Well, you probably should, but No! Stay where you are." Bill swung his seat, looked squarely at Roger.

"I don't want to put you on the spot, Roger, but I'm going to!" He cleared his throat before continuing. "When we announce our initial public offering, a lot of the communications headaches are going to fall squarely on Dan's shoulders." Bill glanced at Dan, a slight smile on his lips.

"Once the announcement is made, and our stock begins trading, we're going to be deluged with calls from financial analysts who will be trying to pick apart our business. There also are likely to be a mountain of calls from the news media, especially business and financial publications, including reporters at the *Plain Dealer.*

"Those calls will not stop, ever! The analysts will press us for quarterly projections, which we won't give them because I don't intend to run our business based on what outside analysts think we do right or wrong. That's our call, not theirs. But, they'll hound us for quarterly conference calls.

"I'm not going to field those calls, and neither are you nor Brad. None of us are going to have the time to train ourselves how best to respond to a million questions, easy and tough, about our business, how terrific we are, what are our plans, why did we screw up thus-and-so. Are you following me? Do you know where I'm heading."

There was a reasonably long pause before Roger spoke.

"Yes, and I concur completely."

"Thank you." Bill turned to face Dan. "Congratulations, Dan, you are now, as of this minute, a corporate officer in this firm with the title of Vice President, Corporate & Financial Communications."

"WHAT!" He jumped to his feet. "Are you serious? I can't believe it."

Both Bill and Roger stood to shake Dan's hand.

"I'm very serious, Dan. You've earned this promotion, and the salary that goes with it. Congratulations!" Bill gave Dan a pat on the shoulder.

"Congratulations, Dan." Roger also gave him a handshake and shoulder pat, they all re-seated. There was a short pause in their conversation as Bill and Roger enjoyed watching Dan smile, pump his fist. "Wow! This is incredible! Wait 'til I tell my wife! We'll probably have sex tonight!" The three of them roared with laughter. "I really can't believe this . . . thank you so much!

"But, Bill, let me raise the question Roger and I came in here to ask you: Can we proceed to make these three announcements with-out compromising your plans regarding the initial public offering?"

"Yes, you may." Bill was impressed that Dan's focus remained on business, despite the surprise announcement. "I'm still meeting with underwriters . . . in fact, it will be good to let them hear what you guys are up to. So, go ahead. Your announcements will help."

"Thank you, Bill, and thanks a million, both of you, for that awesome surprise."

Dan and Roger rose to leave. Dan shook Bill's hand again; Roger gave Bill a wink and big smile. He knew Bill would be on the phone immediately to Brad and Gordon to advise them of the decision he had just made, fully endorsed by Roger. He'll explain why they weren't invited to vote, knew both would be in favor of the move, and would call or visit Dan quickly to extend their best wishes.

On their way back to Roger's office, Dan couldn't refrain from exclaiming about what he had just been told.

"Dan, you've got your marching orders. Now go call your wife and plan your celebration this evening!"

"Thank you, Roger, so much."

"Incidentally, Dan, we didn't talk salary in Bill's office; that will come later this week when we five 'Monarchs' can get together. The five now includes you, don't forget that!"

"Vice President! I still can't believe it. I'm just thrilled that you folks think so highly of me. I will never disappoint you."

"We know that. You've proved it over and over again. Now go call your wife." He gave Dan a pat on the shoulder and a playful shove toward his office

Back in New York, Cecily was again pacing her apartment. She had to find a job, was uncertain how best way to proceed. Under no circumstances would she set foot in a hotel bar; she was going to find a legitimate job, one she could discuss with Roger without shading the truth. Newspaper ads were out, in her judgement; not a smart way to look for the kind of job she wanted. But what did she want? Finance was not her strong suit, despite what she had told Roger. But she was smart, a quick learner, good looking and personable. All of that should work in her favor.

She began by placing another call to Margi, this time at her ad agency office.

"Well, good morning, Cecily. How are you!"

"I'm good, Margi, but I need to begin looking for a job, a real job I can tell Roger about when I see him."

"So where are you going to look?"

"That's my problem. I'm not sure where the heck I should start, Margi.

Circling help wanted ads in the newspaper doesn't really ring my chimes."

"I can understand that." There was a pause. "Well, look, I'm going to call a friend here at the agency who works in Personnel. I'll vouch for you and see if she would be willing to meet with you."

"That'd be great, Margi. Just don't tell her about my past!"

"Don't worry. And you better come up with a logical story about what you've been doing for the past two years . . . maybe you just moved to New York from Boston, and are settling into your new home.

"Okay, something like that." Another pause. "Margi, I'll wait to hear from you or the woman in Personnel, and thanks a million. You really are a very good friend . . the best."

"Stay by your cell phone, Cecily. If this works, you'll probably get a call within the hour."

"Okay, and thanks, again." She hung up, sat back in her chair, and waited expectantly. The call came about an hour later, the personnel woman eager to meet with Cecily on Wednesday morning.

Roger, meanwhile, had had a frantic and exhausting afternoon of meetings and phone calls, didn't get to leave the office until almost eight o'clock, stopped to pick up a bucket of fried chicken on the way home. Marina had fed the kids, who surrounded him with hugs and pleas for a some of his chicken. He sat at the kitchen table, chatting and laughing with Jen and Tommy, admired the gold studs in Jen's pierced ears. She was giddy with delight, kept looking at herself in a handheld mirror.

Roger suddenly pulled his cell phone, dialed Cecily's number.

"Good evening, gal. How are you doing?"

"Roger! I'm so glad to hear from you. I was beginning to think you'd forgotten me."

"No way, Cecily. But things are really hopping here. I've been promoted, and we've agreed that I should hire two Area Managers, one to travel the Far East and Australia, and a second to handle Central and South America. That takes an enormous burden off me. They'll report to me, but I can focus my attention on Europe, where I'll have my hands full for at least the next year."

"Well, congratulations on the promotion, and if you're focusing on Europe it means you'll be passing through New York a lot. Will I be able to see you then, do you think?"

"We'll have to see, Honey. It'll obviously depend on the urgency of my various trips, but I'll certainly try to stop and be with you as often as I can."

("He called me 'Honey' again!")

"That sounds so tenuous, Roger . . so up in the air. Am I supposed to just sit tight and wait . . . .?"

"I told you Cecily, I'm married to my job. That's not going to change anytime soon, and I'm sitting with a couple of wildcats who deserve lots of my attention." His voice was firm, not angry, but firm. "I enjoy your company and love being with you, Honey, I really do. But I'm not in the . . . I'm not in a position to consider a full-time relationship."

There was silence on the phone for several long seconds. He could hear her breathing.

"Cecily, have you begun looking for a new job?"

("Shit! All he wants to talk about is work, work, work. I'm hoping for a lover . . . for more than a lover, and . . . I should just tell him good-bye, but I can't do it.") She began to well up.

"Yes! In fact I have an interview at an ad agency Wednesday morning. They're looking for an administrative assistant in their Art Department and I'm hoping I'm it!" She sniffled.

"Hey! That's great news! Congratulations. I'll keep my fingers crossed for you."

"Thank you." She sniffled again.

"Are you crying, Cecily?"

"Yes! . . . Damn you, I'm crying!"

"I'm sorry, Honey. I really am. I'll phone you often, and see you as soon as I can."

("He called me 'Honey'! Said he 'loves' being with me! That's gotta mean something!")

"Okay. Will you think of me even when you don't call?"

"You bet . . but I'll call. I promise." He paused. "Hang on a minute, I want you to say hello to someone." He placed his hand over the phone to muffle his voice, handed the phone to Jen. "Say hello to this lady, Jen. Her name is Cecily."

"Hello!" There was silence for a few seconds.

"Hello! Is this Jennifer?"

"Yes! I'm Jen. You're Cecily!"

"Yes! I am. It's nice to talk with you. I've heard a lot about you from your Dad. You're his very special girl!"

"Are you his special girl, too?"

"Well, I like to think so, but you'll have to ask him. I hope to meet you sometime soon, Jen."

"That would be great. I love your name, Cecily. It's very pretty."

"Thank you, Jen. I understand you're very pretty, too!"

"Thank you. Well, I'll let you talk to Daddy again, Here he is. Good night." She handed the phone to Roger.

"Oh my gosh, Roger. She sounds so wonderful. I hope I can meet her and Tommy sometime soon. Can we make that happen?"

"I'll bet we'll find a way!"

"Roger . . . I lov . . . I miss you terribly." *("I almost said 'I love you' but couldn't . . not yet . . I think it would frighten him away. But when . . . when can I tell him how I really feel about him? Will that temper what I have to tell him about my past?")*

Roger hesitated before replying, just a second or two, but she knew he knew what she had almost said.

"I miss you very much, Cecily. I'll see you as soon as I can, and call you every evening, okay."

"I guess that will have to do . . . for now."

"Cheer up. Let me hear you smile."

She laughed briefly. "Okay. I'm smiling . . . . Goodnight, Roger."

"Good night. I'll call you tomorrow night."

"Okay. I'll be waiting to hear your voice."

They both hung up.

"You called her 'Honey', Daddy, and said you miss her."

"Yes, I did, and I do, Jen. She's a very close friend of mine who lives in New York City."

"I like her name . . . Cecily."

"And I think you and Tommy will like her, too. She's very nice."

"Is she pretty, Daddy?"

"Yes, Tommy. She's very pretty."

"Does she like to fly?"

"Yes, Tommy, I think she does. In fact I met her on an airplane!"

"Awesome!"

"When do you think we'll meet her, Daddy?"

"Well, I'm not sure, Jen. But I'll try to make it soon, okay!"

"Okay. I'd really like to meet her."

The children, especially Jen, continued to pepper him with more questions, some of which caused him to struggle for a suitable answer. The cross examination ended when he was finally able to tuck them into bed, return to the living room, and dream about what it might be like if Cecily . . . .

The balance of Roger's week, and every day of the week that followed, was dominated by a galaxy of meetings, conference calls, emails, letters, phone calls, correspondence, more meetings, strategy sessions, the usual menu of time-consuming priorities which confront a senior executive with international responsibilities. It was a pace he had become accustomed to after ten years of working extremely hard with his associates to build their company from the ground up, to make it a preeminent success in their industry.

Dan Winslow had issued news stories on all three of the major announcements they had discussed on Roger's first full-day in the office after his European trip. The management executives also had met that Wednesday morning (which they did every Wednesday) to discuss their salary adjustments given their new titles and expanded responsibilities, as well as a variety of other issues important to the business, including the status of the planned initial public offering.

Dan sat in that meeting like a kid in a candy store: excited, quiet, not quite believing he was now part of the inner sanctum that made Aeronautic Supplies the successful and respected company it was. He was beyond fascinated.

Roger had also managed to phone Cecily almost every evening. Their conversations had initially taken about fifteen minutes but had increased in length to the point where they now conversed for over a half hour, often about nothing of particular importance other than their mutual desire to be together.

Then there was the evening . . .

Roger dialed her number. It was pushing eight o'clock and he was still in his office, leaning back in his chair, legs crossed, shoeless feet propped on his desk.

"Hi, Gorgeous! How are you this evening?"

"I'm pretty good, actually, now that you've called. You sound very upbeat. What's happening?"

"Well, I have some interesting news. Are you ready?"

"Stop teasing me, you bum! What's up?"

"I've had a very interesting call from our recruiter for an Area Manager covering Latin and South America. I'm leaving in the morning for Miami to interview the candidate; he's from São Paulo. I'm going to have dinner with him tomorrow night, then fly the next morning to New York because I want to see someone special!"

"Oh, I can't believe it! Roger, you've made my day! Please let me know your exact schedule so I'll know when to expect you. I'm so excited, so eager to see you!"

"I'm eager to see you too, Honey!"

("There's that word again. Does he realize he's calling me 'Honey'?")

"I just can't believe it, Roger. Rush, rush, rush."

"How is your job going?"

"Well my start date isn't until the first of the month. But I've met most of the people I'll be working with, and like them a lot. They're very creative."

"That's awesome. I look forward to hearing all about it."

"Okay, but I'll keep it short, because I don't want to talk only about work, mine or yours!"

He laughed. "Yea, I got it. Well, look, Cecily, I'm still in my office. I've got to close up, go home and spend some time with my kids, then pack. But I really look forward to seeing you Friday."

"Roger?" There was a pause. "Roger, I miss you tons!"

There was a longer pause.

"Cecily, wait until we're together, okay. And I'll tell you exactly how I feel. In fact I'll show you exactly how I feel. Meanwhile, here's a kiss and hug. See ya Friday afternoon, late."

They signed off.

Roger's Thursday morning flight to Miami was uneventful. He spent part of his time reviewing the agenda from yesterday's weekly Management Meeting, re-reading his notes, especially Bill's comments on where he hoped to take the company over the next two years, with an update on the status of their IPO.

Roger used the balance of the flight to review the resume of Jose Grossa, the applicant for the job of VP/Area Manager, South & Central America. He was well educated, currently held a good position with a Brazilian regional airline, his professional credentials seemed superb, and he was obviously conversant in English as well as Portuguese and Spanish.

After checking into a beachfront hotel, Roger changed into a bathing suit and relaxed in the hotel's pool for the better part of an hour; then showered, dressed casually in an open collared short-sleeve shirt, grey slacks, black loafers.

He met Jose in the lobby about six; they walked out to the hotel patio, sat at an umbrella table. Roger hailed a waiter, ordered a bottle of San Pellegrino for himself, and . . . Jose also stuck with the water. They also ordered dinner.

Jose was handsome, about six-three, 180 pounds, dark complexion, black hair, trimmed black mustache, dark eyes, a ready smile, firm handshake. Roger liked him before the guy had said anything other than "Pleased to meet you".

They dispensed with the small talk fairly quickly and got to the meat of their conversation. Roger politely grilled Jose on his professional credentials, his employment history, the specifics of his current job, his reasons for wanting a job change, his attitude about living on airplanes.

How about his family (wife and two kids), and Roger's favorite question: "If you had the power to change your job, what three changes would you make?" That question stumped a lot of applicants because it came from so far out in left field; they never anticipated it.

Jose had the right answers to Roger's questions, including that last one; asked a slew of penetrating questions himself about the scope of Aeronautic's business, its management, its future plans and strategy for continued growth, where he'd be based, his access to Roger and the Cleveland headquarters, where he was likely to be in three-to-five years if the company continued to grow.

Roger couldn't give him precise answers to some of those questions; did not reveal the company was close to an IPO and that Jose, if hired, would be on the receiving end of stock. That was proprietary information

Roger was not in a position to share with an outsider. But when they got to salary, Roger outlined the firm's offer and added that "if" the company ever went public, Jose's position as a VP would "most likely" entitle him to a block of incentive shares.

Jose seemed interested in the company, the job, and the compensation package Roger described. He took the "if" about an IPO as code for "we're heading in that direction."

"Roger, is it okay with you if I think on it overnight?"

"Absolutely, Jose. I have a flight to New York at ten. Please call me about eight, or we could grab a quick bite, if you're so inclined, before I leave for Miami International."

"Let's share a cab to the airport, Roger. I, too, have a flight back to São Paulo."

They shook hands, and parted when they reached the elevator bank. Roger phoned his kids.

Jose was standing at the checkout counter at eight Friday morning when Roger approached him. They exchanged greetings, Jose said he would like to join "Roger's Team".

"You're company sounds very interesting, and it's on a fast track. I like that, and so does my wife. I spoke to her last evening."

"Thank you, Jose. I'm delighted. I know you're heading back home, but I'll phone you Monday to set a date for you to come to Cleveland to meet our management, get a look at our facilities, get some hands-on with our product line."

They grabbed their luggage and headed for the doorman and a taxi. They spoke enthusiastically about the job, the company, and Jose's probable future with Aeronautic.

7

Cecily was beyond excited that Roger was coming to New York to spend the weekend with her. It would be the first time they would spend time together since Rome, which seemed like ages ago.

And a weekend in her co-op almost certainly meant they would make love. She could almost feel his arms around her, his body pressed against hers, lips locked together, hearts beating in unison, passion . . . passion . . . passion! She couldn't wait!

She was deeply concerned, however, about how to tell him about her past. She'd never been a professional hooker, only sold herself for sex a few times, twice with that nut-case who bought her a ticket to Rome so she'd go with him, then didn't show at the airport, thank god! She was *not* prepared to be his arm candy; he could fine himself some Italian prostitutes.

She paced her apartment, thinking.

("How can I describe what I had done without Roger getting the wrong impression? I can't find the words. Do I really need to tell him? Margi said I should, just to make sure he doesn't hear about my past from someone else. But who?

("I can easily pass off the lie about working for a financial firm because when I told Roger that we were complete strangers. We'd only met ten minutes earlier on that flight. But the other stuff, the 'sticky stuff' as Margi described it! I don't know how to phrase it without making it sound like I was a hooker. Which I wasn't!

("Not this weekend! Why should I screw up our first weekend together? No way! We're beginning what has the potential to become a wonderful

relationship and I'm not about to blow it. That crap is history, water over the dam! The hell with it!")

Roger's American Airlines flight touched down at LaGuardia about three o'clock, forty-five minutes later his taxi pulled up to the front of her co-op building, a few doors west of Columbus Avenue on West 77th Street. A green awning stretched from the front door across the sidewalk, anchored at the curb by two polished brass poles. A doorman rushed to open the taxi door and assist Roger with his luggage.

Once inside the building, the doorman asked which apartment he was visiting, requested his name. He punched a button on his desk, spoke briefly into the phone to announce "Mr. Roger Manning is calling." He led Roger across the graciously furnished lobby to an elevator, set his luggage on the floor, pressed button #3.

Cecily was standing in the hall, threw herself into Roger's arms as he stepped out of the elevator. They kissed warmly, their first truly romantic kiss.

"Oh my gosh, I'm so very happy to see you, Roger. I've missed you terribly!"

"I've been eager to see you again, too. I'm glad I'm here with a weekend to spend with you."

"Come on!" She grabbed his hand; he lifted both his overnight bag and briefcase with the other. "Let's get you into my apartment so we can relax." Once inside, he dropped his bags on the floor, kicked off his shoes, removed his tie and suit coat, plopped onto Cecily's sofa. She dropped beside him, he leaned over and kissed her again.

"How about a libation to wet your whistle?"

"No!" He was smiling. "That can wait! I told you Wednesday night that I'd tell you, even show you, how I feel about you . . . so where's your bedroom?" She was surprised, broke into a grin, stood, took his hand, helped him to his feet.

They wasted no time getting undressed and into her queen-size bed for over an hour of passionate love, whispered endearments, soft tender exploration of each other's body. They lay wrapped in each other's arms, eventually fell asleep, made love again about six, slept until after eight. They showered together, returned to her bed for another round of bonding.

It was pushing nine Saturday morning when they showered, dressed, sat side-by-each on her couch to share a pot of coffee.

"Roger . . . I'm falling in love with you!

"The feeling is mutual, Cecily. I'm really surprised at how quickly you've become so important to me." He pulled her close, kissed her, smoothed her long blond hair, caressed her cheeks, gave her a peck on the nose.

"You've got a nice place here, Cecily. How long have you been here?"

"A little over two years. I think I told you I'm from a jerkwater town in New Jersey and got tired very quickly of the commute into the city, so I decided to find myself a small apartment. It's centrally located, and in a great neighborhood. Let's go for a walk in awhile and I'll show you a nice restaurant on Columbus Avenue."

"That sounds like fun! But first . . . ." Roger reached for his cell phone. "I want to tell someone all about you!" He hit two buttons on his phone.

"Hi, Jen!"

"DADDY!" He could feel the excitement as well as hear it in his daughter's voice. "Where are you?"

"I'm in New York, Jen, but I'll be home tomorrow."

"New York? Will you see your friend Cecily?"

"I sure will. In fact, I'm in her apartment right now!"

"Is she there, too?"

"Yes, she is! I'll let you say hello in a minute."

"Can you bring her home with you? We'd really like to meet her!"

"I'm not sure, Jen. She starts a new job here shortly, so I'm not sure she could leave New York right now."

"Yeah, but it would be great if she could come and maybe stay with us . . . to make Tommy and me feel warm and comfortable when you're traveling . . . like a Mommy. Please, Daddy! Ask her!"

Roger was stunned. His eyes began to water, he leaned back into the couch, his head tilted upwards, realized in spades how much his daughter and son missed having a mother, a loving woman in the house. Cecily could see his tears, held his hand, her face expressing deep concern, didn't know what Jennifer had said.

Roger finally spoke.

"Jen . . . I know that would make you very happy, but we're not . . . I just don't think . . . it's just not that easy, Jen." He passed the phone to a surprised and very concerned Cecily. "Say hello to Jen." He retreated to the kitchen for a tissue to wipe his eyes, blow his nose.

"Jennifer?" Cecily's expression was very tentative.

"Hi! Can I call you Cecily! I like your name. I've never known anyone with that name. It's very pretty. And I think you're making Daddy very happy!"

"Yes! You may certainly call me Cecily, Jennifer. And your Daddy makes me happy, too. I look forward to meeting you and Tommy. We'll do that real soon, I promise!"

"Tommy and I would like that. Do you think maybe you could fly home with Daddy tomorrow?"

"Gosh, I don't know, Jen. Let me talk with him and we'll see if we can work something out."

"Okay. Give Daddy a hug from me, and tell him to give you one, too! Cecily, do you call Daddy 'Honey'?"

"No! Why?"

"I bet he'd like that!"

"Jen, you're so wonderful! I can't wait to meet you, and get to know you!"

"Ditto, Cecily! Tell Daddy I'd like it if he'd bring you home."

Cecily laughed. "We'll see, Jen. You take care."

The line went dead. Cecily stood, walked into the kitchen to find Roger. "Are you okay?"

"Yeah, I'll be alright." He put his arms around her, buried his head in her shoulder, began to cry, his body shaking.

Cecily stood gently rubbing has back for several seconds.

"What happened, Roger? What did she say?"

He composed himself, blew his nose again, caught his breath.

"She wanted to know if you could come home with me . . . 'like a Mommy', she said. Live with us 'like Mommy did!' To make her and Tommy 'feel warm and comfortable' when I travel. I just lost it!"

"Well, she just asked me to ask you if you'd bring me home with you tomorrow! And she told me to call you 'Honey' because you'd like that. So cheer up, Honey!"

Roger smiled, his face brightening.

"That's a hell of an idea! Why didn't I think of that? Can you do it? What's your schedule this coming week? Can you break away? I'd love it, too, if you could come to Cleveland with me, spend a lot of time with Jen and Tommy."

"Oh my gosh, Roger." She was beaming. "Probably, I think! I don't start my new job until the first of the month, so I'm pretty much free this next week. Are you serious?"

"I'm serious, and Jen is more than serious. Let's do it!"

"This is unbelievable!"

"Pack tonight and we'll catch an early flight tomorrow morning. The earliest flight we can get. I'll call our company travel agent now to book us tickets and get you a return flight a week from tomorrow!"

"Cleveland! With you! We'll be together all the time! That sounds great, but won't you be married to your job?"

"Yeah, but that won't prevent me from showing you where I live, where I work. I want you to meet the people I work with. I want you to meet their wives, the Country Club where we all hang out and play golf. Bottom line, Cecily: I want to show you off! And I want my kids to know you, really know you, and for you to know them."

"Roger! Oh my gosh! She kissed him warmly. "Clothes! What should I pack?"

"Bring a lot, because we'll be going out every night, or most nights. During the day I'm sure Bill's wife, Toni, Brad's wife, Linda, Josh's wife, Helen -- they're all great gals and you will fit in perfectly."

"Are you sure?"

"Yes, I'm sure, and they'll keep you so busy during the days you'll have trouble staying awake in the evenings so I'll be able to get some sleep!" He smiled broadly.

"I really can't believe this!"

"I'll be jammed up at the office. The guy I just interviewed may be coming in for a day or two to meet my partners, and so on, but I'll make time to spend with you and Jen and Tommy."

"An entire week with you, an entire week together! It'll be like Rome, Roger!"

"No, believe me, Cleveland is nothing like Rome!"

"I'm really excited, but nervous about meeting all of your colleagues, their wives, your children. You really think I'll fit in okay?"

"No problem, I'm positive. They'll love you . . . maybe not the same way I love you, tho!" He pulled her close and they embraced, warm, tight.

They enjoyed a relaxing late afternoon cocktail with soft music on her stereo, sitting side-by-side on her couch. Their conversation revolved around Cleveland, Cecily's new job, Roger's promotion and his job, his trip to Miami to interview Jose Grossa, his anticipated travel schedule in the weeks ahead, his likely movement in and out of New York.

They busied themselves with the *Times*, rattling pages more than devouring stories about traffic accidents, the antics of the City's politicians, School Board arguments involving science texts considered too sexually explicit for high school students!

About 7:00, they walked arm-in-arm a few blocks south on Columbus Avenue to a sushi restaurant, sat at the sushi bar, told the chef to make them whatever he would like to eat for dinner. He produced a meal the ingredients of which neither Roger nor Cecily could identify, but it was fantastic.

Their conversation flowed easily, as it does with two people in love, eager to know everything about their mate, even the small inconsequential stuff: What's your favorite color? Your favorite flower? Your favorite book or TV show?, etc. Once back at her co-op they wasted little time getting into bed to begin the pelvic two-step, finally fell asleep in each other's arms after midnight.

They woke early Sunday morning. Roger made a move to get up, but Cecily pinned him down to the bed with her naked body, massaging Mr. Happy until Roger pleaded for relief.

"You're giving him callouses," he whispered in Cecily's ear.

Cecily burst out laughing, breaking the romantic mood.

"Well he better get used to it!"

They both laughed, stretched, yawned, agreed they should stumble out of the sack, tend to their morning ablations, make themselves sufficiently presentable, and catch a taxi to LaGuardia. It was after noon on Sunday when they pulled into the garage under Roger's condo building. He started to exit the car when Cecily stopped him.

"Roger, I'm very nervous."

"Why? What are you nervous about?"

"Meeting your children. What if they don't like me! What if they object to your bringing another woman into the house?"

"Cecily, please relax. Both kids were very young when Janice died. Tommy was only three; doesn't even remember her. Jen was five; has only a fleeting memory. And it's been almost six years since we lost Janice. You'll be fine, take my word for it. You heard Jen on the phone. She's very eager to meet you, wanted to know if you could live with us! Come on, trust me."

He barely had the apartment door open when he was assaulted by his two young children, yelling, hugging, excited "welcome homes!"

He stepped into the entry foyer followed nervously by Cecily, set his luggage and briefcase on the floor, hugged and kissed the kids, then turned to Cecily, who stood back somewhat overwhelmed by the enthusiastic reception the children gave their Dad.

"Jen and Tommy, I'd like you to meet Cecily. Cecily, I'm happy to present the prides of my life, Jennifer and Tommy."

Jen stepped forward and shook hands. "It's nice to meet you, Cecily. I'm very glad you came home with Daddy."

"Thank you, Jen. I'm happy to be here, and excited to finally meet you."

Tommy initially stood his distance, shy, uncertain, waved and said "Hi", stepped forward to shake her hand.

"Well, 'Hi' to you, Tommy. I've heard a lot about both of you from your Daddy. He's very proud of you, and now I see why."

"Jen, why don't you and Tommy give Cecily a tour of our home while I unpack and make us all some cold refreshments." Jen grabbed Cecily's hand, promised to show her "everything, including where we sleep and where you and Daddy will sleep!" Cecily blushed a little at that last phrase coming out of an eleven-year-old, quickly let it pass as nothing unusual. Roger's daughter obviously was somewhat savvy.

Roger headed for the kitchen to make he and Cecily a drink, cold lemonade for the kids. Following the tour, they all settled in the living room, Roger and Cecily on the couch, the kids on the floor, Jen peppering Cecily about "what's it like in New York?", Tommy struggling to build a house with playing cards like his Dad had done.

"I love your condo, Roger: the layout, your choice of furniture, the decor, the roominess, the large windows, the marvelous views. This is a spectacular apartment, and it is so wonderful to be here with you and the children. I still can't believe it . . . and entire week together." She threw her arms around him and they kissed warmly.

"Wow!" Roger took a deep breath, smiled. "That's what I call a nice welcome home!" Jen winked at him!

"That's nothing," Cecily whispered. "Wait until later!"

Roger laughed, picked up his phone, dialed a number.

"Hi, Bill. It's Roger."

"Hi! Are you home, and how did you make out?"

"Yeah, got home about an hour ago, and I hit the jackpot. This fella Jose Grossa looks even better in person than he does on paper, Bill. I think he is terrific, and I'm sure you'll agree. I'm calling him tomorrow to arrange for him to fly up here so you and the other brass can meet him."

"That's great news, Roger. I'm excited to meet him, and I know it'll be an enormous relief for you to have someone covering that entire area for you. Lot's of potential there."

"You bet." Roger paused briefly. "Also, Bill, I'd like to invite you and Toni to dinner to meet someone special."

"Really!" There was a pause; he could almost hear Bill smiling.

"Who is she?"

"Like I said, someone special. Her name is Cecily Sommers, and I think you both will like *her*, also."

"Sounds great! I'm very happy for you, Roger. Let's make it tonight, Roger, if that's okay. Toni and I will see you at the Country Club at eight. We very much look forward to meeting Miss Sommers."

"Thanks, Bill. We'll see you there."

When Roger hung up, Cecily gave him a nudge.

"So, I'm someone special, huh?"

"You knew that." He gave her a quick kiss, took hold of his drink and downed a swallow.

"So who were you talking to?"

"Bill Enright, our CEO . . . the top banana at Aeronautic Supplies. Bill is a terrific guy, and you'll also love his wife, Toni. She is one of the women who will keep you out of my hair this week!"

"Good luck to her!" Their conversation for the next hour was light and casual, Cecily asking multiple questions about the people Roger worked with and their wives, his schedule during the week, how much time she might be able to spend with him other than evenings.

Marina arrived about 7:00 to spend the evening with Jen and Tommy, tuck them into bed, watch TV until Roger and Cecily came home from dinner with Bill and Toni.

The two couples met at the Country Club, headed straight for a table for four so they could converse easily. Cecily was initially nervous meeting Roger's boss and his wife, but quickly relaxed, very much enjoyed their company, the conversation, the atmosphere, the dinner. They parted after ten, Toni telling Cecily she would pick her up at Roger's apartment in the morning, Bill looked forward to meeting with Roger at the office.

Roger was up at 6:30 Monday, skipped his normal exercise drill, shaved, showered, dressed and was in the kitchen making breakfast for the kids when the phone rang. It wasn't even seven o'clock!

"Hi, Roger. This is Toni Enright."

"Hi, Toni. What's up so early on a Monday?"

"Let me speak with Cecily, please. I want to describe her day and set a time to pick her up."

"Great! Hang on a moment, she's still in the sack." He carried the phone into the bedroom, sat on the edge of the bed, shook Cecily until she groaned, rolled and looked up at him.

"You have a phone call."

"What?" She popped awake. "Who is it?"

"Say hello!"

Cecily grabbed the phone, within a matter of seconds she and Toni were engaged in a rambling conversation involving Toni's plans for the day with Cecily, who rose from the bed, carried the phone as she was talking, continued gabbing with Toni.

"Boy, she's fantastic, Roger. She has the entire day all planned out for us . . . touring, shopping, lunch with some of the other wives. What a nice gal! She's picking me up here at nine."

"Good. You'll be able to leave me alone!"

He laughed, stood, kissed her warmly, and announced he was leaving shortly to drop the kids at school, then hit his office. Coffee, juice and toast ready to eat, bacon and eggs in the fridge. Both children grabbed lunch bags and school books, waved to Cecily as they followed Dad out the door.

Once settled in the BMW, Tommy asked for the roof to go down.

Jen was next to her Dad, touched his arm: "Cecily is very nice, Daddy. You really like her, huh! That's why you call her 'Honey'."

"I really love her, just like I love you and Tommy. That's why I call her 'Honey' and I'll start calling you that, too, on occasion. But Tommy wouldn't like it; it's not a guy thing!" He kissed Jen's nose, smiled as he drove to school.

He was behind his desk by 8:20, shuffled papers into assorted piles, reviewed the mail Dana had organized for him, ultimately opened his briefcase to withdraw a folder marked "The Americas". He glanced at his watch . . . almost nine, eleven in São Paulo . . . buzzed Dana, asked her to put through a call to Jose. He was on the line in less than two minutes.

"Good morning, Jose. It's Roger Manning!"

"Hello, Roger! Great to hear from you! How was your weekend?"

"Awesome! How about yours?"

"Ahhh, Maria and I and our children, we celebrated, big time! We're all very excited about the opportunity you've given us, Roger: not just me, but our entire family! My kids call you 'Ranger', as in Lone Ranger!" Roger laughed uproariously.

"Don't you dare tell them I know how to ride a horse!" He laughed, as did Jose.

"No! I didn't mention silver bullets, either!" still laughing. They discussed a timeframe for Jose to come to Cleveland for a round of interviews with Bill, CFO Brad Lewis, and North American VP/Sales Gordon White. Jose planned to be in New York Wednesday on business, would fly to Cleveland Thursday and head back home Saturday. Roger's admin Dana would handle tickets and local hotel accommodations for Jose.

Roger had a full plate: The Aviana business was picking up steam; tomorrow he was scheduled to speak with the Majestic people regarding a possible contract; Bill was getting closer to a deal on the IPO, which would necessitate a road show by management to speak with financial analysts in several important U.S. markets.

He had phone messages from the recruiter who had found Jose stating he also had candidates ready for preliminary interviews in California for the Far East and Australia sales position. Roger also had his on-going business to manage, and he was pressing Josh Steinberg, the firm's Engineering & Maintenance czar, to complete the important upgrade to the firm's cockpit training facilities so he could advise Aviana to send over its first trio of pilot, co-pilot and first officer for in-depth training.

He began his day by drafting a "By Order Of" document he gave to Dana authorizing her to close his office at 5:30 -- "no matter what" -- and order him to go home to meet Cecily. The Order gave Dana to right to set his suit jacket on fire if he didn't rise, immediately put on the jacket, and head for his car.

So, promptly at 5:30, Dana entered his office, dropped the "Order" on top of the document Roger was reading, told him to close up shop "and get out of here!"

"No can do, Dana. I just need another half hour."

Dana spun on her heels, left his office, returned moments later with a cigarette lighter. She snapped it on, lifted his jacket off the back of his office door, and threatened it with the lighter.

"I am about to follow orders."

Roger looked up, saw she was serious, smiled broadly, rose from his seat and grabbed the jacket.

"You'd really do it, wouldn't you!"

"I have my orders." They both laughed as he slipped on the coat and left his office.

"Don't tempt me again this week!" She yelled after him.

The week's social schedule was almost as hectic and fatiguing as the pace of Roger's work load. Toni Enright had shown Cecily an interesting and busy day, and she and Roger had enjoyed a warm, friendly and relaxing dinner Monday evening at Bill and Toni's home.

Cecily's other weekdays were filled with similar fun excursions with Brad's wife, Linda, and Josh's wife, Helen. They toured the city's upscale shops, fine restaurants, the Rock 'n Roll Hall of Fame, the Cleveland Museum of Art, and other Cleveland highlights. The evenings and nights were occupied by cocktail parties at the homes of various Aeronautic Supplies executives, plus a special evening at the home of the city's mayor, a former college friend of Bill's.

Jose arrived at Roger's office Thursday, mid-morning, as planned.

Roger began his orientation by introducing him to Dana "who runs my life. She'll also run yours while your here this week, and if everything pans out she will be your umbilical cord to anything you need."

"Welcome, Jose, to this zoo we call Aeronautics. And, by the way, I've never thought of myself as an umbilical cord!" They all laughed.

"It's my pleasure to meet you Dana. You're a very attractive umbilical cord!"

"Thank you, Jose, I think! While you're here, please teach Roger the Dodger a little of your Latin grace!" More laughter.

Roger and Jose had a brief meeting in his office, then moved to Bill's, where they spent over an hour in deep conversation about Jose's background, his knowledge of the aircraft industry, the origin and growth of Aeronautic Supplies, with just a hint of Bill's thoughts on growth potential in the next three-to-five years.

Dana then took Jose under her wing, introducing him to CFO Brad Lewis and North American VP/Sales Gordon White for additional interviews. She also toured Jose through the company's R&D and manufacturing facilities, where he spent over an hour in deep conversation with Josh Weinberg, the firm's Director of Engineering and product development.

Jose was psyched by the end of the day, when Dana returned him to Roger's office.

"How'd it go, Jose?"

"Oh! Man, Roger, this is an amazing company. Your key people are spectacular . . . I'm not sending you or them a Valentine, I mean they are on top of their game. I hope to join your team."

"Well, the good news, Jose, is that while you were touring the engineering, R&D and manufacturing facilities, I had a meeting with Bill, Brad and Gordon, and it is my pleasure to offer you a position as Vice President/Sales for South and Central America!"

"Oh! That's awesome, Roger. Thank you very much. You really won't regret your faith in me."

"I'm sure we won't, Jose, and we look forward to having you with us."

They moved on to a discussion of Jose's salary and benefits, and ultimately to his anticipated start date. Jose planned to resign his current job upon his return to Brazil, then take two weeks with his family before beginning with Aeronautics for a couple weeks of orientation and training.

"I suggest you bring your wife with you, Jose, so she can meet the people you'll be working with."

"That's very nice of you, Roger. I'm sure Maria will enjoy that."

Bill, Brad, Gordon and their wives, plus Roger and Cecily, had dinner with Jose that evening. The following morning he met with Dana to complete administrative paperwork, then flew home via Chicago.

By Friday evening, both Roger and Cecily were wrung out and exhausted. They begged off another party, another dinner out, settled for a relaxing evening in Roger's apartment with a bottle of wine and delivered pizzas, which they shared with Jen and Tommy.

They slept late Saturday, took the kids to a nearby Starbucks, settled onto a comfortable couch for a leisurely morning with lattes, pastry, the *Cleveland Plain Dealer* (her) and *The New York Times* (him). He dozed off part way through the *Times;* Cecily enjoyed watching him sleep, smiled, took his hand carefully in hers while he continued to doze and she played with the newspaper, not really digesting the news, thinking instead of the building intensity of their relationship. She was beyond happy. The kids were entertained with games on Cecily's iPad while devouring their third pastry.

That evening, Roger and Cecily dressed casually and enjoyed a relaxing dinner in a little steak house a short walk from Roger's condo building. (Marina fed the children, bedded them down.)

Back in his condo, Cecily pawed through his collection of CDs, popped one in his stereo. The voice of a female singer, tender, romantic, filled the room. Cecily turned to Roger, held out her hand. "Let's dance . . . this is one of my favorite songs."

Roger rose, slipped his arms behind her back to pull her close. She had her arms around his neck, they rocked slowly, their faces only inches apart. When the song ended, Roger released Cecily, walked to the corner, dimmed the living room lights, re-started the same song. He embraced Cecily again, and when the music stopped, he took her by the hand, led her into the master bedroom. They made love, then lay in each other's arms.

"Roger, I wish I didn't have to leave tomorrow."

"Me, too." He caressed her cheek. "This week has flown by much too fast."

"When will I see you again?

"Boy, Cecily, it's hard to say. Jose will be handling the Central and South American territories, which relieves me of a hell of a lot of work and travel. The people I met in the UK called me Tuesday and are coming in next week to meet with us, tour our facilities, look at our equipment, and hopefully discuss a contract."

"Phooey!"

"It may be 'phooey' to you, but it's my bread and butter!" They both laughed. "And there's a lot happening which I can't talk about . . . so I dunno, Cecily. I'll see what I can do to get to New York, and will call you every day, but that's the best I can promise at the moment."

Cecily rolled on top of him, whispered: "Then let's celebrate this past week!" They made slow, passionate love.

Roger and the children drove her to the airport Sunday afternoon. She had to promise Jen and Tommy she would come back to see them soon. They both gave her long hugs, Tommy cried as she exited the car; so did she when she hugged Roger.

8

The Management Meeting the following Wednesday morning was a shocker. After a shortened review and update on the status of Aeronautic's business, Bill announced he was negotiating the acquisition of a company near Boston which he felt would be a logical and profitable adjunct to Aeronautic's core business.

He described the company in brief, negotiations were still on-going, made it clear it was not a hostile takeover: the other firm was interested in being acquired to be part of the Aeronautic family. The owner and some of his management people would depart.

He emphasized that no one outside of the corporate officers were to breath a word of this to anyone, and while this was not yet considered "proprietary information" because Aeronautic Supplies, Inc., was not yet publicly traded company, he was still discussing an IPO and it was important not to muddy the waters.

His also said he was eager to complete the acquisition quickly so the IPO could proceed. If negotiations dragged, he would be required to delay the IPO, which he was determined not to do, or delay the acquisition. Both things could not happen simultaneously without the Securities & Exchange Commission smelling self-promotion to influence the sale of the newly issued stock, a serious No-No.

He also said "This acquisition, when it comes to pass, will not be our last."

There was considerable excitement among the corporate officers in response to his news. It was clear to all they were on the threshold of some substantial growth, personally and professionally.

"I've also made inquiries about the feasibility of forming contractual relations with, or acquisitions of, two companies overseas," Bill continued. "So, brace yourselves, because this firm's future, and yours, are about to explode!" He was smiling broadly. The atmosphere in his office became electric: the executives had just heard a stimulating half-time talk from their coach, and they were prepared to break down walls to win the game.

The meeting over, they rose to leave.

"Roger and Brad, please stay behind for a couple of minutes."

They both settled back into their chairs. "Let's go to Chez Francois for lunch, if your calendars are open. We need to talk. I've secured us a private room. Roger, ask Josh to join us."

That was a surprise, Josh was not yet senior management. Clearly, Bill had something special on his mind.

The private room at Chez Francois was small, but big enough for their needs. A rectangular dining table, capable of seating six dominated the room. There was little else in it except chairs, a sideboard, some artwork on the walls, an antique clock. Four place settings on linen mats graced the table along with crystal water glasses and silverware; no wine glasses or ashtrays.

Bill sat in one of the end chairs with Roger and Brad flanking him and Josh beside Roger. All three produced folded paper on which to make notes; Josh was still trying to figure out why he was attending this meeting. *("Must be good news of some sort!")*

A waiter took drink orders, they each requested a bottle of water. Bill suggested the waiter delay thirty minutes before returning to take lunch orders, another clue to Roger, Brad and Josh that they were in for some serious discussion. Bill cleared his throat, prepared to speak without notes.

"I've asked the you to join me in this meeting because I expect each of you to play a pivotal role in bringing to fruition what I'm about to tell you." He looked intently at each executive, then continued.

"I want to talk about heavy maintenance. Does that mean anything to you?"

"It does to me," said Josh. "That's when a major airline has to subject one of its aircraft to a very prolonged, thorough maintenance teardown. They virtually take the aircraft apart: wing, tail, flaps and rudder are dismantled, and the cables, bolts, wires, etc., are removed and checked. The landing gear is disassembled and checked for hydraulic leaks, cracks, whatever. The interior is gutted, seats, tables, overhead bins, carpeting, side panels, the entire enchilada, and the engines are removed and thoroughly inspected.

"It's an extremely time-consuming, complex and intricate undertaking mandated by the Federal Aviation Administration."

"That's correct, Josh. Where is it done?"

"Well," Josh continued, "ideally in the U.S. But to save money, most big airlines now farm out their heavy maintenance to offshore locations because the labor is vastly cheaper. They deliver their aircraft to heavy maintenance hubs in Mexico, China, El Salvador, or other garden spots around the globe."

"Correct! And the problem with that is?" Bill was pressing

"It's a big safety issue!" Josh replied. "Most of those mechanics don't speak or read English, but the service and repair manuals are written in English. So no one really knows what those foreign mechanics are actually doing: whether they're adequately checking and testing all the component parts, or whether they're re-assembling the aircraft properly. There have been several instances where they didn't!

"Those mechanics can't be licensed by the FAA because they don't understand English. That presents a major safety concern, and the FAA doesn't have sufficient personnel, nor a budget large enough, to base people overseas so they can inspect what's going on in those foreign maintenance hubs."

"Bingo!" Bill was smiling.

"What's got to do with us, Bill?" This was Roger.

"Nothing. Yet!" He sipped his water.

"Yet? You mean you're thinking of us getting into that business!"

"Not the heavy maintenance part, Roger. But I think we can develop a plan to provide the FAA with the kind of inspection help they need overseas. We can do it for less money than the FAA would require, and we can still make a profit."

"Mother of god, Bill! What are you smoking?" They all laughed.

"Hear me out. I'm going to give you the broad outline of my idea, then ask you fellas to fill in the blanks." He was smiling.

Bill began by describing a lunch meeting he had the previous week with an Ohio Congressional Representative. During the course of their conversation, the Congressman mentioned his concern about aircraft safety following two episodes when U.S. mechanics discovered missing parts or malfunctioning instruments on aircraft which had recently undergone heavy maintenance at overseas facilities.

The Representative also was critical of Congress for not providing sufficient funding to the FAA so the agency could transfer licensed professional mechanics to reside abroad, with responsibility for overseeing the work performed by those foreign heavy maintenance hubs.

"That," Bill emphasized, "opened my eyes to an opportunity." He turned to Roger.

"You just returned with a multi-million-dollar contract with Aviana Airlines. How about we sign a service agreement with the FAA to train small groups of foreign aircraft mechanics, those who *do* speak and read English, to become FAA licensed heavy maintenance supervisors.

"Then, you offer Avian the opportunity to have us train some of their mechanics to FAA standards so they can be 'rented' by Aviana to overseas heavy maintenance firms. That's a plus for us, a plus for Aviana, and a plus for those overseas maintenance outfits because the airlines and the FAA will be a hell of a lot happier and secure in the knowledge that the aircraft hauling the public are as safe as humanly possible. That's not the case now!"

"It's a damned interesting idea, Bill," said Josh, the head of Aeronautics maintenance operations.

"But Bill," interjected Roger, "why don't we just offer to train mechanics from the existing maintenance hubs?"

"They don't speak or read English, Roger. Wanna send them to school for a year before we can talk mechanics? I don't think so!"

"Ahhh, gotcha!

"Bill, let us play with this idea and see what kind of workable plan we can develop. Then Roger and Brad can fine tune the strategy and financials so we can make this baby fly, pardon my pun!"

"Okay, Josh, you're on!"

"Thanks, Bill, this is really exciting."

"Well let's take it to the next step. Let's make the same training offer to all of our overseas clients so the FAA has a strong portfolio of properly trained mechanics worldwide, people we've trained under our FAA contract.

"And at some point, Roger," he pointed at the young executive, "we just may decide we're better at heavy maintenance than anybody in China, Mexico or anyplace else except where Aeronautic has an established operations base. *Then*, Yes! We'll consider getting into the heavy maintenance business!"

"Bingo! Bill, to quote you! That's terrific!"

"Thank you, Josh. Now let's eat!"

"What's with the acquisition you mentioned this morning?"

Bill cut Roger short.

"Roger, let's talk about that later. It's a completely different subject."

Their conversation during lunch revolved entirely around Bill's idea for enlarging the scope of the company's business. They didn't focus only on Aviana as a target opportunity, but also other regional airlines they had under contract in the Europe and the Far East. The more they talked, the more excited they became, with Bill pressing for a meeting with FAA officials as quickly as the plan could be polished. Roger's schedule was a blur; his days so full of activity he hardly remembered up from down. The other executives were the same, especially Brad and Josh who, with Roger, became attached to Bill's hips, working closely with him every day as they commenced non-stop acquisition discussions with the Boston firm and long-range planning involving Bill's revelation about the FAA and heavy maintenance of aircraft.

The Majestic Airline executives from London were on board for all of Thursday and Friday, returning to London on an early evening flight Friday via Chicago to Heathrow. The meetings had gone exceptionally well, thanks largely to Josh and his impressive staff of engineers and technicians. Roger played account exec, and Bill functioned as Bill: the CEO very much in charge.

Roger asked Dana to plan an extensive introduction and training schedule for Jose Grossa, who was arriving Sunday evening from Brazil with his wife Maria. Next week, and most likely the week after, would be a horrendous jungle of meetings, lunches, social outings and dinners just like when Cecily was in town. *Bingo!* Roger had an idea.

Cecily answered on the second ring.

"Hi, gorgeous! Are you sitting down?"

"I can be! What's up?"

"YOU, are what's up!"

"What does that mean?" He could sense her excitement.

"Jose Grossa is flying in here Sunday for two weeks of orientation and training. He's bringing his wife, Maria, and since you have already spent a week in Cleveland and know all of the wives and management people here, I think you'd be the perfect hostess to keep Maria entertained while I keep her husband busy! Catch my drift!"

"Oh my god, Roger! Yes! Yes! Yes! I'd love to be Maria's hostess . . . and your concubine!!" She was giggling with delight.

"Okay, you're hired. Jose and his wife arrive Sunday afternoon, so why don't you fly out here tomorrow and plan to stay for a week."

"That's really all I can afford, Roger, because I start my new job at the ad agency the following week. But a week is a week! I'll be there with bells on."

"Okay, Honey. I'll have Dana Fed-X you tickets, and I'll pick you up at the airport. I suspect I won't be alone, because when Jen and Tommy learn you're coming to Cleveland for a week, you'll hear giggling all the way to Central Park!" They both laughed.

"I can't wait to hug them again, Roger. They're wonderful. Please tell Dana to book me on an early flight Saturday so we have the weekend together, or at least part of it. I love you, Roger, and can't wait to hold you."

"I love you too, Cecily, and am very eager to hold you, as well!"

Cecily arrived in Cleveland before noon Saturday, greeted at the airport by Roger and two very excited youngsters. She got a long hug and kiss from Roger, warm hugs from Jen and Tommy. At his apartment Tommy sat in her lap, his head resting on her shoulder as he pestered her with questions about how long she'd be staying, did she really have to go back to New York, etc.

Jen sat next to her, chattered incessantly about how glad she was to see her again, activities at school.

"I got an A on a spelling test because you grilled me, remember! Let's do that again this week cuz I'm going to have a math test! Ugh!"

"First, I have something for you and Tommy." Cecily went to her suitcase, returned a minute later with two wrapped packages, gave a small one to Jen and a larger one to Tommy. Jen tore hers open and exclaimed.

"CECILY! Oh, boy! Look, Daddy, they're gold hoop earrings, pierced earrings! Cecily, thank you so much! I'm going to go put them on!" She gave Cecily a kiss and left for a bathroom mirror.

Tommy meanwhile had unwrapped his package and was hugging a new baseball glove.

"Wow! Cecily, thank you so much. I'm gonna start PeeWee League soon, and this will be perfect!" He stood and gave her a hug.

"Well, honey, I think you've won the hearts of my kids, as well!"

"That's my plan!" She was smiling, gave him a quick kiss.

Jen returned to the living room, stood before Roger and Cecily modeling her new earrings. "I love these, Cecily. Thank you!" Jen again sat next to her, her head resting on Cecily's upper arm.

"I'll be glad to help you again with your school work, Jen, and you, too, Tommy, if you need help with your homework."

"Well . . . I'd rather play Monopoly or Chutes & Ladders!"

Cecily laughed, as did Roger and Jen.

"Boys!" said Roger. "We're all the same, no matter what age!"

Cecily enjoyed a girls' night out that evening, dining with Linda Lewis, Helen Steinberg and Toni Enright to plan a week of touring and entertainment for Maria Grossa, including assorted cocktail parties, dinners involving their husbands and Roger. They opted not to overdue it the first week mindful that Maria and Jose would be in town for two. In Cecily's absence that second week, the other three women would alternate being hostess to Maria to be sure she felt welcomed into the Aeronautic family.

Roger and Cecily met Jose and his wife at Hopkins International Airport Sunday afternoon, drove them to an exclusive hotel in Shaker Heights, close to the office. Dana had booked them a comfortable suite for their two-week stay. Mindful that they had had a very long trip with at least one, perhaps two, stopovers, Roger suggested they relax for the evening, dine in their suite, he and Cecily would meet them for breakfast at eight the next morning. He also handed Jose the keys to a rented sedan parked outside for their use during their stay.

Jose and Maria impressed both Roger and Cecily as charming, funny, very well educated, quick to laugh at themselves. Maria was attractive, five-five with black hair and dark, dashing eyes. She wore fashionable clothes and was clearly in love with her husband. Cecily felt a tinge of jealousy!

Roger brought both Jose and Maria, with Cecily, to the office Monday morning so they could say hello to management and other key employees in the company. Bill's wife, Toni, joined Cecily to shepherd Maria on a tour of Shaker Heights and Cleveland itself, focusing on a variety of upscale shops, the theatre, lunch with an influential group of women friends (some of whom Cecily knew) who immediately took to Maria.

Roger, meanwhile, began Jose's orientation, connecting him with Dana.

"She's the one who's really in control, Jose. Not me. Whatever you or Maria may need, any questions you may have, Dana's your source." All three laughed.

"Well, Dana, it is good to see you again, and know to whom I report!"

"We'll get along just fine, Jose. I'm a real easy boss!"

"Seriously, Jose, Dana has compiled your orientation schedule over the next two weeks, and will direct you to the people with whom you have appointments. You've already met a lot of them. I'm also here as a fall back for you, and I know Cecily and I would welcome an opportunity to kickback with you and Maria. Let's plan on dinner this evening."

"That would be great, Roger. Thank you. And now, Dana, lead the charge, please." Jose sat next to Dana as she began walking him through his orientation and training schedule, a blur of meetings, new acquaintances, questions, answers, notes taken and discarded, briefing papers, a prolonged customer review, strategies for securing prospect appointments, and a plethora of other opportunities and issues Jose would need to understand in order to operate effectively in about fifteen countries.

He had been in the industry for several years, knew the competitors and the territories. He was a very quick study on the why's and way's of Aeronautic Supplies approach to the business.

In addition to the dinner with Roger and Cecily, there had been several other social evenings during the week, one at Bill and Toni's home, another at the home of Brad and his wife, Linda, and a couple at restaurants. On Saturday, Roger, Jose, Bill and Brad played a foursome at the Shaker Heights Country Club. Toni, Maria, Linda and Cecily, who drove a cart but didn't know a putter from a potter, played behind the men. All eight showered and changed in the Club's locker rooms and had dinner in the Club's impressive dining-room.

Cecily bid farewell to all when they parted Saturday night, and to Roger when she flew back to New York Sunday afternoon. There were tears at the airport before her flight, as well as promises to talk by phone every day and meet again ASAP. Jen and Tommy tried to convince her not to leave, had to settle for a promise to return soon.

The following week Jose was left largely in Dana's care, spent four days traveling with Gordon White, EVP/Domestic Sales, visiting customers in Chicago, St. Louis and Atlanta. Roger, meanwhile, had narrowed the resumes he received from applicants for the Far East Area Manager's position, flew to San Francisco to meet with two different candidates and the executive recruiter who found them.

He enjoyed dinner at one of his favorite San Francisco restaurants, a spot in Japan Town. The following morning, he met with the recruiter, then with the two applicants. The first candidate, an American engineer with extensive business and residency experience in China and Japan, didn't strike Roger as a good fit for Aeronautic. His professional credentials were impressive, he spoke Mandarin, but there was something about his personality that Roger found . . . "disturbing."

The second applicant impressed Roger as another Jose. Frank Chang was Asian-American, 32, a slim five-nine, beaming smile, bright eyes, sharp as a whip. His experience and professional credentials were superb, he spoke four languages, still had relatives in China, had been traveling the Far East on business for five years, based out of Singapore. He and Roger clicked within minutes.

Roger had probed Frank in depth, even asking: "How did you get the name Frank?"

"That came in grammar school, an English language class. The teacher went around the room and gave each of us an American sounding first name, and mine stuck. It's been a great asset to me in business!" He smiled.

"I'll bet it has! So you don't object if my colleagues and I call you Frank?"

"You wouldn't even want to try my Asian name, so Yes! Frank is fine."

Roger was impressed that Frank knew so much about Aeronautic Supplies. He had obviously done his homework, knew the names of the principal players, details of the firm's product line, had read about the new Aviana Airline contract. His last question stopped Roger cold.

"Are you folks planning to go public?"

Roger paused, framing his answer before responding.

"Frank, that's a possibility. We've been entertaining the idea, and when the timing is right, we may elect to go ahead with it."

His pause had been long enough to alert Frank that he had hit a nerve; that management was probably planning an IPO soon, but Roger wouldn't/couldn't admit it. *("Nice dodge, Roger. That's a 'Yes' without you saying it!")*

Roger quickly changed the subject to describe the Area Manager position in detail and the orientation and training program Frank would endure in Cleveland. He advised Frank that another fella who will handle Latin and South America was currently training.

He detailed the company's compensation package, offered Frank the same deal they had given Jose. Frank thought for only a few minutes before accepting, knowing deep in his heart that the company was preparing and IPO and he would most certainly be a beneficiary. He wanted assurance of that.

"Roger, I like what I'm hearing and Yes! I'd like to be part of your team. Can you give me any assurance that when, or if, you undertake an IPO that I will be on the list for shares?"

"That would be a definite consideration if we do issue an IPO."

("Clever answer, Roger. I'll take that as a definite Yes!")

They shook hands, moved to a discussion of a probable start date, with Frank intending to give notice to his current employer the following morning. He was not married -- "I don't have time in my life now for romance!" -- so would be coming to Cleveland alone.

("God, I can relate to that, Pal. Where is Cecily? What's she doing?")

"Frank, I'm delighted. I think you'll enjoy it, we're a fine group of people, treat our employees well. You'll work your ass off, but you have a very good chance of getting rich while you do it. We have some aggressive plans in place to make that happen. I'd like you to come to Cleveland to meet the other executive managers. When would that be convenient for you?"

"I can make it next week."

"That's terrific, Frank. I won't be there because our CEO and I are negotiating a . . . an arrangement." He smiled; Frank got the message. "But, I'll have my admin, Dana, call you to set you up with everything you'll require: airline tickets, hotel, rental car, and a meeting with key managers. Late in the week I'll be back and will catch up with you.

"This also will give you an opportunity to meet Jose Grossa, who will be handling the Americas. He's Brazilian, lives in São Paulo. His wife, Maria, is with him. They're a wonderful couple. You'll like them, and vice versa. He's going through an orientation and training program now.

"I'll send you a letter confirming our interest in having you as part of our team. Meanwhile, let's have a drink to celebrate."

Roger returned to his hotel room after dinner with Frank, opened his laptop and began drafting emails: one to the management executives announcing his desire to hire Frank Chang; he included a summary of Frank's resume and details of compensation package. A second to Dana asking her to provide Frank with airline tickets, arrange his hotel and rental car, and set up confirmed appointments with Bill and Brad.

It was well after midnight before Roger was able to slide between the sheets. He was too tired to phone Cecily or his children.

PART 2

Heartbreak

9

He called Cecily at five Friday morning (8:00 o'clock in New York) and caught her just before she was leaving for her ad agency job.

"Guess where I am."

"Please tell me you're in New York!" He could hear the excitement in her voice.

"Not yet, Honey. I'm in San Francisco, and I've decided not to go home. I'm going to fly to New York so I can spend the weekend with you!"

"Are you serious? Oh my gosh, I can't wait! What time will you get here?

"I won't arrive until late this afternoon, and I'll take a cab to your apartment."

"Oh, Roger. Call me when you land at LaGuardia and I'll leave the office to meet you at home. What a great surprise!"

"I love you, Kiddo. See you in a few hours."

Their reunion was very passionate, in her vestibule, in her living room on the way to her bedroom, where they enjoyed each other's company for well over an hour.

They rose, showered and dressed for dinner. Roger had ordered a TownCar, waiting for them at eight. They held hands in the back seat while the driver wound his way to an exclusive French restaurant on Park Avenue, Roger's favorite from his many trips into and through New York. The restaurant doorman opened the car's rear door, gave them a very polite greeting, especially when he recognized Roger.

"Good evening, Mr. Manning. It's a pleasure to welcome you again."

"Thank you, Andre. It's good to be back."

Andre beat them to the entrance, swung open a heavy oak door with glass inserts. Cecily was awed by the atmosphere, the decor, the dining room illuminated by enormous cut glass chandeliers, a lit candle on every table. The thick carpeting, soft, the walls dark wood, the tables dressed in pale green linens with sparkling white napkins, brilliant sterling place settings, fine crystal glassware. A trio in one corner played soft mood music, customers engaged in quiet conversations. Tuxedoed waiters hustled silently among the tables, disappeared into a passageway leading to the kitchen.

Dinner was a marvelous French-cuisine feast, commencing with escargot, a salad, main course (tender roast beef for him, pan fried Dover sole for her), dessert and coffee. Lots of eye contact, fingers entwined at mid-table, toasts with their bottle of French wine, which Roger drank sparingly before switching to ice water.

They opted to have an after-dinner drink at the restaurant's elegant bar. Orderly racks of polished glasses of various sizes suspended above the bar, a long mirror behind the vast array of liquor bottles reflected the dining room behind them as they sat on the upholstered bar stools. A tuxedoed bartender laid linen cocktail napkins in front of them, took their drink orders, returned within a minute or so with their beverages of choice.

They whispered softly to each other, smiling, lots of tender eye contact, occasionally sipped their drinks, when Roger noticed a fellow at the corner of the bar staring at them.

He ignored the guy initially, but every time he glanced up and looked beyond Cecily, the guy was still staring at them. At one point he winked at Roger, who couldn't help thinking the fella was gay, perhaps trying to make a move on him despite the fact that Roger was accompanying a gorgeous woman.

The man paid his bill and rose as if to leave, but instead came up behind Cecily, called her by name! Cecily turned abruptly and looked at him.

"Remember me?"

"No, I'm sorry, but I don't." Cecily's answer was soft, hesitant.

"We met about three months ago at a hotel bar." The fella's speech was slurred; too much alcohol. "You told me you were in the entertainment business, helping guys like me relax so we could enter the lion's cage on

Monday morning. I've never forgotten that."

"I'm really sorry, but I think . . .

"Yeah, okay, I get it. Well, it's good seeing you anyway." He began to back way, looked at Roger, winked. "Have a nice night, sir." He turned and was gone.

Cecily stared into her glass.

"Who the hell was that?"

"I don't know, Roger. I really don't . . . ."

Roger wasn't buying, and she sensed it.

"I take it he isn't a former boyfriend!"

"No! Not at all. I don't even know him."

"You may not remember, but you've obviously met him before."

"Roger, I have no memory . . . ."

"Is that your line, a line you've used in a hotel bar: 'I'll help you relax so you're ready to enter the lion's cage on Monday'?"

"Roger, please." She was flustered, embarrassed, her face flushed the color of beets. "Let me explain . . . ."

"Not here!" He was suddenly angry, she could tell. His face, too, was flushed, his eyes cold, his voice even colder. He hailed the bartender and asked for his bill. Stood to pay: "Let's go!"

"We haven't finished our drinks."

"Now!" It was a command, not a request.

Cecily gathered up her purse, walked with Roger toward the entrance. Andre hailed them a taxi, opened the rear door. Roger gave the driver Cecily's address.

"Roger, please let me explain . . . ."

"Not here. Hold up until we're in your apartment." His voice was ice. They rode in silence. Once in her apartment, Roger sat on the sofa, Cecily beside him.

"How much financial experience do you have?"

"What?"

"You told me you worked for a financial firm on Wall Street and got laid off. So I'm asking how much financial experience do you have?" Roger was pressing, pressing hard.

"Roger . . . ."

"You lied to me, didn't you!" No answer. "DIDN'T YOU!"

Cecily nodded her head slightly.

"DAMMIT, ROGER! I LIED TO YOU ON THAT AIRPLANE BECAUSE I DIDN'T EVEN KNOW YOU. YOU WERE JUST A GUY TRYING TO MAKE A MOVE ON ME. SO I LIED TO A STRANGER! SO WHAT!"

"OKAY! I understand that! But how long did you hang out in bars?"

"Roger . . . please . . . ."

"I asked you how often you hung out in bars!" Cecily began to well up, tears rolling down her cheeks.

"What the hell were you doing . . . or can I guess correctly?"

"It's not what you think, Roger. It really isn't!" Tears were streaming down her cheeks.

"How many men . . . never mind, I don't want to know."

He stood, paced her living room.

"'Entertainment business!' Jesus, Cecily, do I wanna know how you entertained those guys? How many guys . . . THAT S.O.B . . . did you let him slam your ass like a screen door in a hurricane? Is that what 'entertaining' means?" He slapped a fist into his open palm.

"Roger, please believe me, I am not what you're thinking, and I haven't been in any bar since I met you."

"Wonderful!" His response was sarcastic. He sat in a chair, his elbows on his knees, his face buried in his hands. "Oh my god, Cecily. I can't believe the mess we're in." He looked up at her. "My kids, my job! Why the hell did you let me fall in love with you!"

"Because I love you with my whole heart, Roger. I want to spend the rest of my life with you."

"That's not going to happen, Cecily." He drew a deep breath. "You know I'm in a fiercely competitive business. And if people know I'm dating a . . . what? What do you call yourself? Prostitute? Call girl? Entertainer? Whatever the fuck . . . if people learn I'm dating whatever the hell you are, I'll be the laughing stock of the industry. I may as well go to barber school!"

"Dammit, Roger, it's not what you think." She was crying, hard. "Most times the guy just bought me a drink or two . . . ."

"'Most times?' How about the other times? What did they buy then? A wrestling match? A blow job? What was your specialty . . . never mind, don't tell me!"

"Roger, I've been trying to find a way to tell you about my past . . . what it was and what it wasn't." She was crying so hard it was difficult for her to speak. "Please . . . please forgive me for lying to you on the airplane about that financial thing . . . I didn't even know you then, didn't know what to say . . . god, I'm so sorry I lied to you, Roger. I never would have if I had any idea our relationship would become what it has."

"Oh, the hell with the lie! That doesn't matter. But this other stuff, selling yourself for sex with strangers. That's a really big deal, a really big deal *breaker*!"

"Please, Roger. I don't want to lose you, I'll do whatever you want me to, but please don't leave me . . . please, Roger, I love you . . . . you said you love me!"

"Hell!" His cold eyes starred at her. "It's one thing to have lied about a stupid job . . . but this 'entertainment' shit! What was that all about? You can't tell me it wasn't what I know damned well it was! So don't talk to me about love, for chrissake!" He turned away from her, then snapped back to face her.

"You *dare* talk to me about love! Jesus, if you had told me the truth on that flight to Rome we wouldn't be in this mess because I would never have been with you. If you'd just told me your fucking price I never would have sat with you!"

She was sobbing. He stood in front of her, she reached for him but he brushed her aside.

"Cecily, I've been breaking my back for ten years to get where I am." He used his finger to lift her chin, forcing her to look at him, tears streaming down her cheeks. "For ten years I've been working sixty- seventy- eighty-hour weeks with my partners to build our company. I've sacrificed time with my kids. I've lived on airplanes and in goddamn hotels until I could puke." He stood, angrily.

"And now . . . we're about to reach our goal, to go international, to broaden our commercial footprint. I shouldn't tell you this, Cecily, but we are about to go public, to sell shares on the stock exchange, and I'll be President of the entire ballgame" He was pacing, flailing his arms, turned and leaned close to her face.

"I'll be damned if I'll permit a call girl, a whore, to ask me to throw all that away. It's not fair to me, it's not fair to my children!" His eyes also began to well up. "And it's not fair to the company, for that matter."

Cecily sprang to her feet, her arms stiffly by her sides, her fists balled.

"I AM *NOT* A WHORE, DAMN YOU!'" She flashed a fist at him. "Stop belittling me! Listen to me! I am *not* what you think I am, and I never have been!"

"Horse shit! You've admitted selling yourself for sex, so what the hell do you call that? As for belittling you, I'm not belittling you any more than your behavior has belittled yourselfI" He walked away, stared at a wall, then turned to address her again.

"My god, Cecily! Think of the position you've put me in. How many other guys, in how many other restaurants, are going to walk up to you and say 'Hi, Cecily! Remember me?' Jesus, woman, I'm telling you I can't risk being with you if that's going to happen!"

"It won't!."

"Well, it happened tonight, so how the hell can you sit there and tell me it won't happen again! And think of my children. Granted, they don't know the meaning of prostitution now, but they will in a few short years. I don't want them teased unmercifully by other kids in school . . . 'You're Daddy loves a whore!' . . . 'How much does she charge?' . . . 'My Daddy would like to meet her!' Kids can be very cruel, and I just won't have it!"

Cecily sat, her face buried in her hands, her body shaking as she sobbed. A minute passed, then another. He was standing stock still, head hanging, looking at the floor. She looked up at him, her face a mess of tears, running eye makeup.

"Please, Roger. Please give me another chance."

He sat next to her, not close, not comforting.

"Another chance to do what? Embarrass the shit out of me? What the hell would have happened if we were entertaining one of my clients, or a prospect, and his wife? What the holy hell do you think their reaction would be? I'd be mortified beyond belief . . . I'd be dead in the water. 'Oh, you know that Roger Manning! He dates a whore'!"

That word again. It had a devastating impact on Cecily. She slid off the couch onto the floor, lay sobbing, her body contorted into the fetal position.

Roger stood, walked into her bedroom, returned carrying his overnight bag and briefcase. Cecily looked up, arms reaching for him. He avoided her.

"Where are you going, Roger?"

"I'm going to LaGuardia, goddamn you! I'll either sleep in the airport, or if I'm lucky I'll get a room at an airport motel."

"NoNoNo! Please, oh please, don't walk out on me, Roger. Give me a chance to explain."

He moved toward the apartment door.

"Look, Cecily. I suggest you throw away my phone number, because I'm going to throw away yours." He opened the door, exited, slammed it behind him.

Cecily fell flat on her carpet and sobbed. She sobbed well into the night, awoke early Saturday morning still sprawled on her living room rug. She struggled up off the floor, went into the bathroom, shocked at her image in the mirror. She looked and felt like ten miles of bad road. She washed and dried her face, picked up her phone, dialed Roger's cell phone. She let it ring and ring; no answer. She began crying again, couldn't stop.

She called her friend Margi, who answered in a sleepy haze.

"Margi!" Cecily could hardly speak coherently. "I need help!"

"Jesus, Cecily! What happened? It's only 6:30!"

"He left me!" She struggled through her tears. "He walked out last night, Margi! I need help!"

"Okay, Cecily, I'll get dressed and come right over. You try to calm down. Take a shower or something, and I'll be there as quick as I can." Margi walked into her apartment twenty minutes later to find Cecily lying on her sofa, crying uncontrollably.

"Good Lord, Cecily." Margi knelt on the floor next to Cecily's face, began to stroke her hair. "What on earth happened?"

"He told me he loved me . . . and then . . . and then . . . I don't believe what I've done!"

She proceeded to tell Margi, in detail, about the prior evening, the guy at the bar, Roger's immediate reaction, everything he asked and said about her past and what it could mean to him if his firm, his customers or prospects, his children found out.

"He called me a whore, Margi. And I deserve it . . . but I can't live without him . . . I can't . . . I can't!"

"Yes, you can, Cecily. Yes you can, and you're going to figure out how. It's not going to be easy, but time . . . ."

"Screw time! I want him now!"

"Well, it sounds like that's not in the cards. So, you're going to have to grow up and start over. But, for chrissake, stay out of cocktail lounges!"

Margi stayed with Cecily all day Saturday, slept on Cecily's couch that night, left at eight Sunday morning to go home, freshen up. Cecily was still asleep when Margi left.

Roger had lucked out. Despite the late hour, he had secured a room in a motel near the airport. He fell onto the bed, couldn't sleep. He kept thinking of Cecily . . . her damned past. He really did love her, but couldn't afford the potential for a disaster. What would Bill say . . . the other executives? He did the right thing walking out . . .he had to learn to forget her . . . that wouldn't be easy . . . he'd do what he always did, bury himself in business.

He dozed off well after midnight, woke with a start at 6:15, his cell phone was ringing. Christ, it was Cecily. He refused to answer, shut the phone off so he wouldn't have to hear it again.

But he couldn't go back to sleep, finally shaved, showered, dressed and took a taxi to the airport. He checked onto a nine o'clock flight to Cleveland, got a seat: tourist, but didn't give a damn. He wanted out of New York.

When he got home, he opened his briefcase and slammed it shut. He couldn't work. He was too upset, too distressed. The first time in years he had allowed himself to think about something other than business, and it blew up in his face. Never again. Never, never again. At least in business you could understand what you were getting into . . . but this love shit . . . never again.

His kids were surprised to see him home and Marina gone. They could tell he was very upset, face drawn and dark, temper close to exploding. He poured himself a double Chivas on the rocks, sipped some, dumped the rest down the kitchen sink.

"What's wrong, Daddy?" Jen. She climbed onto his lap, lay her head on his chest, felt it heaving as he cried. "Can I help you, Daddy?"

"I wish you could, Honey. But, No! I'll be okay." He lied.

"Did you see Cecily?"

"We won't be seeing her any more, Jen. She and I broke up."

"Oh, NO! What happened? Tommy and I like her. Can't you make friends again, Daddy!"

"It's not easy, Jen. I'm sorry, but it isn't. Something bad happened that has forced me to end our relationship. In the long run, it will be best for all of us, including you and Tommy. I promise."

"But, Daddy . . . .!" She, too, began to cry.

"I know it's difficult now, Jen, but we have each other, and it's better for Cecily and me, and for all of us, that she and I separate."

"I was hoping . . . Tommy and I were hoping . . . that Cecily could be with us . . . ." She sniffled.

"I know, Jen. I was, too." He kissed her forehead. "But I'm hiring a couple of guys to do a lot of my traveling so I'll be able to spend more time with you and Tommy. We'll be fine, I promise."

"She's really nice, Daddy. What went wrong?"

"Well, it's an adult sort of thing, Honey. Just take my word that I have done the right thing, okay."

"Okay, but it's not easy."

"I know, Jen. It's not easy for any of us, but sometimes life is like that."

She left his lap, ran into her bedroom, still sniffling.

He was a bear all weekend, Jen and Tommy pretty much staying in their bedrooms, engaged in games or books, didn't relish spending time with Daddy. He was angry, sad, depressed. Jen had shared with Tommy what Roger had told her earlier. They, too, were sad that the woman they hoped would live with them . . . become part of the family, keep them warm and comfortable when their Daddy traveled . . . that was not going to happen. They didn't know why, and Daddy wouldn't explain.

He didn't sleep well Saturday or Sunday night, three nights in a row without proper rest. He got up early Monday and was behind his desk at seven (Marina arrived to make the kids breakfast and drop them at school). He sat in his chair, swiveled away from his desk, stared out the window without seeing anything . . . just thinking . . . about her . . . what could have been but never would be. Damn, he loved that woman, had to stop thinking about her.

Dana entered his office at eight, was shocked when she saw his appearance: open collar, no tie, his face drained, melancholy, obviously sleep deprived, not the Roger she had worked with for so many years.

"Are you okay, Roger?"

"NO! I'M NOT!" His response was stern, angry, shouted. "I'm sorry, Dana, I've had a terrible weekend, but give me some time and I'll be alright," he lied.

"You don't look it. Is everything okay with Jen and Tommy?"

"Yes! Thank you. They're fine, or will be."

Dana rose and settled behind her own desk, shielded from the open office area by a metal-and-glass partition. She saw CEO Bill Enright enter his office, walked in behind him.

"Good morning, Bill."

"Hi, Dana! How's it going?"

"I'm concerned about Roger, Bill. He looks awful. I think something terrible happened to him this weekend."

"Okay, thanks for the heads up, Dana. I'll check him out." Bill rose from behind his massive desk, a marine *("once a marine, always a marine")* still in good shape, five-eleven, graying hair, about thirty-five years Roger's senior. He carried himself like the guy in charge.

He rapped on Roger's doorframe, settled into a visitor's chair across the desk.

"I've seen 'before' and 'after', but you look like 'in the process'! What's going on, Roger?"

Roger didn't answer right away. Looked at Bill, looked away, shook his head, struggled for composure. Then he unloaded. Didn't mean to share half of what he said, but once he got rolling he couldn't stop, told Bill everything, from the Rome flight to the devastating events of Friday evening. He choked up, looked at the floor.

"I'm sorry to hear that, Roger."

"I can't sleep, Bill. I haven't slept since Thursday night in San Fran. I can't stop thinking about her. We were so close, the first woman I've loved since I lost Janice." His eyes were watering. "Even my kids love her . . . but I know I did the right thing for us, for the business."

"Yeah, but was it the right thing for you? Or your children? Think of your children, Roger. They haven't had a woman in their lives since they were toddlers. You're denying yourself the comfort of a woman you love, and your children a chance to grow up with someone who could fill the vacuum left by Janice's death. Is that fair to them, to you, or to Cecily?

"Only you can decide that, Roger. I'm not saying you did the wrong thing, but I urge you to think very carefully before you burn that bridge. Once it's gone, there is very little likelihood it can be rebuilt. And take it from me, there are some decisions in life which should be made from your heart, not your head."

Roger swung back and forth in his chair.

"Bill, I just can't risk the chance that something like that would happen when I'm with a client or prospect . . . when she and I are together entertaining one of our customers. That would be a calamity of staggering proportions. And my kids . . . god, what would they think . . . they could be teased terribly if their friends found out."

"Maybe, maybe not. But always remember, Roger, that we all have things in our past we'd rather not have anyone else know. You're a great guy, but you're thirty-four, and you can't tell me you haven't fallen once or twice."

"I'm not, but I wasn't for sale as a pimp or paid boy-toy, either."

"I understand, Roger. But it may not be as bad as it's struck you. I'm sure it was a staggering blow, a real shocker. But, it also sounds like you didn't give her much of a chance to explain anything. I gather that was a part-time endeavor which happened long before she knew you. After all, she lied to you on an airplane after knowing you for only ten minutes.

"It's not my business to judge, Roger" Bill stood to leave. "If you're comfortable you've made the right decision, that's all that counts. But please think carefully before you slam the door, okay! And you do look like hell. Why don't you go home and get some rest."

"No, I'll be better off if I stay here."

"Well, we might not be!" He stood, headed for the door, turned back to Roger.

"I read that you found a fella in San Francisco to handle the Far East. That's great news, Roger, very positive. I look forward to meeting him later this week. Something to be happy about. Now give me a smile, will ya!"

Roger tried to smile.

"That's my boy. Have a better day, Tiger!" Bill left for his own office.

("A better day! I've just lost the only woman I've loved in so many years, and I'm supposed to have a better day. Shit!")

10

Things were not rosy in New York either. When Cecily finally woke Sunday morning Margi was gone, the apartment was deathly quiet. She washed her face, combed her hair, slipped on a housecoat, kept it on all day. She could not think of going out, had no desire to see anyone or do anything but sit in her apartment and mope.

She found Roger's toothbrush in her bathroom, threw it in the waste basket, then retrieved it and sat on her couch holding it, occasionally crying. She dialed Roger's cell phone once during the morning, got a busy signal; dialed again in the afternoon, got his voicemail and left him a message. He never called back. She didn't eat all day, wasn't hungry, didn't think she could hold down food.

She phoned Margi at six, brief conversation; Margi was meeting someone for dinner; did Cecily wish to join them? No way, thanks.

Cecily went to bed early, holding Roger's toothbrush. She cried herself to sleep; woke up about eleven, tried to sit up, fell back on her pillow and stared at the ceiling. Headlights occasionally flashed through her windows, briefly illuminated her bedroom. The world was still moving forward, nobody knows how I feel, nobody cares.

She fell asleep and woke again about two. She was slept out, lying in bed was not the answer. She stood, threw Roger's toothbrush out her bedroom window, brewed a strong pot of coffee, sat in her living room to make a resolution: she would get the hell out of New York. Too many lousy memories.

She found a pad and pen in her end table, wrote Roger a note to tell him she was sorry, then tore it up. Took another piece of paper, wrote "New

York SUCKS" and lay it on her coffee table so she would see it later in the morning and recall her resolution to get out.

("Where to go? Who the hell knows? Who the hell cares? Margi's right! Forget the son-of-a-bitch and get on with life.")

Then she suddenly spoke out loud, to no one: "Roger! Please forgive me for even thinking you're an S.O.B. You're not. I love you! Please accept my phone call. . . please, Roger, come back to me."

She phoned her office, feigned sickness, stayed home all day, never dressed, barely ate, threw up. She really was sick.

Roger buried himself in work, meetings, phone calls, reports, correspondence, more meetings, strategy proposals, he had so much on his plate, kept his head spinning, his mind occupied.

But he never stopped thinking of her. Cecily! What was she doing . . . how was she doing . . . why, for god's sake, why!

He picked up Frank Chang at the airport Thursday morning, got him checked into the hotel, brought him to the office for a meeting with Bill, then Brad. Gordon was traveling. He dropped Frank off with Josh in engineering, then he re-joined Bill and Brad, got a thumbs up on Frank, pulled him away from Josh and offered him the job as VP/Sales covering Asia and Australia. Frank was psyched, planned to fly back to Singapore on the weekend, quit his job Monday and return to Cleveland in two weeks to commence his orientation and training.

Roger found Jose and Maria and the four of them dined at a local restaurant that evening. The two new Area Managers hit if off, which pleased Roger. Maria was her usual vivacious self, helped the evening immensely. She asked about Cecily, awkward moment which Roger stumbled through, not very convincingly.

He took both Jose and Frank to the office Friday morning, leaving the rented car for Maria and whatever her plans were for the day. She had a full schedule, thanks to Toni, Linda, Helen and their broad assortment of good friends.

He met first with Dana to catch up on the status of his on-going business, especially the Aviana account and the agenda for the UK people from Majestic Airlines. He sat with Frank to dispatch with personnel matters, leaving Jose to embark on his schedule for the day. Roger and

Frank then met again with Bill Enright, and Roger drove Frank to the Airport for his long trip home to Singapore.

Roger closed out his week in a lengthy meeting with Brad Lewis to plan their Monday trip to Boston for their meeting with the owner of Custom Marine Upholstery.

The company was located in a small box-store building in a gritty section of Chelsea, across the Mystic River from downtown Boston. The building was old, unimpressive, with rolls of material and scraps of fabric strewn all over the floors and work tables. A half- dozen employees labored over sewing machines, another four or five worked at cutting tables.

It impressed Brad as a fire trap waiting to flare.

The firm had no outside sales force, generated its business from walk-in marine traffic or customers developed at recreational boat shows. The sales volume was iffy, the profit margins lower than ideal, the growth potential extraordinary if the business expanded to another industry and was marketed aggressively.

Hence, Bill's interest in owning it. He had said their first priority was to make "the joint" presentable, then think about structuring an outside sales program.

With their marching orders in hand, Roger and Brad had commenced discussions with Custom Marine Upholstery's owner. Most of the 'i's and 't's were already agreed upon: their mission was to sign the acquisition papers and arrange for Aeronautic's bank to transfer funds to the seller.

They also wanted to meet immediately with all of Custom's employees, advise them what had just happened, assure them there would be no layoffs.

Once back in their rental car, Brad turned to Roger.

"What the hell have we just done?" He was smiling, sort of!

"What do you mean?"

"Roger, that place is a dump! We'll never make that 'joint', as Bill described it, into anything approaching presentable."

"Right. But Bill wanted to buy, we got it at a fire sale price, and all it needs is for you and Josh to clean it up so you can perform an accurate inventory, and prepare to enhance the bottom line."

"You think that's all it needs?" Brad was incredulous. "What the hell are we going to do with it?"

"Brad, that's just the backend of a new business. We can't operate out of that place. We bought the business, not the building. It isn't at all compatible with the image we want for our company."

"So what's your angle?"

"We need a first class interior design presence. This place is just a production outlet, but it does need to be cleaned up, put on a solid financial footing. You and Josh prepare an accurate inventory of its assets. I can't worry about that.

"So, let's go look at some property suitable for an exquisite, first class fabric and design studio . . . something that drips elegance . . . screams upscale fashion . . . shouts expensive. Bear in mind, our customer base is people who spend millions on jets and very large, fancy yachts."

"Got it. So where do we look for this space?"

"On Newbury Street in downtown Boston. But not just any-where. We need to be within a block of Boston Common. That's the really upscale block on Newbury. So, you and I are about to meet with a commercial real estate guru who says she has just the spot we're looking for!"

"My god, Roger, you are some kinda operator."

"You just learning that?" They both laughed.

The real estate agent showed them three different properties which seemed to fit their criteria. It was the third one that rang their chimes: large glass fronted retail space right on upscale Newbury Street, less than a block from Boston Common and a luxury hotel.

The retail space had the potential for an elaborate carpeted and elegant showroom, dramatic lighting, a lounge, coffee bar, glass enclosed "consulting" offices, and an artistic gallery of color photos of aircraft and mega yachts decorated by AeroMarine Design.

It would be staffed, not by sales people, but by "interior decorators" with a strong sense of design, effective use of color, sensitivity to the decor and ambiance preferred by each marine or aircraft client. And the retail space itself: Roger made it clear to Brad he intended to spend whatever amount it took to make it look like Steve Jobs had envisioned it: lots of glass, open floor plan, light ambiance, a welcoming atmosphere.

They signed a rental agreement with the proviso that it take effect only after they had secured the approval of Aeronautic's CEO. They assured the selling agent that would occur within twenty-four hours.

With an extraordinary day behind them, the two execs headed for Logan Airport and a flight home to Cleveland. They chatted excitedly in the car, in an airport bar prior to their flight, and on the flight itself.

"How'd it go?" Bill asked Tuesday morning, even before the two executives had sat around Bill's conference table.

"Outstanding, Bill. We closed on the acquisition of Custom Marine Upholstery, and we'll file papers with the Massachusetts government today to register the name AeroMarine Design.

"We also met with all of the employees, about ten or eleven people, and advised them of the ownership change and our intent to appoint a new production manager from the inside, if one is qualified. That's up to Josh."

"That's great news, Roger. Thank you, both of you, for all you've done to successfully conclude this expansion of our business."

"He's not done, Bill. Wait until you hear part two!" Brad was smiling.

Bill starred at Roger, a questioning look on his face.

"Bill, since we were in that neck of the woods, we met with a commercial real estate gal who showed us some excellent retail properties in downtown Boston. One, in particular, struck our fancy as an ideal showroom for a very upscale design and fabric studio in which to show customers our expertise in helping them select the right fabrics and designs for their upholstery, carpeting, walls, whatever the hell they want covered. It's on Newbury Street, just one block from Boston Common and a fancy hotel. . . ideal location.

"That's where the money really is, as you know. The Chelsea firm is just a battery of sewing machines to handle production once we've made the sale. The sales will come from our new showcase gallery on Newbury Street, maybe an outside sales person if we find that's necessary. I'd like to wait on that to avoid the expense.

"The Chelsea place needs some serious organization, cleaning up, which Brad and Josh can handle, primarily so they can perform an accurate inventory valuation."

"And you . . . .?"

"I've got to find the stylists, fashionistas, whatever, to design and run the showroom. I think I'm going to find the head guy or gal in Rome, either working for or with Aviana, and turn him/her loose on the showroom decor, inventory selection, staffing, and so on. The Italian accent will, in my judgement, be a big asset."

"Is it smart to raid Aviana for that person?"

"I don't think I'll have to, but I can use them as a resource."

"Then what do we do with the Chelsea operation?"

"We only bought the business, Bill, not the building. Once Josh and Brad get the business end squared away, we're going to move the people and equipment to the back end of the Newbury Street outlet. Plenty of room in what was a retail stockroom. That way we consolidate the entire operation in one location. . . one rent, with a senior retail manager to oversee the entire shooting match."

"All we need from you, is a nod of your head Bill so we can sign the lease. Are you nodding, Bill?"

Bill started laughing. "Go for it, Roger. I trust your judgement. Get everything off the ground as quickly as you can so AeroMarine Design is up and running sooner rather than later. I'll handle the Board. I want to proceed as quickly as possible with the IPO. I want our stock on the street, actively trading."

"Thank you, Bill. Consider it done!"

The days were not anywhere near as exhilarating for Cecily. She never left her apartment until Wednesday morning, and that was just a brief walk on Columbus Avenue to pick up a few groceries so she didn't starve, although that idea also had some appeal! She had dialed Roger's cell number three more times, but all she got was his voicemail, he never called back. Still, she heard his voice.

She was having enormous difficulty letting go. She hoped in her heart of hearts he would call, or answer when she called him. She refused to accept that it was really over. He had become so important to her, said he loved her, but that was before! Could he, would he, ever resume contact. She could not take him as just a friend . . . not after all they had shared together . . . but even friendship, that seemed doomed.

The idea of leaving New York was growing on her. There were too many memories, not all of them pleasant, certainly not the other evening. She was starting to hate her co-op, couldn't stand looking at the bed where she and Roger had made love. Decided to sell that even if she didn't move. But she was going to move, if she only knew where.

She had a dinner date with Margi that night; intended to tell her of her plans to vacate the City. Maybe she could help Cecily figure out where, and how, to find a job in a strange city. Doing what?

They met at the same restaurant where Margi had told her she better fess up to Roger in person before their relationship went too far. "It's important to tell him yourself," Margi had said. Well, she didn't follow that advice, and look where it got her. She was sitting at an outdoor table with a glass of wine when Margi walked up, sat opposite her, and said: "You look like you've been hit by a train."

"I have been. That's how I feel."

"Look, Cecily, you've got to let go. You've had plenty of time to cry and get it -- get him -- out of your system. You've got to go back to work, begin to go out, live life. This is not a dress rehearsal."

"I know, I know. But I still love him, Margi. I can't forget that, I can't let go of that." Her eyes began to well up. "I can't believe I didn't follow your advice, and I screwed myself. I've lost the only man I've really and truly loved." She began crying.

"Oh, Cecily. I know it must be devastating for you, and I wish I could help. But I don't know what to do for you, other than offer you a shoulder to lean on. And you have to stop crying on it or I'll drown!" Her attempt at humor flopped, although Cecily did try to smile through tears.

"I'm going to leave New York."

"What! You have friends here, a nice apartment in a great location. You love it here."

"I *hate* it here! Too many lousy memories. And I'll make friends someplace else. I hate my apartment, I hate the bed where we made love. If I need to start over . . . I'm going to start over someplace else." Tears rolling down her cheeks.

"But where?"

"Well, my Dad lives outside of Boston. He moved there to be near his brother after my Mom died two years ago. I'm thinking of moving in with him until I get on my feet, then get my own place in the city."

"That might be a great idea, Cecily! Will your Dad be up for that? Sometimes parents don't want their kids screwing up their lives again!"

"Oh, I think Dad would love it. I might not, but he would. And it would just be temporary, until I land a job and find my own place."

"Well do it, then! Give it a shot, Girl. It's better than sticking around here, threatening to hang yourself! And you'd still be close enough for us to get together there or here."

"Okay, I think I will."

"Well, great. See, you feel better already. Let me order a drink, and we can have dinner and talk more about it. It's a wonderful idea."

Margo paused, looked directly into Cecily's eyes.

"And, I want to introduce you to a friend . . . a *male* friend."

Several nights later, Cecily and Margi were seated at a cozy table for four in an attractive rustic/contemporary restaurant on a corner of West 12th in the West Village. They were nursing glasses of wine while they waited for their dates: Margi in anticipation of seeing her boyfriend; Cecily very nervous, almost dreading the arrival of her blind date. She didn't feel ready to "be with" another guy, especially a stranger. Margi insisted.

The two men walked in together, both in tailored suits and carrying briefcases, casually laughing at something, obviously associates in the same office. Margi's date bent and kissed her on the lips, then straightened, reached across the table and introduced himself to Cecily. Mike Donaldson stood near six feet, slim, ready smile, firm handshake, very out-going.

Margi then introduced Cecily and her date for the evening: Dave Michaels, about five-eleven, mid-thirties, easy smile, warm personality. He shook Cecily's hand, sat in the chair to her left.

"I'm very pleased to meet you, Cecily. I've heard about you from Mike via Margi. I work with Mike, and have known Margi for several years."

"Margi says you're lawyers."

"Yeah, Mike and I are with the same firm. Some people might say we're sharks! I'm in corporate law, and Mike is into wills and trusts and 'death-do-us-part' kind of stuff!" He was smiling, gave a friendly wink to Mike and Margi. Cecily was laughing. It felt good.

"How about you, Cecily?"

"At the moment, I'm between jobs." She glanced quickly at Margi. "But I expect to be relocating to Boston shortly, and I'll end up doing whatever pays my bills."

"Why Boston? What's there? Why not stay in New York?"

Margi interrupted so Cecily wouldn't have to answer.

"Cecily has recently broken up with someone, Dave, and it has hit her particularly hard. She wants a change of scenery, and I think it's a smart idea. She needs the break, and she has family near Boston, so that's a logical place for her to settle."

"I'm very sorry to hear about your breakup, Cecily. I know from experience that kind of thing can be devastatingly difficult. I wish you luck, and I hope you won't hesitate to call on me if there is any way I can help."

"Thank you, Dave. I'm sure I'll grow up."

"Aaahhh, it's not a question of growing up, Cecily. It's just a matter of getting on with life . . . of realizing that your world has not come to a screeching halt! I know, I've been there myself not too long ago."

Cecily was eager to pry, to ask when, how, what did you do, what *are* you doing, how long did it all take? But she kept her mouth shut, sipped her wine, hoped the moment would pass quickly. But the thought of Roger stuck in her mind. *("Will I ever forget him? I wouldn't bet on it!")*

Dinner was excellent, conversation among the four was light, gay, funny, not at all prying. The two lawyers argued over the bill, finally agreed to split it. They all rose to leave, Mike and Margi making it clear they intended to share a cab uptown to Margi's apartment.

"Well, Cecily, I cannot in good conscience permit you to cab it alone to wherever you live," Dave said. "Please let me escort you that far. I promise I won't pressure you to invite me in, or suggest we go to my digs."

Cecily laughed.

"You're a knight in shining armor, Dave. But I can find my way home, honestly."

"Won't hear of it. We'll cab to your place so I can make sure you get into your building safely, and then I'll disappear like dust if that's what you wish." He was secretly hoping that wouldn't happen.

They talked all the way uptown. Dave got out of the cab with Cecily in front of her building, left the taxi door open so he could get back in if she did not extend an invitation. He reached for her hand.

"It's been a delightful evening, Cecily. You're everything Margi had told Mike you were. I'd like to see you again." He began to pull her close, but she balked.

"Please, Dave. I'm just not ready for another relationship. I enjoyed this evening very much, and I'd welcome an opportunity to see you again. Can we leave it at that . . . for now?"

"Absolutely. But I'm going to get your phone number from Margi, and I *will* call you, I promise."

"Thank you, Dave. And thank you for understanding."

She turned to enter her building, he re-entered the taxi. Once in her apartment, Cecily sat in her living-room . . . and cried.

She phoned her father the next morning to say she was coming home "for awhile" and could he tolerate her company. He, of course, was thrilled, eagerly anticipated her arrival and visit.

She took a bus to Boston, transferred to the subway, rode the Green Line to Wellesley. Her Dad met her at the station. Once settled into the living-room of his home, Howard Sommers fixed his daughter and himself cold drinks, and prepared for a serious conversation. He could tell by looking at her something was wrong.

"What is it, Cess? Something is really bothering you."

She burst into tears. Howard put his arm around her, felt her body shaking, held her tight until she was composed enough to speak. She proceeded to tell him everything about her flight to Rome, her time in Rome, the guy she met and fell in love with, their time in New York and Cleveland, his quick departure. She left out the exact reason, felt her Dad did not need to hear she had occasionally acted as a call girl in a hotel bar. That wouldn't go over too well.

Howard tried his best to comfort his daughter. It wasn't easy.

She finally told him she had put her co-op in New York on the market: "I don't want to see that apartment again, and I don't want to be in New York; too many lousy memories." She announced her desire to "bunk in" with him until she could find a job in Boston and get her own digs. He assured her she was more than welcome.

"Thank you, Dad. You're very understanding."

"Hey, you're my daughter, and I stand ready to help you any way I can. Would you like me to phone this young man and . . . ."

"Good lord, No! Dad, it's over, he made that abundantly clear.
I'm just having a hard time coming to grips with that. I think getting out of New York will be a big help to me . . . the change of scenery, new digs, a new job, new people."

"Well, then, you settle in here and stay as long as you'd like." He kissed his daughter on the forehead. "That guy may no longer love you, for whatever reason, but I sure as heck do."

"Thank you, Dad. I love you, too."

Cecily stood, picked up her suitcase, climbed the stairs to the second floor, entered the spare bedroom. It looked different than her bedroom in New Jersey, new furniture, new curtains. But her old stuffed animal still sat on the dresser along with a framed photograph of her parents and brother. She felt comfortable, welcomed, safe.

She lay on her bed: could not stop thinking about Roger; smiled at the thought of her Dad calling him! What on earth would he say! What would Roger say!

She rose and opened the closet door, shoved aside her university cheerleader's outfit *("I can't believe Mom saved that!"),* hung the clothes from her suitcase. She thumbed through a couple of her old books, a textbook from college, a novel, her yearbook. She picked up the photograph of her family, the smiling faces of her Mom, Dad, brother William: Mom and brother deceased. That brought a tear to her eyes, she replaced the framed picture, flopped face down onto the bed, buried herself in the pillow, tears wetting the cover.

Several minutes later there was a soft knock on her doorframe and Howard entered her room.

"Look, Cecily, I realize your loss of this fella has hit you very hard. I'll do whatever I can to help you get over it. I suggest we begin by going out for a pizza!"

Cecily turned, looked up at her Dad, and burst out laughing.

"Pizza! Why didn't I think of that! You're a genius, Dad, I'd love to share a pizza with you."

She dried her eyes, followed him down the stairs, minutes later they were sitting at a table in a Wellesley Center pizza joint, laughing about old times.

Bill had pulled Roger and Brad into his conference room for what would normally be a regular Wednesday morning business discussion. However, he had made it known to both executives that he intended to discuss a major reorganization of the company. Anticipation was high as the two senior managers settled into chairs, as was concern about who or what was about to be "reorganized."

"Let me begin by telling you that at the Board meeting yesterday, I told the Directors I intend to retire by the end of the year. I'm pushing sixty-nine. I've been at the helm of this company since you fellas were in high school, and I intend to spend the balance of my life with Toni, our children and grandchildren."

Roger and Brad expressed dismay at Bill's news. Bill continued.

"I also told the Board that before I retire, I intend to broaden the footprint, the focus, and the reputation of this company to make it a world-class player. I do not want to abandon our core business, but I believe we're in a perfect position to expand our horizon. Our discussion of heavy maintenance the other day is an example of what I mean.

"The Board has endorsed my vision, beginning with the formation of a holding company, AeroMarine International, Inc. (AMI). The present company, Aeronautic Supplies, Inc., will change its name to AeroMarine Supplies (AMS), and becomes a wholly-owned subsidiary of the holding company.

"Also under the AMI umbrella will be two new subsidiaries: AeroMarine Diversified Operations (ADO), which will run all future acquisitions including AeroMarine Design, and AeroMarine Global Finance (AGF), which assumes responsibility for financial planning, currency and cash management, investment strategies and related financial operations worldwide."

"Bill, you're completely remaking the company!"

"Yes, we are Brad. Our financial position is strong, and soon will be a lot stronger. More importantly, our skills base is first class, and a lot of that is due to the two of you and your competence in managing the business and hiring the right people." He took a swig of water, then continued.

"Roger, you're being promoted to President of the holding company, AeroMarine International, and President of AeroMarine Diversified Operations. You will supervise all of our acquisitions in support of our core business. You'll need to begin thinking of people to replace you as President of Diversified and your current job at AeroMarine Supplies. As President of the holding company, you will be running the entire shooting match so you cannot devote a lot of time to those subordinate operations.

"And you're going to do this at a salary of one-million-dollars annually."

"WOW! My god, Bill! What can I say! . . . This is an unbelievably exciting and generous opportunity you and the Board are giving me. I can't wait to get started!"

You'll report to the Board, on which I will remain Chairman and CEO, temporarily CEO, which you'll own in a few months."

"Your first acquisition" Bill continued, "will be the Boston-based company, a leader in decorating custom-built mega yachts, the 200- and 300-foot privately- and corporately-owned yachts. If they can upholster, carpet and drape a 300-foot yacht, they sure as hell can do it to a privately or corporately owned jet, or a *fleet* of jets. That's how I want to expand their business under our direction.

"I see no reason for us to farm out to subordinate firms our upholstery and interior decoration requirements. If you two hire the right people, and position *our* subsidiary as a high fashion, interior decor resource, we can keep the business in-house, and make good money doing it."

Roger and Brad smiled at each other; Bill resumed his briefing.

"FYI, I'm also discussing, through a couple of intermediaries, the potential acquisition of a company in The Netherlands. If we find we can manufacture behind the European Union's tariff barriers, our pricing becomes a lot more attractive to our European prospects and customers, shipping costs will be negligible compared with trans-Atlantic rates, and we can establish cockpit simulator facilities in Europe.

"Also, there's a couple of excellent naval architectural firms in Holland who design and manufacture the mega-yachts we're talking about. If we buy the electronics firm, we can expand the profile of its business overnight. And, like Aviana, it just might open the door for an FAA consulting agreement for us to train Dutch mechanics so they get licensed by the FAA and rented out by their employer, our subsidiary!"

"This all very exciting, Bill, but where do you fit in all of this corporate expansion and re-organization?"

"As I said, I will be CEO of AeroMarine International, the holding company, and Chairman of the Board of Directors. But remember, I'm only good for the next several months. Then you fellas take the helm."

"My god, I'm glad you've given us some warning!!"

All three laughed at Brad's remark.

"Now, Roger, you are clearly going to have a plateful. I want you by my side constantly to help me identify compatible acquisition opportunities, and negotiate our purchases. We -- the Board and I — are not interested in any hostile takeovers because of the expense and time involved. We also don't want reluctant employees."

"Brad, your financial expertise will be crucial, not only in terms of the acquisitions, but in bringing all of our diversified operations on line financially so we maximize our return for the benefit our people, ourselves, and our soon-to-be shareholders. I expect you to play a pivotal role in making this happen, and in managing it financially.

"Your new job as President of AeroMarine Global Finance, puts you in charge of all of our financial operations, worldwide. You will be responsible for the staffing and organization of Global Finance, as well as blueprinting all of the financial schedules, investing and reporting for maximum benefit to all concerned. You will report to Roger at a starting salary of eight-hundred-thousand per year!" Bill smiled.

Brad was shocked. It took several seconds for what Bill had just said to register, and when it did . . . . "Good lord, Bill! What a surprise! What a fantastic opportunity! I can't begin to thank you. This is awesome!"

"You can also thank our Board. As I said, all of this has been Board approved."

"Man, what a thrill. What a challenge! I can't believe it!" The two young executives gave each other high fives, back pats, beaming smiles.

"Good! Let's think about lunch." Bill buzzed for the waiter.

The lunch conversation was extremely upbeat. Bill had just made his two senior executives so happy, so primed, so ready to walk on water! He sat back and enjoyed their excitement, satisfied and proud himself that the Board had supported him in this endeavor.

"Bill, what about Josh? He's very valuable to our company, I think, and to our growth. Where does he fit in all of this?

"What do you have in mind, Roger?"

"At the very least, he should be made an EVP. We just promoted Dan Winslow, and Josh is equally important to us."

"You're right. I'm sorry I didn't think of that. Consider it done. Why don't you tell Josh this afternoon?"

"I think it would mean a lot more coming from you."

"Okay, I'm on it."

While Roger and his colleagues were buying a company and leasing an upscale showroom facility in downtown Boston, Cecily was being interviewed for a job as receptionist and billing clerk at a large dental practice in Boston's Copley Square, a stone's throw away!

She had seen the practice's ad in the *Boston Globe* and had already been moved to the head of their applicant list because of her maturity, administrative experience, and drop-dead good looks. The interview, with two of the five oral surgeons who owned the practice, was penetrating but not particularly difficult for her.

She had held a similar position in New Jersey before moving to Manhattan; covered her time in the Big Apple by suggesting she had tried modeling but "got fed up with starving myself and being treated like a hunk of meat." She was moving to Boston -- Wellesley, actually -- to be with her elderly widowed father.

"When can you start, Cecily?"

"Tomorrow morning, if you'd like!"

The balance of her two-hour visit dealt with her salary, working hours, and a tour of the practice's facilities, introductions to the medical records staff, an IT specialist, dental hygienists. She would meet the other three oral surgeons when they weren't busy with patients.

"Welcome, Cecily. We are delighted to have you with us."

"Thank you, Doctor. I'm pleased to be working with you, your associates, and your staff. I'll do my best to make sure you remain convinced you've made a good decision."

Cecily was humming to herself as she walked to the nearby subway station, eager to tell her Dad about her new job, determined to find an apartment in Boston ASAP.

After two weeks on the job, she could honestly say she loved it. She got along extremely well with the five surgeons who owned the practice, their surgical nurses, dental hygienists and the other women in the spread of offices who handled medical records and a variety of administrative duties.

Her salary was good, she was meeting a lot of new people; she was thrilled not to be living in New York any longer. Her New York co-op had sold, leaving her with $200,000 in cash after she paid off the mortgage, so she had begun looking for a Boston condo or rental apartment.

As she did every morning, she settled into a seat on the subway and thumbed through the morning's *Boston Globe*. She normally didn't pay much attention to the business section, but today something caught her eye. It was a brief item in the "People" section:

> Roger A. Manning has been appointed President of a newly-formed subsidiary of AeroMarine International, Inc., a leading aircraft supplier based in Cleveland
>
> Manning is also President of AeroMarine Diversified Operations, responsible for acquiring a variety of companies here and abroad which will complement and expand AeroMarine's business globally.
>
> The firm has already acquired a small upholstery company in Chelsea and is merging it into a newly-formed upscale fashion outlet on Newbury Street. It serves the interior decorating needs of private and regional aircraft and multi-million-dollar yachts. The name of the new company is AeroMarine Design.

("Oh my god, it can't be it! Roger will be spending time in Boston! I'm trying to get over him, and now he'll be working here! Should I try to call him? No! No! No! Forget it!")

But she couldn't. The thought was like glue, consumed her thinking all day. She didn't tell her father when she got home that evening; thought of calling Margi in New York; *("What should I do, Margi?").* Thought better of that, too.

Could she stand to be so close to him and not make contact. What would she say? What would *he* say? She lost him once, why risk another episode? She'd be better off if she hadn't even seen the news item. But she had, and she couldn't forget it. Really didn't want to forget it.

She lay in bed that night, could not fall asleep thinking of Roger, the time they had together in Rome, New York, Cleveland before . . . before! Could that happen again? Did she *want* it to happen again? Yes, but would it. He's probably dating someone special; maybe engaged. Better to let go . . . she began crying, softly at first, then uncontrollably.

She did not get a lot of sleep; could not get him out of her mind, even during her busy workdays. She had been so happy in her new environment, making new friends, meeting new people . . . but now! She thought constantly of him, wanted him back, didn't know what to do, so did nothing but mope. And hope.

Two weeks later, she saw another item in the *Globe:*

> AeroMarine Design is opening an upscale design and fashion boutique on Newbury Street which will cater to the interior decor needs of the owners of private and commercial aircraft and large motor yachts, according to Roger A. Manning, President of AeroMarine Diversified Operations,
>
> Manning said he is looking for a manager "with extensive fashion or interior design credentials" to properly counsel yacht and aircraft owners on the "look and appeal" of their vessels.
>
> This is the first of several acquisitions planned by AeroMarine Diversified Operations in the U.S. and abroad, Manning said.

("Good lord! If Roger ever gets on the subway we're bound to bump into each other! What then? I've got to find an apartment in Boston quick. Can't stay so close; can't risk an occasional meeting; couldn't stand it. And I don't want to see him riding with another woman!")

That evening she did tell her Dad she intended to spend the weekend looking for her own place in Boston.

"I have to move, Dad. I need to be on my on."

"Well, I'm going to miss you, Cess, so I hope you won't be a stranger."

"I won't, Dad. I promise, but I just need my own space."

She didn't tell him why.

The following weekend she was back in New York, nervous, didn't feel comfortable, especially when the cab dropped her in front of Margi's co-op building, across West 81st Street from the north side of the Museum of Natural History. Her co-op had been on West 77th, facing the south side of the same Museum. Same neighborhood, same lousy memories.

Margi opened her door in response to Cecily's rap and the two women embraced as close friends do. She led Cecily into her living room, they both settled onto the couch.

"Margi, I think I'm going crazy."

"It's that guy, isn't it? I thought you were making good progress forgetting about him."

"Well, I kinda was, but in the past three weeks there have been two articles in the *Boston Globe* mentioning his name, even quoting him, because his firm is opening some kind of design firm on Newbury Street. I've even seen him interviewed on local television. Gawd, Margi, if he's going to be spending time in Boston I'm afraid I'll bump into him, or meet him on the subway! I think I should move to Philadelphia or St. Louis!"

"That's nonsense, Cecily. You've made a commitment with your Dad to locate to Boston, and you've found yourself a good job. You can't permit the memory of this guy to dictate where you live."

"That's easy for you to say."

"Let me make some coffee and we'll talk." Margi rose, walked into her kitchen, leaving Cecily alone on the couch to think. When she returned, Cecily was dabbing at her eyes with a tissue to wipe away tears. Margi set the coffeepot and cups on her coffee table, again sat next to Cecily, put her arms around her shoulders and pulled her close, could feel Cecily's body shake as she cried for a minute or two.

"Look, Cecily, you *will* go crazy if you don't get over this guy. You've got to put him behind you. It's over, all over. And it doesn't do you any good to keep dwelling on it . . . him."

"I blew it, Margi, didn't I? I blew it!"

"Yes, I'm afraid you did. But that's history, Cecily. There's a whole world out in front of you. Embrace it. There's another fella out there looking for you, and he'll find you. Just give it some time, and try to stop thinking about the guy who walked out. He's gone!"

"Well, he's *not* gone if I'm going to keep reading about him in the newspaper, or see him on television, or bump into him in a restaurant. What if he's with another woman? I couldn't handle that, Margi, I really couldn't."

Margi paused long enough to pour them both a cup of coffee.

"Look, Cecily." She held her friend's hands. "You're very good looking . . . when you're not crying." Cecily tried to smile, failed. "You're smart, you have a very good job, you're close to your Dad, you're making new friends, and you're looking for an apartment in the center of a very vibrant city. The world is your oyster, so forget the dead fish!"

Cecily did laugh at that line.

"I'll try to remember that: oysters, not dead fish!"

"There! See, you feel better already. Let's enjoy our coffee, then you freshen up, and we'll have a girl's day out in *my* vibrant city: lunch, maybe a show or art museum, and then a fancy dinner. How does that sound?"

"It sounds like heaven." Cecily sniffled, then embraced her close friend. "I don't know how I'd be able to get by if it weren't for you, Margi. You're such a wonderful friend."

Dan Winslow, the Corporate Communications VP, had issued a series of press releases announcing AeroMarine International's new corporate organization, and the promotions of Roger Manning and Brad Lewis to positions of responsibility for management of the firm's worldwide business expansion.

He had achieved substantial coverage in the business pages of the most important dailies nationally, as well as the leading business publications and major aviation professional journals in the U.S. and abroad. His phone was beginning to ring off the hook with calls from financial analysts eager for additional information on the company's plans and a "hint" of the firm's anticipated quarterly revenue and net earnings.

He didn't provide any "hints" despite unrelenting pressure for more information than he was authorized to release about the company's plans moving forward, the companies or industries it was targeting for acquisition, could the analysts expect a quarterly meeting or at least a quarterly on-line conference call with management?

Dan's world was literally turning upside down.

Those calls and the dozens which followed in subsequent weeks were the result of the trans-continental road show Bill, Roger and Brad had undertaken at the request of, and with planning by, the lead securities underwriter in order to meet with financial analysts in key markets to discuss their initial public offering. They had taken the road show to the West Coast first, holding meetings in Los Angeles, San Francisco and Seattle on three consecutive days.

They took two days in Cleveland to rest, fine tune their presentations, then headed to the East Coast to meet with the financial communities in

New York, Boston and Philadelphia.

The New York meeting, the largest by far, was held in the ballroom of a Park Avenue hotel for more than 200 financial analysts and business reporters. Roger was somewhat uneasy going to the hotel on the off chance he might see Cecily sitting at the bar. If he did, he wasn't sure what he'd do; wasn't sure he'd even give her a glance or modest wave; also wasn't sure what *she* would do -- certainly might make his life awkward if she approached and said "Hi, Roger. Remember me!"

Boston also had been a large meeting, not as large as New York, but large, primarily because of Roger's involvement in the organization of AeroMarine Design and his continuing search for other businesses, foreign and domestic; businesses that would fit within the framework of the worldwide conglomerate AMI was intent on forming under his and Bill's direction.

This had resulted in another headline story in the *Boston Globe,* which again caught Cecily's eye. Roger was quoted in the paper's story, and interviewed on local TV news that evening. He looked exactly as she remembered him, his voice mellow and smooth, his eyes bright, focused, smiling. She felt a strong pang of yearning; he had been so close, yet so far away.

AeroMarine's stock had done extremely well on the stock exchange since its initial introduction; newspaper and business magazine stories about the company were frequent and glowing in their appraisal of the firm's management and its commercial opportunities.

Cecily was tempted to phone Roger, if she could find him, and extend congratulations that his years of hard work had paid off so handsomely. But she thought better of it, wasn't sure he'd even answer her call. Besides, he's "dead fish" according to Margi.

When the AeroMarine team held its Philadelphia meeting on its way home to Cleveland, Roger had planned to reverse course and head back to Boston to monitor construction of the Newbury Street showroom. Bill, however, insisted he return to Cleveland to meet with Jose to help plan his travel itinerary for the next several weeks in key markets in Latin and South America.

Bill also told Roger he wanted him in town Saturday evening for a large party he and Toni were hosting for all AeroMarine salaried employees to celebrate the successful formation of AeroMarine Design and the very successful IPO. It wasn't just an invitation; it was a command, mindful that Roger had played an important role in the IPO and the initial expansion of the firm's global reach.

It had taken awhile, but Cecily had found a two-bedroom, two-bath condo in a building on Exeter Street not far from her Copley Square office. It was affordable, comfortable, and centrally located. She was surrounded by a menagerie of marvelous shops, restaurants, cafes and the Boston Public Library. She couldn't believe her luck.

Her furniture arrived relatively quickly from storage in New York. She bought a new bed. She was very comfortable, dined out at least two nights a week with colleagues from her office, phoned her Dad a couple of times a week, had entertained her close friend Margi her third weekend in her new home.

She had succeeded, somewhat, in recovering from the loss of Roger, found it far easier to be in her new surroundings in Boston as opposed to the many lousy memories of New York. However, her comfort was upset by the newspaper stories, the TV interviews, which rekindled her longing for the relationship they had enjoyed just a few months earlier.

She couldn't shake those memories no matter how hard she tried, despite the oyster/dead fish counsel from Margi. She frequently thought of phoning Roger's office, always gave up the idea, but not without remorse. Thought of walking into the AeroMarine Design showroom on Newbury Street and asking for him; nope, that, too, was a lousy idea.

("Would he talk to me? What would he say? What would I say? Is there even a remote possibility of our getting back together? Do I really want that? Would he? I'd probably just be depressed.")

And then her phone rang.

"Hi, Cecily. It's Dave Michaels in New York."

She almost fell over.

"My gosh, Dave! How did you find me?"

"You have a friend named Margi, remember? Well I've been her friend longer than you, and what are friends for? In fact she told me you had been in New York several weekends ago and she then visited you in your new digs. That's how I got your Boston number!" He was laughing, and

Cecily joined in.

"It's really good to hear from you, Dave."

Their conversation rambled on a variety of subjects for more than twenty minutes: her job, her new apartment, his job, what's new with Margi and Mike.

"Cecily, I may have to be in Boston in a couple of weeks to meet with a new client, and I'd like to see you if that's okay."

"Yes, Dave, that would be fine. I look forward to seeing you."

"Where are you, Cecily? I'll be staying at a hotel in Copley Square."

"I'm very close to the hotel, Dave. Give me a call once you're in town and we can arrange to meet. I look forward to it."

"Thanks. I do, too!"

They continued to chat for several minutes, then rung off. Cecily sat staring at the phone, wrapped her arms around her midsection, didn't know whether to laugh or cry. A date! With a fella who liked her. An oyster? The hell with dead fish!

11

Bill and Toni's home in Shaker Heights was really a mansion, a huge red brick three-story with floor-to-ceiling windows and the impression that it would require roller skates to go from one end to the other. Manicured lawns and gardens lined both sides of the long cobblestone driveway embraced by ground level lights from the automatic gate to the mansion's front entrance, a large double door standing between four huge columns, five steps above ground level.

The house was lit like a cruise ship, blazing chandeliers visible through every first floor window and a few on the second floor, the front entrance illuminated by overhead lights. Visible from the circular car park were lit tennis courts and a large swimming pool.

Roger was greeted by a butler who welcomed him to the Enright's home, directed him to either the bar in the library or the assembled guests in the mammoth living room. He chose the library, where a hostess passed a tray of champagne flutes. He accepted one, stayed to admire the library itself. Several other colleagues from the office also were gawking at three walls of floor-to-ceiling shelves stacked with leather-bound rare editions, a collection Roger pegged as worth multiple thousands of dollars. The fourth wall featured an enormous picture window overlooking the illuminated pool and tennis courts.

After several minutes Roger left the library, entered the step down living room abuzz with a multitude of people. The room itself was magnificent, walls glistening with expensive art, furniture tasteful with so much room between chairs, sofas, end tables and coffee tables, guests had no difficulty maneuvering. The floor was inlaid wood with occasional antique scatter rugs; a musician at a grand piano played soft background music. Lots of floral bouquets.

Toni was the first to see him, greeted him enthusiastically.

"Roger! Welcome to our home. It is so good to see you!"

"Thank you, Toni. I can never get over what a beautiful home you and Bill have here."

"Thank you. I understand you'll be spending some time in Boston, but I hope you won't be a stranger. We'd love to have you visit anytime. And bring your children so they can swim and splash in our pool. We don't often get to enjoy the laughter of little children."

"Thank you, Toni. I'd welcome that, and I know Jen and Tommy would love it! Thank you so much. As for Boston, Cleveland owns my heart, so I don't intend to spend too much time away from the home office. Besides, my job won't allow it!"

"Yes, I understand. Congratulations!" She was smiling broadly.

"Well, enjoy yourself this evening, and I'm serious about bringing your children here for a swim. We'd love to have you all."

She moved on to other guests and Roger, too, began circulating to greet colleagues and their wives. Jose and Maria were there, dazzled by the opulence so tastefully decorated, combined with the gracious hospitality of their hosts.

Roger conversed with Josh and Helen and Brad and Linda; he was collared by Dan Winslow and his wife, Barbara; Dan peppering Roger with questions about the news reporters who attended the analysts' meetings and the extraordinary volume of telephone calls he was receiving.

"I don't hold a receiver anymore, Roger. I've got myself a small headset which I wear all day, and when my phone rings I just punch a button and I don't have to lift the phone. Saves me a lot of time, and I have both hands free to scratch my ass!"

"That's wonderful, Dan. I'm sure your ass appreciates it! And I think our medical plan covers loss of hearing!" They all laughed, Barbara slapped Dan's arm. "Men!"

Dana was standing near the piano, drifted over to Roger when she saw him, clinked glasses and offered him a toast.

"Well, Chief, you've had an extraordinary couple of months. I just heard you will soon be the top banana in this zoo!"

"Hey, let's not go around talking like that, okay," he was smiling, but serious. "I have a full plate, Dana, and I'm not eyeing Bill's job. He's a great guy, a terrific visionary, and the company needs him. I'm just in the wings."

"Bullshit, Roger. You know damned well you're being groomed, and Bill is your chief groomer." She had leaned close, kept her voice low. "You've just made him disgustingly rich, as well as yourself, by the way. And I happen to know he's eager to put his feet up in that awesome library and relax."

"Please, Dana, don't keep talking like that, especially to anyone else. I don't want people thinking I'm trying to shove him out. I'm not."

"I'm *not* talking like that to anyone else, Roger . . . but Toni is, and she's obviously not making that stuff up on her own."

"Oh, god, you've got to be kidding me!"

"Wanna bet?"

"Please, Dana. No more, okay!"

"Get me another drink and I'll behave."

He left her to find a waitress; could not stop thinking about what she had said. Did she hear that stuff from Toni?

He rejoined Dana who was engaged in conversation with Gordon White and an engineer whom Roger didn't recognize. The engineer introduced himself, congratulated Roger on all he had accomplished for the company in the past couple of months, left to join a small group of his colleagues.

"So, Roger." Dana, again, leaning close, voice low. "Since we're not going to talk shop, I want to ask you a personal question."

"Dana, you're impossible."

"No, but you are. You're 34, drop-dead good looking, newly rich, you drive a BMW 650 convertible, and you show up at a party like this without a date. *That's* impossible!" She was smiling. "So, where is she . . . Cecily, I mean?"

"Dana, please. I'd rather not talk about it."

"*It!* You mean her! You came back from California and NewYork with your tail between your legs, and it's taken you a damned long time to come out of your funk. If you recall, I'm your umbilical cord. So feed me." She was only partially teasing.

Roger looked at his feet, then glanced around the room, took Dana by the hand.

"Let's find a seat on the deck and I'll tell you a little."

They did, and he did. In fact, he unburdened a lot more than he had intended, even disclosed to Dana why he had called if off with Cecily. His tale of woe took more than twenty minutes. When he finished, Dana took his hand in hers, looked him in the eye, her matronly instincts in full throttle.

"Roger, do you love that woman."

"Yes, I do . . . did. But I just couldn't risk . . . ."

"But you still think of her, correct?"

"Yes, Dana. I do. But . . . ."

"You jerk!" She interrupted him. "You damned jerk! I'm sorry to speak to you like that, but Jesus Christ, Roger, what possessed you to walk out on someone you love! Screw what other people think, Roger. What *you* think is all that's important. If you have half a brain you'll find her and see if she'll take you back.

"Think of your children, Roger. I know they think the world of Cecily. They were really excited about having a women in the house, something they can hardly remember because they were so young when you lost your wife."

"I was thinking of my kids, Dana. How would they react, when they're older, and understand the woman their Dad romanced was a prostitute before I met her? Gawd, Dana!"

"Do you *really* believe that? I don't think so, or you wouldn't be so interested in finding her. So she tumbled with a few horny pricks. That does *not* make her a prostitute, which implies that's how she made her living. As I understand it, from *you,* Big Guy, it was an occasional fling. Mis-directed perhaps, but occasional. Not her real occupation."

"Yes! That's right, but still the label is viable."

"Don't tell anyone. Cecily wasn't very good at that profession, certainly wasn't committed to it. So she stumbled a few times. You haven't? And with the passage of time, there's very little likelihood some drunk will pull the same shit that other bastard did."

Roger looked startled, had never heard Dana use so many four-letter words to make a point. She was wound up, working hard to bring him to his senses, make him rethink his decision to dump Cecily like the unclean.

He looked down at his shoes, thought for several seconds about what Dana had just said. Then looked at her.

"Honestly, I'd love to find her, Dana. I want to apologize and plead for her to take me back, although I doubt that she would. I was a really big ass! I realize that now. We had a great thing going between us, and I blew it. My fucking ego . . . ."

"No! That wasn't it, Roger. You were broadsided, hit in the chest with a hammer. You had no warning, not even the slightest indication. And WHAM-O! I can understand why you were shocked, but you didn't take time to think rationally. That's not like you, but I believe that's what happened.

"So, you're miserable, you're kids are miserable, and I'll bet Cecily is miserable. That's a problem you know how to solve, Roger. You're very accomplished at solving problems. So find a way to solve this one and end everybody's misery!" She smiled, he did as well.

"I don't even know where to look, Dana. Her New York numbers have been disconnected."

"Put an ad in the newspaper. Google her. You'll find her!"

"But if she tells me to pound sand . . . I couldn't take that, Dana."

"Well, *she* had to take it, so grow up!"

Roger starred at his shoes again, fiddled with his empty glass. Sat quietly thinking. Dana broke the silence.

"I'll tell you what, Boss," she continued. "You're so damned busy, I'll bet you fifty bucks and lunch at a restaurant of my choosing that *I* can find her. No arguing with me, because you know you'll lose. Just leave it to me!"

She gave him a hug, stood, walked back into the crowded living room. Roger sat alone for almost five minutes reflecting on what Dana had said, especially her bet.

("Maybe she's right! Maybe she can find Cecily. It would be worth fifty bucks and a lunch if Dana's successful, and I wouldn't bet against her! Why not let her try? I treated Cecily like shit. What will she say if Dana does *find her? Also, my kids won't leave me alone, pester me all the time about why Cecily doesn't come to Cleveland any more. And I don't phone her, don't call her 'Honey'. What's wrong, Daddy? What the hell can I tell them?")*

Roger heard Bill's voice calling his name, rose and went back into the living room. Bill was standing near the piano, champagne flute in one hand, a portable microphone in the other. He called for the crowd to calm down, asked those in the library and dining room to wend their way into the living room. When all were assembled, Bill began to speak, no notes. He knew exactly what he intended to say.

"I want to personally welcome you on behalf of Toni and myself to our home, and to this terrific celebration of our recent successes.

"We have embarked on an entirely new chapter in the history of our company. It is a very aggressive plan, involving expansion into a variety of related industries compatible with our core business. We will not, ever, abandon that core business, which has meant so much to our growth over the years.

"All of us, and I mean this sincerely, all of *you* have a unique opportunity to grow and succeed in the new AeroMarine International we have embarked upon building. There will be new jobs, new kinds of jobs, new management opportunities, and everybody in this room has an opportunity to take advantage of that. *You* are the core of what has been our core business, and *you* will have first crack at opportunities our new strategy will present."

There was applause, a few shouts, lots of clapping. Bill was no BS artist; he meant what he was saying.

"There are a few people I want to thank for our extraordinary success in the past several months. Brad Lewis . . . where are you Brad? Brad has played an integral role in the planning and execution of our first acquisition and our recent stock offering. He deserves a combat medal for all the time he had to wrestle with our underwriters. Thank you, Brad." There was considerable applause.

"Josh Steinberg, over there, has been immensely important in our negotiations with Aviana Air in Italy, which represents the largest and most profitable contract in our history. Josh also will be running our new facility in Boston to get it organized while Roger handles the showroom side of the business and scouts more targets to stuff under Josh's wings!"

Laughter and another round of loud applause.

"Oh! One other piece of news about Josh." He turned to face the man and his wife, Helen. "As many of you know, the Board recently voted to make him a Senior Vice President! A well-deserved promotion. Congratulations! Josh." The crowd cheered very loud, and very long. Josh hugged and kissed his wife, big smiles on both their faces.

"Dan Winslow, another new VP." Bill raised his glass in Dan's direction. "Dan had no idea what was in store for him when he joined our organization. Well, he's learned darned quickly. I think he's fielded repeated phone calls from every financial analyst and stock broker in the northern hemisphere. He claims he's going deaf, but when his lovely wife, Barbara, whispers 'I love you' in Dan's ear, he has no trouble hearing her!" There was loud laughter and equally loud applause. Dan, and Barbara, blushed, hugged, kissed.

"Now!" Bill paused to swallow his champagne. "None of this would be possible if it were not for one guy . . . the guy who has put our company on the map internationally . . . the same guy who has successfully begun our aggressive acquisition plan . . . the same guy who has been very instrumental in our successful stock offering.

"I'm sure you know to whom I refer. Roger Manning . . . ."

He was interrupted by loud applause, sustained boisterous cheering.

"Roger," Bill continued, "was instrumental in successfully negotiating the Aviana Air contract, his latest in a string of such successes. He returned from Europe and promptly hired two very smart and talented Area Managers, Jose Grossa and Frank Chang. Jose is with us this evening, along with his lovely wife, Maria. I hope you all have had an opportunity to meet them here tonight, outside the stiffness of the office. Be sure to extend a warm welcome to our corporate family."

More applause in honor of the two new hires. Jose and Maria waved their thanks.

"And Roger didn't stop. He no sooner had those fellas on board, then he and Brad went to Boston and concluded our acquisition of Marine Upholstery, changed the name to AeroMarine Design, found us an exciting new showroom facility in downtown Boston. And typical of Roger, he intends to hire a beautiful fashion model to run the place." Lots of laughter and applause.

"Roger and Brad then came back home to Cleveland to take over responsibility for the road show we've been running to introduce the company and our very bright future to financial analysts, brokers and business reporters in the nation's top markets. That initiative is still continuing.

"Ladies and gentlemen, let's hear it for Roger Manning!"

The room erupted in applause, cheering, loud whistles, which lasted for almost three minutes, to the point where Roger was embarrassed and Bill gave him a hug, whispered in his ear; "Hang tough for another few minutes."

When the crowd calmed down, Bill again used his microphone.

"Now, Toni and I have an announcement which will surprise you all." He paused for effect, then resumed speaking.

"I intend to retire before the end of this year." There were audible gasps throughout the room, people leaning closer to hear all that Bill said.

"I've had a twenty year run as the top dog at Aeronautic, have seen it grow from a fledgling local supplier to an international firm on the verge of becoming a worldwide leader. I was smart enough to surround myself with outstanding talent. I'm damn proud of that, and all of you."

There was polite applause.

"But, as you can see around you, Toni and I have a very comfortable home, which we're eager to enjoy without the pressure of business. We've also just become financially well off, and want to travel domestically to see our children and grandchildren, and internationally to simply enjoy each other's company. And Toni is demanding that I devote my time to the charitable causes she's been undertaking through her private foundation."

More laughter. He paused, took a swig of champagne.

"Now, for some *really* interesting news. Effective immediately, Roger takes over management of the entire company, with me by his side as Chairman of the Board!"

The crowd went nuts, hollering, cheering, applauding, high fives. Roger, on the other hand, stood in shocked silence, was not expecting Bill to make that announcement. Bill turned, shook Roger's hand and embraced him. Next in line was Toni, who hugged him, kissed him on both cheeks, whispered congratulations.

Then it was Dana. She gave him a hug, whispered "I told ya." She whispered again: "I'm not the woman you should be hugging!", kissed him on the cheek, stood back and raised his arm in victory. The crowd went crazy! After several minutes, Bill calmed the assembled group, resumed talking.

"You know we have formed a holding company called AeroMarine International, Inc. Our existing company will be a subsidiary of the holding company, as will our two new organizations: AeroMarine Diversified Operations, and AeroMarine Global Finance.

"It should come as no surprise that Roger will be President and Chief Executive Officer of AeroMarine International. Temporarily, he will retain his leadership role at Aeronautic Supplies until he finds his replacement as EVP/International Sales. He'll also manage AeroMarine Diversified Operations, the company which will handle all of our aircraft and marine acquisitions, until he can identify a replacement for *that* position, as well. I suspect those people are in this room with us this evening."

That comment produced a murmur of excitement, lots of smiles, glances left and right.

"Roger's going to be a busy son-of-a-gun. He'll be running the entire show immediately, with me in his pocket as a silent resource." Again there was loud applause and cheering until Bill quieted the crowd, continued speaking.

"It also should come as no surprise that Brad will be Executive Vice President of AeroMarine International and President of AeroMarine Global Finance, reporting to Roger. This is a promotion and recognition for Brad, well earned and well deserved." More cheering and applause, Bill held both Roger's and Brad's arms aloft in a victory salute. Roger shook hands with dozens of people to accept their congratulations, couldn't bring himself to speak.

He ultimately turned to face Bill, grabbed him in a bear-hug, whispered: "My god, Bill! I hope you know what you're doing!"

"I know damned well what I'm doing, Roger. You'll do just fine. The Board has unanimously approved all of this, as you know. The company is yours, Roger. I'll stick around for several months as a resource, but you're going to run the place."

"Bill, I just can't believe this is happening so quickly."

"By Monday morning, reality will sink in." Bill began laughing, turned Roger over to the many employees who still pressed to shake his hand or pat him on the back. What had been a relatively calm cocktail party had suddenly become engulfed in loud laughter, animated conversations in every corner of every room

12

Cecily's apartment phone rang earlier that same Saturday afternoon, late. She picked it up almost immediately.

"Hi, Cecily! It's Dave."

"Hi, Dave." She began smiling. "Are you at the hotel?"

"Yes, just checked in. I flew up this morning for a client meeting which lasted a lot longer than I anticipated. Can we still get together this evening as planned?"

"Yes, Dave, I'd love to see you. What's a good time to meet?"

"Awesome, Cecily. I've missed you. Let me take a shower and change. Why don't I pick you up at seven?"

"Actually, Dave, I live only minutes from the hotel. I'll meet you in the lobby at seven . . . really look forward to seeing you."

"That's terrific, Cecily. I understand the hotel has turned the ballroom into a 1940s style dance hall with a real big band playing romantic tunes of that era. I'll reserve us a table and we can dine and dance 'til dawn, or whatever!"

"Fantastic, Dave! That sounds like a lot of fun"

"Great, Cecily! I'll see you at 7:00!"

Cecily's taxi pulled up to the front entrance of the hotel. As she stepped out of the cab she saw Dave standing next to the doorman, wearing the doorman's hat. She burst out laughing.

"Good evening, Madam. Welcome to Boston's finest!" Dave stepped forward to take her arm, Cecily still laughing. She wore a navy blue dress with a plunging neckline, broad gold choker necklace and matching earrings, stiletto heals: she was drop dead gorgeous. Dave stopped to admire her. She grabbed the hat off his head, put it on her own, returned it to the doorman as they entered the hotel, both of them laughing, Dave trying not to drool!

He slipped his arm around her waist as they were led to a cozy table for two in a corner of the massive ballroom, chandeliers set on low, lighted candles on every table. A thirty-piece orchestra was set in one corner, close but not so close Dave and Cecily would have difficulty conversing comfortably. He immediately ordered a bottle of Sir Winston Churchill Champagne.

"What are we celebrating, Dave?

"Our first real date!"

"What about that evening in New York?"

"That was a crowd, four of us. I think of that as an occasion, but tonight, this as a real date!"

Cecily joined in his laughter, they raised their champagne flutes, toasted their first date. Moments later Dave rose, took Cecily's hand, moved to the dance floor where he held her tight, dancing cheek-to-cheek to the romantic big band music. His kissed her passionately; a minute later she kissed him the same way.

"Cecily!" Dave was whispering, looking into her eyes. "I've thought of you a lot since New York. I'm very happy we can be together this evening."

"Thank you, Dave. I've also thought of you, and I'm very glad to see you, glad you called me."

Their dinner was delicious and intimate, the dancing romantic, they kissed twice more on the dance floor. That would not be their last kiss, nor last dance, of the evening. They stayed until the 1:00 AM closing time, when Dave insisted on escorting Cecily home in a taxi. He eagerly accepted her invitation to come up to her condo for a nightcap.

They sat together on her couch, enjoyed a half hour of light conversation. Dave moved close to her, slipped an arm around her shoulders, pulled her close. They kissed, warm, passionate. *("Gawd, this feels good! Haven't kissed like this since Roger!")* Dave reached for her breast but she pulled away, took his hand, stood and began walking toward her bedroom.

He began to hurriedly undress, she was slower, let her dress slide to the floor, was unhooking her bra when she suddenly stopped, said: "Dave, I can't! I'm sorry, but I just can't do this!"

He stopped, surprised, confused.

"What's wrong, Cecily?"

"I just can't do this, Dave. I'm very sorry." She sat on the side of her bed, tears forming on her cheeks.

"Is it something I said or did? I'm really sorry! What was it?"

"It's not you, Dave. It's me. I'm an emotional train wreck. I'm sorry, I really am. It's not you . . . you're a terrific guy, very sweet and kind. But me . . . I'm just not ready. I can't do this now!"

"Okay, I understand Cecily. I'm sorry to push you, won't do it again until you give me an all clear! It's okay, Honey! Really."

("My god, he called me Honey!")

She blushed, they both then smiled. He got re-dressed and they moved to the apartment door, she in her bra and panties. They embraced once again, but did not kiss. She thanked him for a delightful evening.

"I'm going to be back soon, Cecily. I think of you a lot, and I don't want too much time to pass before I can hold you again."

She kissed him quickly, and he left.

With Dave gone, Cecily sat back on her couch, relived the evening. *("It was truly fun, romantic. He's an interesting guy, not as gracious as Roger, but an interesting guy just the same. Besides, Roger is history, it felt great to go out with a really nice fella, to feel his arms around me, to kiss and kiss again. But it wasn't the same!")*

She slipped into bed, lay thinking about her next date with Dave, maybe seeing Roger if only from a distance, slowly drifted off to sleep.

As Bill had predicted, reality did sink in when Roger entered the office Monday morning and everyone stood to applaud. He waved, very embarrassed, quickly entered his office. Dana walked in behind him."Good morning, Big Fella. Is your ego bigger than your head?" She was smiling broadly.

"You knew all that was coming, didn't you? You knew and didn't warn me!" He also was smiling.

"I did to! I said you were being groomed, and that Bill was your chief groomer. But you didn't want to believe me! That'll teach ya!"

"Yeah, but I didn't know it was coming Saturday night!" He smiled broadly, gave Dana a hug. "God, you're impossible!"

"No! I also said *you* are impossible!" She settled into one of the guest chairs facing his desk. "So, have you thought about her this weekend? Do you have the courage to take my bet?" She was smiling broadly.

"Dana . . . ." He rummaged through some papers on his desk. "Yes! Damn you, I thought about her this weekend, and I thought of her this morning, and I'll think of her tonight."

"And . . . ?"

"And, Yes! I want to accept your bet. But if she says she never wants to hear from me, I don't want you to tell me that. Just say you won, and I'll figure out the rest on my own. And I'll want you to mind your own business after that and leave me alone, or I'll cut our umbilical cord!" He continued smiling.

"No! You won't! I'm not worried about that, because you're going to need me more than ever now that you're wearing the White Stetson around here!" She also smiled while he continued to shuffle papers on his desk. He looked up, still smiling.

"Regrettably you're absolutely right. Now, will you get out of here, please. I need to meet with Bill!"

"Only if you say 'thank you'."

"Thank you." He smiled. "You really are very special."

Dana rose and left his office, extremely pleased that she had pushed him to acknowledge he was thinking seriously about Cecily, wherever she was. And her own job was very secure.

Roger walked into Bill's office. "Good morning, Bill.

"Well, hello! Has reality set in? Would you like to sit behind this desk and try it out for size?" He was glowing.

"Bill, please, not you, too! I've just had a cupful from Dana, and when I arrived this morning the entire office staff applauded. It's embarrassing."

"Oh, come on! You love it. Get used to it. They have terrific admiration for you as a person and a leader. And they're thrilled that the Old Codger has given his throne to the Young Tiger!"

"Okay, enough, please, Bill." He sat at Bill's conference table.

Roger briefed his boss on his planned trip to Europe with Josh the following week to introduce the AeroMarine's maintenance chief to the Aviana Airlines management and staff, along with the engineers Josh had appointed to work in Milan with the Aviana technicians. They needed to be a good fit. He also intended to ask Aviana's guidance on finding a bright Italian fashion czar who might be interested in relocating to run AeroMarine Design.

On their return trip to the States, Roger said he intended to stop in London to meet with the Majestic Airlines people and probe their interest in signing a contract with AeroMarine International, and also meet with an executive recruiter regarding an area manager to handle the UK and Western Europe.

He would be gone eight days, max.

"Okay, Roger, but don't forget your primary responsibilities now lie right here in Cleveland. You're captain of this ship and I don't want you running all over hell's half acre. Start hiring, or promoting from within."

"I hear you, Bill. I've already got my eye on someone top run AeroMarine Diversified Operations, and will make that happen when I get back."

"Josh, right?"

"Boy, you can read my mind!"

"How about a replacement for your current job as EVP of our international operations?"

"I'd also like to fill that from inside, Bill. I'm leaning toward Jose Grossa, but I've got to give him a few months in his territory to make certain my instinct is correct."

"Okay, but get back from Europe quickly. I want you to live in my hip pocket for the next several months, or more correctly, I want to live in yours! We'll begin with a presentation to the Board on your plans for this company. I'll organize that for the next Board meeting. You and I will need to caucus a lot, but I want that presentation to be *your* plan, not mine. You're now the driver, Roger. I'm just an advisor to you."

"Wow! That sounds strange, but exciting. My plan, though, will be remarkably similar to yours. You already have us headed in the right direction!"

They both smiled and Roger left to jump on his priorities for the balance of the week until Sunday afternoon's departure for Europe.

Saturday afternoon he sat on his living room couch reviewing files for his trip to Europe the next day. Jen and Tommy played a board game of some sort on the floor close to his feet, laughing uproariously when not accusing the other of cheating!

Jen suddenly looked up at her Dad.

"Hey, Daddy Wanna play this game with us? I'll bet we can beat you!"

Roger looked at his smiling children, dropped his files on the cushion next to him, slipped onto the floor and sat cross-legged between the kids.

"Oh, yeah! Well I'm the biggest cheat in this family, so I don't think you'll be able to whip me!"

"Liar, liar, pants on fire!" This was Jen, and both kids broke into loud giggles. Some kind of cards were shuffled, dice were thrown, and Roger was losing before the game even started. Jen then popped a question she and Tommy had been eager to ask.

"Daddy, how come you don't talk about Cecily anymore, or even talk to her on the phone? Are you still mad at her?"

Roger was caught short. How to you explain to an 11-year-old and her 8-year-old brother?

"Well, Honey, as I told you Cecily and I had a disagreement, a serious disagreement, and I'm not sure if we'll be friends any more."

"But you were more than just friends, Daddy. We heard you call her 'Honey' lots of times. And when she was here she slept in bed with you. And you and she kissed a lot!"

"Wow! You're an observant little mouse, aren't you!"

"I wasn't spying, Daddy. You two kissed right in front of us!"

"I know, Jen. We were more than friends . . . a lot closer than just friends. But sometimes, when adults are really close, something happens that causes them to stop, to pull back and say 'Wait a minute; this might not be alright.'"

"So what happened between you and Cecily? Will we ever see her again? She's really nice, and Tommy and I both like her a lot, isn't that right, Tommy."

"Yeah, guess so!"

"Not 'guess so!' You like her a lot, you know you do."

"Okay."

"So, Daddy, what happened? We were hoping she'd come and stay with us . . . to be with us when you travel, Daddy. You travel so much . . . I know you're leaving again tomorrow, and we wish Cecily could stay with us!" Her face crumpled, tears rolled down her cheeks. Tommy got up, plopped into Roger's lap, he too was crying, wrapped an arm around Roger's neck.

Roger sat still, cuddling both children, gave them each a kiss.

"It's a complicated issue, kids. I'm glad to hear that you both like Cecily. Maybe she and I *will* get back together, and if we do, she will be thrilled to know how much you both think of her. But that may not happen. It depends upon her, and me, and time. We'll all have to wait and see."

Jen reached over and hugged her father, wiggled onto his lap across from her brother, placed a palm on his cheek and looked him in the eyes. Tears streaming down her young cheeks.

"It's just that Tommy and I haven't had a Mommy as long as we can remember, Daddy. We know Cecily wouldn't be our Mommy, but I think she likes us and we like her. So we hope that whatever happened between you two . . . that you can work it out and call her 'Honey' again."

Roger was truly shaken, swallowed hard as he struggled to maintain his composure.

"I understand, Jen." He paused. "Cecily apparently has moved and I don't know how to find her. But Dana has agreed to help me search, so we'll have to wait and see what happens."

"You said you loved her. Do you still love her?"

"Yes, Honey, I think I do . . . and I hope she still has strong feelings for me, but I don't know if she does. If I can find her, we'll all find out soon enough, and then she and I will have to resolve our differences and see if we can work things out. But all of that is going to take time, Jen. So give us time, okay?"

"Okay, Daddy. We just wanted to let you know how we feel, so if that helps you decide, that's good. We'll keep our fingers crossed."

Roger got to his feet, went into the kitchen under the pretext of getting a glass of water. He stood at the sink, looked up at the ceiling, whispered: *"Janice, what do I do? Your absence has created such a hole in our family, such a whopping great hole, for me, for our children. What do I do? God help me, Janice, what do I do?"*

Roger's trip to Europe was his typical rat race. First stop was Rome, where he, Josh and four Aeronautic engineers met with Giancarlo Mello and Guiseppi Valenti on Monday to review the vastly superior electronic instrumentation they had brought to update Aviana's simulator and related training equipment, the prelude to actual installation in Aviana's fleet of active aircraft.

The meeting went smoothly, the four engineers fit in well with the Airline's culture, enhanced, no doubt, by the fact that one of the AeroMarine engineers had an Italian heritage and spoke the language. Their Italian counterparts were amazed at the sophistication of the three-dimensional visualization embodied in the unique AeroMarine simulator electronics.

Roger and Josh also had a successful meeting Tuesday with Millo Salicini, Avian's Chief of Maintenance, who was eager to work with the Aviana employees to develop an appreciation for their equipment, its operating features, servicing requirements, backup systems, etc. A team of Signore Salicini's staff was due to fly to Cleveland with two engineers in two weeks to work in the AeroMarine labs.

Roger and Josh split off from the group later that afternoon for a meeting with Carlo Meola, Aviana's Chief Financial Officer, to discuss AeroMarine's performance to date, review all of the contract terms and financial payments, and agree on the next round of priorities. And on Wednesday they enjoyed a relaxed and friendly lunch with Aviana's CEO Fabio Mazzetti and Carlo. The two Aviana executives expressed "satisfaction and pleasure" that the working relationship between the two companies was proceeding so well.

Roger also spent a portion of the lunchtime conversation describing the fashionable interior decoration showroom they were building in Boston to service regionals like Aviana as well as owners of huge mega yachts. He dwelt especially on the goal of providing AeroMarine's customers with a one-stop shop capable of not only designing and manufacturing customized interiors, but also providing superior fabric installation under the direction of professional fashion and interior decorators sensitive to the customer's preferences.

Mazzetti was impressed with the idea, wondered aloud if AeroMarine could handle the upholstery of the new aircraft seats Aviana already had on order. He also pressed on the design and assembly of new cabin attendant uniforms and interior upholstery. Clearly, Aviana had not yet taken steps to have those assignments handled by Italian fabric and fashion companies, as Roger had been led to believe.

"The answer is Yes, Fabio, but with a qualifier. We do not yet have AeroMarine Design staffed, so we'll need some time. I was hoping perhaps you could point us in the direction of someone we might consider as manager of the firm, someone who knows the interior decoration and fashion business a heck of a lot better than Josh or me.

"We'll want that person to help us with the interior design of our retail showroom . . . a very upscale showroom . . . and then hire the experienced associates we want staffing the place under the manager's direction."

Fabio was quick to offer the names of three people Roger and Josh should meet while in Rome, expressing confidence that one of them would be ideal for the job Roger had described. He was dead on; they hired the first candidate they met, a gorgeous Italian brunette with impeccable credentials. Victoria Mojana had been a popular Milanese high fashion model, entered the world of interior decorating when walking the runway no longer had any appeal.

Victoria was fluent in English as well as French and Spanish, her attractive Italian accent was precisely what Roger was looking for, and she had a strong desire to relocate to Boston. She had relatives in the Hub's north end Italian neighborhood, a bastion of spectacular ethnic restaurants. She would relocate as soon as all of the government paperwork was completed, which Roger vowed to accomplish quickly.

Senore Mazzetti had also planted a seed in Roger's mind: hire, through Aviana Airlines, an Italian fashion house to design and supply the fabrics used by AeroMarine Design. It was an interesting concept which Roger promised to give considerable thought. He also wanted Victoria's participation in the decision; knew immediately that Mazzetti would talk to Victoria before she left Italy!

Then it was Roger's turn to plant a seed with Fabio. He began a discussion of heavy maintenance, outlined the problem of overseas maintenance locations with unlicensed mechanics because they did not speak English and could not pass the FAA licensing tests. Would Aviana like to have four or five of its mechanics trained by AeroMarine Internatinal, then certified by the FAA so Aviana could rent them to foreign heavy maintenance hubs?

"Absolutely, Roger! Sit with Carlo and work out the financials and scheduling, and we are all in favor. Another great opportunity for both of us!"

Wednesday evening, Roger and Josh boarded a flight to London, slept their way to the U.K.

This stop was an introductory meeting so Josh could get to know senior electonics and maintenance players at Majestic Airlines. He would be responsible for working with Majestic cockpit and maintenance people if/when they came to Cleveland for their first exposure to the AeroMarine training labs and the unique electronic equipment. Roger's goal was to press Geoffrey Butler and Ian Pedrick, the Majestic senior executives, to arrive at a decision to sign a contract with AeroMarine International, a deal Roger could almost taste, a gift he wanted to present to Bill upon his return from this European trip.

The two British execs engaged Roger and Josh in lengthy discussions Thursday and Friday regarding the possible terms for an agreement between the two companies. They reviewed all they had heard from Roger during his first meeting with them, as well as all they had seen and heard when they visited AeroMarine's home offices a couple of weeks earlier.

The executives in London, as well as those in Rome, also were surprised and pleased to learn of Roger's selection as the President and CEO of AeroMarine International, a position he was inheriting immediately. Executives at both companies stated they would be relying on Roger, as CEO, to make certain there were no delays or screw-ups as projects moved forward. Geoffrey Butler made their position very clear: "You wear the crown, Roger, so you're the guy we'll hold ultimately responsible for anything that goes wrong."

The contract discussions actually went smoothly: Roger and Josh left with an "assignment" to have their corporate attorneys draft an agreement for review by Majestic's management and legal staff. Once the i's and t's were cleared, there could be a signing ceremony in London, probably within the next two weeks. The dollars were pushing twenty-one million annually for three years.

That was nearly as good as an actual contract signing, a gift Roger knew Bill would relish!

He also stopped to interview an executive recruiter, described the type of person and specific qualifications he was looking for in an Area Manager/Europe. Josh had spent a few hours shopping for his wife while Roger gassed with the recruiting firm. They caught up with each other about six, shared a couple of celebratory drinks, then enjoyed dinner at a well known steak house near Berkeley Square. They were smiling throughout as they thought of briefing Bill and Brad on the success of their European appointments.

They retired early, rose about seven Saturday morning, hopped a cab to Heathrow Airport for their ten o'clock flight to Boston. They would land about three, planned to spend a whirlwind afternoon during which Roger would meet with the contractor to check on the progress of the Newbury Street showroom. It was supposed to be completed, ready for an opening splash.

Josh, meanwhile, would spend a few hours at the Chelsea sewing facility, most likely his last visit before management swung from the previous owner of the business to Josh. He was eager to review the assembly part of the AeroMarine Design operation to make certain it was being reorganized and streamlined according to instructions the owner had received from he and Brad. Then he could relocate the entire she-bang to the back end of the Newbury Street location.

Roger's time at Newbury Street left him in a positive mood. The showroom structure was making exceptional progress, Victoria Mojana would be in Boston shortly on a recruiting trip, interviewing potential staff. She expected to relocate in a month or two.

Josh's time in Chelsea had not been as rewarding. He found the facility as screwed up and dumpy as Brad had initially described it. When he and Roger met for dinner that evening, he was clearly anguished about "the mess" and what would be required to prepare it for a move to Newbury Street.

"Screw it, Josh! The showroom structure is damned close to being completed. We can move that stuff sooner than expected, and it won't get in the way of Victoria's plans for the design treatment of the showroom itself. Sort out the production stuff and fabric inventory as your installing it in Boston. Let's drink to progress and get this damned thing done." They did.

They flew to Cleveland on Sunday. It was late afternoon when Roger reached his condo, hugged and played with his children for a couple of hours, took them out for a steak and fries, fielded a minefield of questions about Cecily: Did you see her? Why not? Are you still friends? Will we ever see her again? She's very nice, Daddy! How come you don't phone Honey?!

He felt drained, hit the sheets shortly after his kids went to bed.

Cecily and her office friend, Hannah, were enjoying after work cocktails seated at the bar in a Boston hot spot close to their office. The place was jammed with twenty-somethings engaged in loud conversations and laughter, occasional cheering, some arguments, lots of drinking, mostly beer. Piped rock music and a loud wall-mounted TV set featuring a basketball replay added to the raucous environment.

The two women agreed to have one drink in this place, then move to a quieter, more adult restaurant for dinner. They were engaged in conversation about their jobs and social life, or lack of it, when a young man rose from the table behind them, stood between them with his hands on their shoulders.

"Hello ladies! Ready for some company?" It was obvious the fella was swilling his second six-pack!

"No, actually, we're not," said Cecily.

"Aw, come on! It's mating season!" With that his hand slid off Hannah's left shoulder and drifted toward her breast. Before he could react, Hannah slammed him in the throat with a karate-like knuckle chop that knocked him backwards. He flew against the chair he had been sitting in, which followed him to the floor in a loud entangled heap. He was gasping, trying to breath.

His colleague yelled "Hey!" and approached Hannah, both hands balled into fists. He stood about five-eight, and when Hannah stood she was a head taller than he: her dress covering a lithe six-foot body with strength developed from eight years of soccer and long distance running in high school and college.

The guy stood looking up at her, hesitant to hit a woman but eager to show the crowd he intended to defend his buddy, who lay writhing on the floor.

"Pick up your friend and get out of here," Hannah said.

"Fuck you!" The fella moved toward Hannah, but two other men stepped in front of him. One placed his hand on the guy's chest.

"You heard the woman. Pick up your friend and leave before you both get seriously hurt." He pushed gently against the fella's chest. The guy back peddled, threw a ten-spot on the table, bent to help his gasping friend to his feet, and they both fled the bar.

"Are you two okay?"

"Yes! Thank you very much," Hannah replied. You're a knight!"

"I've been called a lot of things, but never a knight. Maybe if I was carrying a shield and sword!"

"I thought you were," said Cecily laughing.

"My name is Dick, and this is my friend Jack. Do you suppose the four of us might occupy the table those idiots just vacated, and we'll buy you gals a drink. No strings attached."

Cecily and Hannah exchanged glances. They both said "Yes", lifted their drinks, and moved to the table, Dick and Jack held chairs for them. The men were dressed in suits and ties, obviously older than the young crowd, employed, both married judging from the wedding rings on their left hands.

The four enjoyed a half hour of easy conversation, no attempt by either guy to suggest anything improper. They were financial execs employed by a large Boston mutual fund, lived in separate suburbs of the city, both had children in grammar school. Dick said they often stopped after work for a "jolt" before boarding the subway, but not usually at this hot spot.

"Well, we're glad you chose this place today or things might have gotten uglier for us," Hannah said.

"Not for you, Gal. You leveled that fella real sweet," Jack replied. "I'm sure as hell not ready to tangle with you!" All four laughed.

Cecily could not stop herself from looking alternately at Dick and then Jack, comparing them to Roger. They appeared to be about his age, maybe a year or two younger. They both were good looking, not handsome like Roger, but far from homely. They each had an outgoing personality, sparkling eyes, quick smile, and evidenced a can-do attitude which undoubtedly helped make them successful executives.

("Roger! Gawd how I miss him! I wish . . . I wish I could forget him! Not really . . . but really. Has he found another woman? Is he even looking? Margi's friend Dave. He's no Roger, but he's really nice. Roger! Roger!")

She had to leave, began to feel uncomfortable sitting with these two men, neither one the guy she wanted to be with. Jack suddenly gave her an out

"Man! It's too damned loud in here," he said. "A joint I might have enjoyed a decade ago when I was faking my way through my senior year at Harvard."

"Well, we're leaving for a quieter atmosphere to enjoy dinner. But I want to thank you both for stepping in when Hannah played Wonder Woman, and for these cocktails. You're very kind."

"Yes! Let me echo Cecily's thanks. You fellas have been true gentlemen, and it's been a pleasure to meet you."

"Thank you Hannah, and you, Cecily. I know I speak for Dick when I say we've enjoyed your company, as well. Have an enjoyable dinner, and maybe we'll see you again at some quieter watering hole."

The women rose, shook hands with the men, left for a restaurant.

After shuffling through his office mail first thing Monday morning, Roger drifted into Bill's office, dropped into a visitor's chair facing Bill's desk. They each gripped a steaming cup of coffee.

"So, what do you have to say for yourself?" Bill was smiling.

"Rome was fantastic, Bill." Roger stopped to sip his brew. "And I'm not talking about the city, I'm talking about our time and our meetings with the Aviana people."

Roger went on to heap praise on Josh and his engineering team who had impressed the airline's technical people, especially when one of Josh's guys started speaking in Italian, had relatives inItaly! He also told Bill that Mazzetti and Carlo were pleased with the progress being made under the contract terms.

He also discussed AeroMarine Design and Mazzetti's recommendation of a former Milanese fashion model, Victoria Mojana, as a potential studio manager, whom Roger hired. And he shared Mazzetti's inquiry about upholstering aircraft seats as well as cabin carpeting, bulkheads, and so on. Plus Mazzetti's suggestion that AeroMarine Design contract, through Aviana, with an Italian manufacturer to buy high-fashion fabrics.

"That's an interesting idea! Does he know AeroMarine isn't even off the ground yet?"

"Yes, he does, and he's giving us time to get it up and running. He'll be AeroMarine Design's first customer."

"Superb!"

"That's not all, Bill. He also jumped at the chance to let us train some of his aircraft mechanics so they can become FAA certified. Brad and I have to pull together our training fees and schedules and send them on to Carlo Meola, but it's a done deal. Mazzetti's eager to begin renting his mechanics to the heavy maintenance outfits because, being an airline exec, he knows having FAA certified mechanics overseeing the maintenance will make the major airlines far more comfortable."

"Wow! That's awesome, Roger! Well done!"

Roger then reported on his productive meeting with Majestic Airlines, praising Josh for handling technical questions "with grace and superior knowledge that really impressed the British executives. They want us to draft a contract for a potential signing in London in two or three weeks: twenty-one million annually for three years, renewable for another three.

"And I also met with an executive recruiter in London and have him searching for our European manager. And finally, Bill, we stopped in Boston. The Newbury Street facility is ninety-nine percent completed, at least the back room is. Victoria needs to provide her input on the showroom design. Josh is ready to re-locate the production side from Chelsea."

"Wow! I should let you guys travel together more often! You're hitting home runs everyplace! And I'm eager to meet Victoria."

"Bill, she'll be an enormous asset in that job, and I'm willing to bet that before long Josh will begin grooming her to take over full management of AeroMarine Design."

Roger sipped his cooling coffee again.

"That brings me to another opportunity, Bill. I want to promote Josh to President of AeroMarine Diversified Operations. I want his appointment to become effective immediately with an appropriate increase in compensation. He'll oversee all of our subsidiary companies worldwide, since they'll be primarily R&D and production firms. That's his specialty, and he's damned good at it."

"It sounds very good to me, Roger. Why don't you tell him this morning and I'll clear it with the Board."

Roger shared the news with Josh, who was walking on clouds as he entered Bill's office a short time later, still overwhelmed by the scope of his new job, his job title, his new salary. Kept repeating "I don't believe it" and "Thank you."

Bill and Roger suggested he phone his wife to share the good news; their plan was to make an internal announcement to all employees immediately, which they did, by memo, email, and public address system, resulting in a stream of colleagues filing into Josh's office to offer their congratulations.

Part 3

Lonely

13

Dan Winslow spent several weeks planning a major media rollout to announce the opening of AeroMarine Design's showroom on Boston's exclusive Newbury Street.

His kick-off campaign included a significant photo spread on the firm's web site; a full-page photo spread in the Sunday *Boston Globe;* magazine; major stories with pictures in the leading aircraft and yachting magazines; a full-color mailer to a long list of financial analysts in key markets nationally; and two huge billboards: one near Logan International Airport and the other in Chelsea at the entrance to Constitution Marina.

Victoria, meanwhile, had done an amazing job getting the showroom designed. It featured a bright, upscale, high fashion photographic presentation of aircraft and mega yacht interiors, an elegant customer lounge, coffee bar, and high tech work station where a variety of fabrics and colors could be "placed" electronically on aircraft or yacht furniture, draped from windows, viewed on a large flatscreen TV, and caressed on demo rolls.

The atmosphere was lively, colorful, inviting, precisely what Roger had hoped for.

Next on Dan's agenda was a series of By Invitation Only receptions in the showroom: one targeting an FAA list of registered private aircraft owners; another directed to New England regional airline brass; a third for a Coast Guard list of registered mega yacht owners; a fourth for the Boston heavyweights responsible for managing the local facilities of national and international airlines.

Those receptions were scattered over a three-week period, hosted by Victoria, assisted by Roger, Brad and Josh. They were attended by large crowds of the mink and black tie set, people with sizable disposable incomes they were anxious to "invest' in their new or updated private aircraft or mega yachts.

The "noise" level of Dan's media campaign was not lost on Cecily, who read the *Globe* and saw live coverage on local Boston television outlets. She knew this was a newly-formed business of AeroMarine International, recalled reading about it earlier, resisted sticking her nose in the showroom although she was bursting with curiosity, had often walked past the large design showroom windows.

On this particular lunch hour she gave in to temptation, pulled open the door despite the small "By Appointment Only" sign. As she stepped inside, she was overwhelmed by the bright open decor, the extensive use of glass, the comfortable lounge where a middle age couple was seated on a couch talking with an attractive, young brunette. That woman stood, walked toward Cecily.

"Good afternoon, Miss. My name is Victoria Mojana. May I assist you?" Lovely Italian accent.

"Oh, no thank you. I've walked past this showroom several times and decided to take a peek. I used to know one of the senior executives at Aeronautic."

"May I ask who that was?"

"Roger Manning."

"Oh, Yes! Mr. manning is now President of AeroMarine International. In fact, he's in the back office. Shall I call him for you?"

"Lord, No!" Cecily began retreating toward the door. "I don't wish to bother him."

"Well, may I tell him who stopped by?"

"No, thank you. I'll just be on my way." She turned, raced for the door, began walking briskly up Newbury Street.

Victoria excused herself from the couple with whom she had been conversing, walked to the office, gently knocked on the doorframe.

"Roger, there was a very pretty young woman in here just now who said she knows you, but she did not wish to disturb you and would not leave her name."

"Really! What did she look like!"

"She was late twenties, my height, long blonde hair and sparkling blue eyes."

"Oh my god, Cecily!"

He rose from behind the desk, strode quickly across the showroom, exited onto the sidewalk and began walking slowly up the street, looking into retail stores for any sign of Cecily. He finally spotted her, seated with her back to him at an outdoor cafe having a cup of coffee. He walked up behind her, gently touched her shoulder.

"Cecily!"

She jumped at his touch: "Roger!"

"I'm so very glad to find you, Cecily. I've been looking for you for more weeks than I can count. Several months, actually! You're in Boston!"

"Yes, I moved here shortly after . . . . I wanted to escape New York and move closer to my dad. He's getting older, and lives in Wellesley, not far from here."

"Yes, I know where Wellesley is. I went to BU, dated a few Wellesley girls in my day!"

"I'll bet you did."

"May I join you for a coffee?"

Cecily hesitated before answering. "Yes, of course."

"Cecily, let me tell you what I've wanted to say for months."

"First, tell me about Jen and Tommy. How are they?"

"Oh, they're terrific, Cecily. They ask about you constantly. 'Do you see her, Daddy? When will *we* see her? Is she going to come to Cleveland?' They're driving me nuts so I'm glad I'll finally be able to say I've seen you."

Cecily smiled. "Please give them a hug for me."

"Yes, I will." Roger's coffee arrived, he ignored it.

"Cecily, I've been anxious to find you for months. I regret enormously the ass I made of myself that evening in your apartment. I'm extremely sorry for the pain I've caused you, and will do whatever it takes to convince you to forgive me and take me back. I know now, knew even then, that I love you and want to spend my life with you. Can I have a second chance? Can you find it in your heart to forgive me!"

Cecily looked down at the table for several long moments, composed herself, looked up and addressed him.

"Roger, it has taken me several months to try to get over you. It hasn't been easy, and meeting you like this today isn't helping. I've also read your name in the *Globe* and seen you on Boston TV. It's like being haunted, and knowing you will occasionally be in Boston on business won't help either."

She paused briefly, caught her breath and continued.

"You were very explicit that night in describing an issue in my past which made it impossible for you to continue our relationship. You even called me a whore, three times! That issue is still there, Roger. It's an indelible part of my past, it won't go away. So am I supposed to believe you suddenly want a relationship with someone you consider a whore?

"I don't believe it. I'm terrified of becoming involved with you knowing that some day you might walk out on me again. I honestly, really couldn't handle that a second time.

"Also, that lady told me you are now President of the company, which tells me you're probably even more married to your job. I wouldn't be happy playing second fiddle to Aeronautic whatever it's now called. And besides, I'm dating a fella from New York whom I like quite a bit, and he seems to like me."

Roger was stunned, hurt by her attitude, her comments, her icy demeanor. He stared at his cup, pulled himself together.

"Cecily, I'd be lying if I didn't say that revelation about your past blew my mind, actually stopped my heart. I felt that night like I'd been shot in the chest. I couldn't believe it, felt like I'd been played for a sucker. Maybe if you had said something . . . given me some hint, so it didn't hit me like a sledge hammer.

"I've tried desperately to forget you, but I can't do it . . . I don't even *want* to do it. I think about you all the time. Please don't shut me out. I've had a long time to realize the mistake I made. I didn't listen to you; all I could hear was that bastard in the bar. But now, now I don't give a damn about your past. It's your *future* . . . *our* future together . . that interests me. That's *all* that interests me. I want you to be with me.

"Yes, I'm President of the company. But my international travel is just about over. I've hired two area managers to take the Asian and Latin and South American markets and I have a search firm looking for a manager in Europe. I will no longer be pressured to deal with the acute demands of all those foreign markets. I have enormous corporate responsibility and can't even think about the minutia involved in our overseas business. Someone

I've yet to hire will be responsible for that.

"And remember, you accepted my challenge to make me interested in something . . . *someone* . . . other than work. You succeeded more than you know. I'm no longer married to my job, Cecily. I spend half my days thinking about you, wanting you back in my life. You told me once I would find someone to love and get married again. Well, I did . . . it's you, and I *do* want to marry you.

"And I don't wish to play second fiddle, to use your words, to a guy from New York or any place else.

"I'm telling you, Cecily, I'm in love with you, I want you to be my wife, I want us to share our lives together. And as far as my job is concerned, I want you to be by my side, like Bill and Toni, a stable part of my life, as I will be in yours. *You* are what is most important in my life . . . you and Jen and Tommy."

Cecily was looking at him, wavered, sipped her cold coffee, knew she was losing her composure.

"Dammit, Roger, that's a hell of a romantic proposal. Spoken like a high-powered executive." She burst into tears.

"Cecily, please don't belittle me, don't make fun of me! I'm begging you . . . please take me back. Please let me show you how intensely I love you. Please don't reject me outright. Take some time to think about what I've said. Please." He tried to hold her hand, but she pulled back to gently wipe her eyes with a tissue, careful to not smear her make-up; glanced at her watch, then back at Roger.

"Roger, you know I was very much in love with you. I told you that repeatedly. But you walked out on me. You called me a whore, damn you." She began crying again. "Damn you! I'm very sorry I didn't have the guts to tell you about my past . . . that you had to find out about it the hard way. That you were scared. I was scared, too!"

She sucked for air. "I was terrified that if I told you, you'd leave me . . . and that's exactly what you did. And you called me a whore!"

She couldn't continue, grabbed her face in both hands, weeped for several long seconds before speaking. "I know I hurt you." She sniffled. "And I was seriously wounded by you, Roger, and I understand now how wounded you were by me. But I vowed I will never permit myself to be so terribly hurt again."

Roger took hold of one of her hands. She didn't resist.

"I also don't want to be that hurt again, Cecily. You just said you made an error in not telling me about your past . . . let me find out from a drunk in a bar! And I just said I made an error in walking out on you, on not listening, on jumping to a conclusion too goddamned fast. And I insulted you terribly. I didn't mean it, Honey. I was just to goddamned hurt and shocked and scared shitless!

"So we both erred, Cecily. We hurt each other. Do we each have to live with that hurt for the rest of our lives? That doesn't make sense to me. I have missed you more than words can convey. And I gather you still have feelings for me.

"You can't forget me. I can't forget you. I don't *want* to forget you. What I want *both* of us to forget is the hurt we caused each other. Can't we put that behind us, and fall in love, again? I *know* we can do it if you'll just give us a chance. Let's start over."

Cecily straightened, wiped her face again, both tears and running eye makeup. She gathered her purse with her free hand, left the other in Roger's, looked at him.

"I'm still scared and hurt, Roger." She sniffled and again wiped her eyes. "I'm very scared of us becoming involved."

"Do you not trust me, Cecily? Do you not believe what I'm telling you?"

"Yes! I believe you. But that's now. What happens if . . . if some other jerk in a bar . . . oh, Roger, I'm so scared you'd change your mind and dump me again. I'm so ashamed of my past, what it was for such a short span of time, but that didn't matter to you. What matters to you is what your customers or prospects would think of you for dating me, or marrying me." She broke down completely.

He watched her cry for several minutes.

"Cecily!" He held her hand, caressed her fingers until she regained some composure. "I know I didn't even stop to listen to you . . . to understand what you had done was not your career. I just goddamn blew it because it came out of the blue, hit me right between the eyes. God, I loved you so much, and to hear that bastard . . . that goddamn bastard . . . . and I still love you very much, Cecily. Please believe me."

She straightened, removed her hand from his, prepared to stand.

"Let's leave it that I've heard what you have to say, Roger. I'll think it over, but I make no promises. It might be best for both of us to move on with our lives."

"Oh, god, Cecily. That sounds so damned final. Please don't leave me with those as your last words."

She stood, sniffling.

"I told you I'll think about all you've said. That's the best I can offer. I have to get back to work now. Goodbye, Roger. I wish you success in your new position." She backed away from the table, her eyes locked on his, she then turned and walked away.

Roger sat in the cafe for almost fifteen minutes, didn't know if he'd accomplished anything. Cecily had been cold, very upset, borderline frosty, not a good omen. She promised him an answer, but it didn't look good. He was crushed.

("Why on god's green earth did I call her a whore! The heat of the moment, the shock, the fear for my damn job. I think I've lost her because of my big mouth. If she'd only said something, given me some kind of hint. What else can I say, what else can I do?")

Once back at her office, Cecily entered the ladies room, slipped into a stall, cried very hard, all alone, for a long time.

It had been two weeks since Roger had talked with Cecily in Boston. He had not heard a word from her. He was in Europe again, with Brad and Josh, for a meeting in London with the Majestic people to sign a contract: $21,000,000 annually for three years. He should have been over the moon, but he was extremely disturbed by Cecily's silence, no word, no reaction to his proposal, nada.

Still, Josh and Brad were thrilled with the outcome of their London meetings, and at the signing itself Roger also was gracious, thankful, shared in the congratulations and joy of a lengthy negotiating process successfully concluded. The Majestic people insisted on inviting the three AeroMarine executives to a five course dinner at an exclusive private club on The Bank in Central London.

The following morning the AeroMarine trio caught a flight to Rome to meet with the Aviana management and engineering staff to check on the installation of the state of the art electronics brought over earlier, and the progress of cockpit training on the equipment. All was proceeding on schedule. Brad signed an FAA training contract with Carlo, and they all enjoyed a cordial dinner and several toasts as the guests of Signore Mazzetti at his private club with several of the other Aviana executives.

Their final European stop was with an electronics firm in Amsterdam, a company Bill had identified as a potential acquisition. The firm, Electronique, N.V., was housed in an ultramodern factory on the banks of one of the city's canals. Everything in the place seemed very modern: equipment, test labs, work stations, offices.

Their primary contact was Hans Essen, a fifty-ish, blond haired engineer who founded the company and functioned as it's Managing Director. Initially, he was not interested in being acquired, preferred a consulting arrangement whereby he would sell the R&D expertise of his staff to AeroMarine Diversified Operations on a project basis.

"That's not going to work for us, Hans." Roger was adamant. "We're moving too fast to negotiate contracts every fifteen minutes. We need to know that with a single phone call or email we have your undivided attention and immediate agreement to proceed, technically and financially. And that goes both ways.

"I understand, Roger, but look at what I have here."

"We *have* looked, and we're impressed or we wouldn't be talking acquisition. But think about what you'll lose if we walk and go somewhere else, if not The Netherlands, then somewhere else in Europe.

"We can throw you more business than you've ever handled, and we can start tomorrow. We can offer you a combination of cash and stock, will include some of your management people, if that's important to you. Brad also will structure a profit sharing plan for you and your people based on your net earnings as our subsidiary."

"That sounds very interesting, Roger. I want to think on it, and if it does make sense to me we can discuss the financials in detail."

"Okay, but we're leaving for the States tomorrow morning. We will want you to come over anyway, at our expense, to discuss financials with Brad and Josh. Brad runs our worldwide financial operations, Hans. He's an easy dude to talk with, not a pushover, smart as hell. And Josh is a tiger, President of AeroMarine Diversified Operations. He'll be your direct report, but Brad and I won't be uninvolved, I assure you."

Brad entered the conversation.

"Hans, I want to stress that we're eager to move quickly, so I urge you to not take too long," Brad added by way of timing. "We have too much riding on our decision to make a European acquisition so we can slip behind the European Union tariff barriers. We want to get started."

"Let me add, Hans," said Josh, "that we're very anxious to build a cockpit simulator system in whatever company we acquire so we can offer full-service training to cockpit crews right here in Europe. That will be an enormous benefit to us and the airlines we service."We expect to have a cockpit training contract with Majestic Airlines in London," Josh continued, "If we could build an advanced simulator here in your facilities, it would be good business for you, good business for us, and a hell of a lot more economical for everybody than it is flying crews to Cleveland or to an airline in London for familiarization with our instrumentation."

"Yes, I certainly understand that, Josh. Well, okay, gentlemen, I promise you a phone call next week with my answer. You have certainly given me a lot to think about."

They shook hands, Brad, Josh and Roger left for their hotel and their flight to Chicago the next morning, connecting to Cleveland.

Almost as soon as Roger, Brad and Josh had left on their European trip, Dana had begun plotting a way to reconnect Roger with the love of his life. With him out of the office, she was free to pursue whatever direction caught her fancy. Besides, she was determined to win their fifty-dollar-plus-lunch bet. She could almost taste the steak.

When Roger had told her of his accidental meeting with Cecily in Boston, there was one word he mentioned that kept coming back to her: "Wellesley". That was the Boston suburb where Cecily said her father resided. So Dana dialed Information, told the operator she was searching for a man living in Wellesley with the last name Sommers. She was connected in seconds.

"Hello, Mr. Sommers?"

"Yes!"

"My name is Dana McBride. I'm with a company in Cleveland, Ohio. I work for an executive named Roger Manning, who used to date your daughter, Cecily, whom I also know quite well. Neither one of them knows I'm calling you."

"I see. Yes, I've heard Cecily refer to that guy. I have the impression they were in love, or at least she was, but that fella Manning dumped her for some reason and she's still very upset. I'm concerned for her."

"Well, I have interesting news!" Dana spent several minutes briefing Howard Sommers on the surprise meeting Roger and Cecily had in Boston two weeks earlier, the substance of their conversation as related by Roger, including his marriage proposal.

"WHAT!" Sommers was obviously shocked. "I didn't even know they'd met, let alone that he had proposed. She hasn't said anything to me!"

"Well, she hasn't said anything to Roger, either, and he's going nuts waiting for her answer. I can assure you he really loves her, and wishes he had never broken off their relationship."

"Yeah, well I have no idea why he did. He must have had, or thought he had, a very good reason, but I'll tell you he did some really tough damage to my daughter. She still cries about him at the drop of a hat, and frankly I'm worried about her emotional stability. If he's proposing marriage, he better be damned serious or he's going to answer to me, and *that* he will not enjoy!"

"I understand your concern, Sir. Apparently, Cecily also hurt Roger pretty seriously. I know Roger very well, have worked with him for almost ten years. I'm not a young chic, Sir. I'm a mature, middle-aged woman, and in addition to serving Roger as his administrative assistant, I'm also somewhat of a mother hen.

"He talks to me very openly, not just about business, but also about his private life, what there is of it! I can assure you he loves your daughter. He's said to me, and to Cecily, that he'll do anything to get her back. I'm telling you all of this because when he comes back into the office -- he's in Europe with two colleagues -- I'd like to tell him, with your permission, that you and I have talked, and suggest he phone you to see if there's something you can do or say to Cecily, or to Roger, to help her make a decision, and not keep Roger waiting any longer. It's eating him alive."

"I see."

"I fondly hope she says 'Yes' because it will make him very happy. But if her answer is 'No', at least he can get back to focusing on his job. He can't go much longer in never-never land. I'm sure Cecily is scared. So is Roger. I probably shouldn't be saying this, but she's the one who has to cut and run, or not."

"Well, I hear you, Dana. May I call you Dana? But despite all you've said, I'm sure as hell not going to pressure Cecily one way or the other into another relationship with this guy. She was hurt really bad by him once; probably fears it happening again."

"Yes, Sir! I certainly understand. My advice is that you not tell Cecily we've had this conversation. But I would ask that, without her knowing, you agree to accept a call from Roger so you can judge for yourself the depth of his sincerity."

"Okay, that sounds fine. I won't mention anything to Cecily until after I've spoken to Mr. Manning. Even then I might keep my mouth shut."

"That may be best, Sir. Thank you for speaking with me. I hope to have the pleasure of meeting you in person one day."

"Thank you for your concern for my daughter, and your boss. I'll wait to hear from him. Tell him I'm eager to hear what he has to say."

14

Dave had been calling Cecily three, sometimes four times a week. Their conversations were social, short, no overt romantic overtones, but the message was developing quite clearly.

Dave kept promising to visit, but client and prospect needs always seemed to prevent him from coming to Boston. Cecily had visions of another suitor married to his job, a nice guy but lacking in any sense of commitment. She wasn't eager to go through that again. More importantly, she could not get Roger out of her mind.

Then, Friday evening, her apartment phone rang as she was preparing a simple dinner.

"Hello, Cecily!"

"Hello." She paused. "Who is this?"

"It's Jennifer, Cecily! Jennifer Manning!"

Cecily was stunned, didn't know how to respond, finally caught her breath.

"My lord, Jennifer! How are you? How did you find my phone number?"

"I found it in Daddy's telephone log on his desk. How are you, Cecily?"

"I'm okay. Where are you, Jen? Does your Dad know you're calling me?"

"I'm home, in Cleveland. No! Daddy's in Europe again, and I'm very lonely so I thought I'd give you a call. I miss you, Cecily."

Cecily chocked up, finally spoke.

"It's such a surprise to hear from you, Jen. How are you and Tommy?"

"We're OK. But, we haven't seen you in a long time. Daddy says you and he have had some kind of disagreement and he's not sure the two of you will get back together again. I hope that's not true."

Tears began to well in Cecily's eyes. She struggled to maintain her composure, didn't want the young girl to know she was upset.

"Yes, well that's true, Jen. But we did meet and talk about three weeks ago. That sort of cleared the air a little, but . . . ."

"Daddy told me that. But also told me he still loves you and wants you to come back to him, but he isn't sure you will. I hope you and Daddy make up. It would be awesome if you did. Tommy and I really miss you, and it's so nice to hear your voice again. I wish you were here."

"Oh, Jen. I miss you kids, too, and it's wonderful to hear your voice. It's such a treat to speak with you."

"I hope you can come to Cleveland sometime soon, Cecily. You made Daddy so happy . . . he was smiling all the time with you, happier than he's been since Mommy died."

Cecily was struggling, took several seconds to regroup.

"Oh, we'll have to wait and see, Jen." She paused. "Jen, it's awfully nice of you to call me. I've missed you and Tommy. Give him a hug for me, and you, too, okay."

"Yep, will do! I like hearing your voice, Cecily. I may call you again if you don't get to Cleveland soon. Would that be okay?"

"Yes, Honey. That would be fine. But I suggest you clear it with your Dad first."

"I . . . I'm afraid what he'd say if you two are still not speaking. He told me not to interfere, but I really like talking with you, Cecily, so I may call anyway. I hope that's okay with you."

"Yes! Jen. I'll enjoy hearing from you, anytime."

"Awesome! Well, Tommy and I hope you come to Cleveland soon . . . we'd like you to stay with us!"

"Oh, Jen!" Cecily lost it, burst out crying.

"I'm sorry to make you cry, Cecily. I didn't mean to do that."

"That's okay, Honey." She sniffled. "I miss you both very much. You take care."

"I will. Please talk to Daddy, as a favor to Tommy and me. We both really miss you, Cecily."

"I will, Jen. When the time is right. I promise."

"Good night, Cecily."

"Good night, Jen." She lowered the receiver onto its cradle, stood staring at the phone, tears streaking her cheeks as she thought of those two kids. Would she see them again? Was it up to her, or to Roger? Or both?

She forgot dinner, sat in her living room, thought of that cafe conversation with Roger. He seemed so sincere in his expressed love for her, his flat out proposal of marriage, his promise that he was no longer a captive of the company. She had to admit he looked fantastic, still caused her heart to flutter, still prompted dreams of his holding her, kissing her, rolling her on top of him so their hearts beat in unison.

What to do? She couldn't speak with her father. But Margi....

She picked up her phone, dialed New York.

"Well, Hi, Cecily! How's Boston?"

"Margi, you will never guess who I bumped into here a few weeks ago."

"That guy from Rome and Cleveland!"

"How did you know?"

"By the tone of your voice! You melt when you talk about him."

"I just got off the phone with his daughter, Jennifer. Roger is in Europe, and Jen called to say she misses me and asked when I was coming to Cleveland again."

"Well that's a good sign."

"His firm opened a design center on Newbury Street, so out of curiosity I stock my nose in it. The gal who runs it said he was in an office in back, so I beat a hasty retreat, but Roger came looking for me and we had coffee and talked.

"I had no idea Roger was in Boston, and he didn't know I had moved here. He said he'd been trying to find me for weeks. He apologized all over the place for being such an ass, said he wants to spend the rest of his life with me, asked me to marry him!"

"Great! So have you set a date?"

"Don't be silly, Margi! I can't forget that he called me a whore that night in New York. Now he suddenly wants to marry someone he thinks of as a whore!"

"Oh, Cecily! You've got to let that go! He was very upset and very hurt. Most likely didn't even know what he was saying. It was such a shock for him to hear that guy at the bar, and I warned you to fess up or you'd lose him."

"I know, I know. I should have, but I didn't, and he did exactly what you said he'd do. He walked out, and he did it thinking I was a prostitute. He's now President of the company, but says he has staff to do all the traveling overseas, and that I did convince him to commit to something, some*one*, other than his job."

"Well, that's a big step in the right direction."

"Yeah, well I told him he hurt me terribly and I'm not about to expose myself to even the hint of that again. I also reminded him that he had made a big deal of my past and how it would not reflect well on his reputation in business, and it is *still* my past and always will be. And, to be fair, I admitted that my not telling him about my past was a big mistake on my part. He said hearing about it from 'a drunk in a bar' was like being shot in the chest."

"So are you folks back together?"

"No!"

"For god's sake, Cecily! Did you tell him to shove it?"

"No, I told him I'd think about it and let him know."

"How long have you been thinking?"

"Three weeks!"

"Oh my god, Cecily. You love that guy, you know you do. What the hell is holding you back? You hurt him as much as he hurt you. Wake up! You never told him anything, so he found out the hard way.

"You knew that would be a mistake. If he's now on his knees begging you to forgive him and take him back . . . proposing marriage. . . . what are you waiting for? What's your problem?"

"I'm very scared, Margi. I'm very scared. And by the way, Dave and I have had a couple of dates. He's a nice guy."

"Oh, screw Dave. He doesn't hold a candle to that guy you really love. Yeah, Dave's a nice guy, but he's nothing next to Mr. Right. If you wanna be scared, be scared of Dave; commitment is not his strong suit. I know, as do my women friends here in the city."

"I'm so confused, Margi."

"No you're not. You're scared, but get over it and give that guy Roger a call before you lose him for good. You love him, you know you do! Let him hug you, kiss you, and he'll be your oyster, no longer a dead fish."

"You and your oyster/dead fish! Okay, I'll think about it."

"No! Cecily! No! Sounds to me like that's all you've been doing, thinking! Make a move, Cecily, you have to make a move. The guy loves you, he's apologized all over the place. What more do you expect him to say? Don't turn your back on him, or you'll regret that for the rest of your life. Call him!"

"Okay, Margi. I assume that's what you'd do if you were me."

"Actually, I'd be on a plane to Cleveland!"

They both laughed, Cecily thanked her again for her advise and friendship, and they hung up. Cecily paced her apartment, promised herself she would get the courage to phone AeroMarine International when Roger was back in his office. But she forgot to ask Jen when that would be!

Roger paused before entering the office building Monday morning, stopped to admire the new sign above the entrance, large letters in white against the red brick building: AeroMarine International, Inc. He smiled, his chest swelled with pride, there was a jauntiness to his stride as he walked up the front steps, opened the door.

He stopped dead in his tracks. There was a beautiful new reception area, carpeted, large reception desk, comfortable chairs and attractive walnut end tables, large round coffee table. The receptionist greeted him, pressed a button and Dana appeared as if by magic.

"Right this way, Sir!" She laughed, led Roger to a new section of offices, walked into her own: reasonably big mahogany desk, credenza, upholstered visitors' chairs, a door that opened into a large L-shaped executive office with his name on the door. The first area held his desk, credenza, several upholstered chairs; the larger wing held a magnificent walnut conference table surrounded by a dozen upholstered chairs, warm carpeting throughout.

"Wow! Who did this, Dana?"

"Bill! He wants your office accommodations to reflect the fact that you're the CEO of an international company. It works, don't you think, Mr. President?"

He spent a few minutes admiring his new digs, the layout, the furniture, the large corner windows, the lighting, even the door into Dana's office one had to pass through to reach his spacious facilities. He opened his briefcase, stacked folders on the corner of his new desk, called to Dana.

"I've got to have a Corporate Officer's Committee meeting this morning, Dana. Would you round up the others and ask them to join me. Is Gordon White here today? If so, be sure to include him.

"Also, Dana, I want you to attend all of these meetings, not just as my admin, but as my reference guide as we move to different items on the agenda. Today's agenda will be loose, but in the future I'd like you to prepare and circulate a typed agenda for all of the COCs."

Dana left to round up the "brass"; Roger stood at the head of his conference table juggling folders as the executives filed in and settled into chairs, including Bill. Dan Winslow sat at Roger's right, but he made Dan move, reserving that chair for Dana.

"Good morning. Thank you for joining me for our first Corporate Officer's Committee meeting under my so-called reign." There was considerable laughter. "I feel somewhat awkward sitting at the head of the table, still feel this seat belongs to Bill." More laughter.

"Get used to it!" from Bill.

"I want us to meet every Monday promptly at 10:00. Also, no cell phones. The only phone in this room will be mounted under this table, beside Dana's knee, and she's the only one that will be allowed to use it. She will take notes and issue confidential minutes to all of us. She'll serve as my resource, providing me with whatever briefing material I might need as we move through each week's agenda.

"She'll prepare a typed agenda for each meeting. You may submit to Dana by Friday morning items you would like to discuss. The meetings stay with us: the agenda, the minutes, everything. Nothing is for public dissemination. Whatever we discuss herestays here. And we should feel free to discuss any subject except our individual compensation packages. Those will be handled by the Board. Now, let's get down to business."

Roger opened the discussion with a summary of the meetings he, Brad and Josh had had in London, Rome and Amsterdam.

There was considerable excitement among the corporate executives because of the signed $21,000,000 annual contract with Majestic Airlines; the progress and positive feedback from management at Aviana Airlines on that $23,000,000 contract and their interest in expanding the company's assignment via AeroMarine Design; the Aviana agreement to have AeroMarine train a group of mechanics for FAA certification; the potential acquisition of Electronique, N.V., in Amsterdam. The status of that possibility would be known with the phone call tomorrow from The Netherlands. They had their fingers crossed.

Josh added a verbal report on the activities being undertaken at Aviana and the gearing up for U.K. and Cleveland training of Majestic engineering, maintenance and cockpit crews. He also voiced optimism that the Electronique acquisition was a close reality, enabling them to install a company-owned cockpit simulator in Western Europe.

He noted that he, Brad and Roger were preparing for a visit from Hans Eeten to commence acquisition discussions.

Roger than closed his remarks with a report on his meeting with a London executive recruiter to find an Area Manager for Europe.

Dan and Brad presented a performance review of the AeroMarine Design showroom in Boston, the superb credentials of the facility's manager, Victoria Mojana. Josh discussed the upcoming move of the Chelsea production facilities into the Newbury Street location; Brad also expanded on the positive financial impact of the $63,000,000 contract with Majestic over the next three years.

Gordon White gave an encouraging report on potential sales in the U.S. and Canada, including successful first meetings with large regional carriers in California and Michigan.

Bill spoke briefly about the success of the stock offering. He also confirmed that the Wednesday Partner's Meetings he had been holding would be discontinued in favor of Roger's preference for the Monday Corporate Officers Committee meetings. He noted that Monday was a more productive day, monthly Board meetings were held on the first Wednesday, providing Roger with sufficient time to prepare after the preceding Monday Corporate Officers' meeting.

The meeting adjourned after ninety minutes.

Once the others had left, Dana sat across Roger's desk and briefed him on her telephone conversation with Cecily's father. Roger's first impulse was to hit the roof.

"Jesus, Dana, what the hell are you doing talking to her father? I've got enough problems with her already. I don't need her to know that *you* -- not me, but *you* -- have been talking to her father in my absence."

"Calm down, Roger. Neither her Dad nor I are dumb enough to tell her we've been talking. I called him because I'm concerned about you, and he's concerned about his daughter. The two of us want to see you and Cecily reunite or call it quits. But neither of you can keep up this mooning."

"Mooning? *Mooning!* What the hell are you talking about?"

"I'm talking about you! You miss that woman terribly, you know you do. You've told me you'll do anything to get her back. You said you've proposed marriage to her. And you spend part of every day sitting on your butt wistfully thinking about her. And, apparently, she does the same. Her father says so!

"You've got to cut that out and focus . . . focus on the enormous responsibilities Bill has thrown in your lap, the extraordinary opportunity, Roger. You know you have to concentrate all of your energy on business when you're here. I don't mean to lecture you, Roger, but when you're so often distracted . . . well, it's not fair to you, or to the company, or to our employees and stockholders.

"To do that, you have to either get that woman back into your life, or get her *out* of it. She has to tell you to disappear. That won't be easy for you to accept, but at least it will be over . . . . and, besides, either way, I'll win our bet!" She was smiling, Roger could not help smiling with her.

"Dana, Dana, Dana! What am I going to do with you?"

"You're going to thank me profusely, and then dial this number. His name is Howard Sommers." She stood and walked out of his office as Roger picked up his telephone receiver.

"Mr. Sommers, this is Roger Manning in Cleveland. I just learned that you and my assistant, Dana, had a phone conversation recently about Cecily and me."

"Yes! Yes! I've looked forward to hearing from you. Thank you for calling."

"I apologize for the tardiness of my call, Sir, but I've been out of the country, just got back this past weekend."

"Yes! Dana said you were in Europe. Did you have a good trip?"

"Yes, Sir, it was very good. But let's talk about Cecily and me. We met unexpectedly in Boston over three weeks ago. I had been trying to find her for weeks, didn't realize she had moved to Boston."

"Yes! She relocated shortly after the two of you broke up."

"As I'm sure you've heard, I walked out on her after . . . well, after something which bothered me enormously, and which I thought might interfere with my business career. My wife died several years ago, and since I lost her I've been pretty much married to my job. I have two young children, and have been devoting all of my free time to them."

"I see."

"Then I met Cecily. We met on a flight to Rome, and we very quickly fell in love. I mean, *deeply* in love. I don't have to tell you that your daughter is someone very special."

"No! You don't!"

"Well, I've felt terrible since I left her. I know I caused her a lot of pain, which I regret more than words can convey. And frankly, Sir, she caused me some real heartache as well, which is what prompted me to end our relationship. However, I still love her, Sir. I told her that when we met in Boston. I proposed to her, said I want to share the rest of my life with her."

"Yes! Dana told me that. I was surprised because Cecily hadn't even told me she had met you. She keeps the details of your relationship pretty close to her chest."

"Well, she told me she'd think about what I said, and get back to me. However, I haven't heard a word from her, so I'm beginning to think she'd rather I just disappeared. I really hope that isn't true."

"I don't believe it is, Roger. May I call you Roger? I can assure you she's still in love with you, but is terrified you may walk out on her again. She's scared stiff. I do know she has spoken with a good friend of hers in New York, a female friend, who has counseled her to call you, but she remains scared to become involved with you again. And I'm not about to push her one way or the other because I don't know you from a hole in the wall, so I don't know if she should trust your proposal of marriage."

"Mr. Sommers, I'm not interested in making life difficult for Cecily. I love her, for god's sake. I want her to be part of my family, even my kids want her to be part of our family. They're always asking me when they'll see her again. I just don't know how to convince her that I'm dead serious. What the hell else can I say to her?"

"I don't know, Roger. All I can tell you is she still carries a torch for you, even the mention of your name causes her heart to flutter. So I suggest you find a way to get your message across in such a manner that her concern, her fear, will go away and she'll listen to her heart."

"Okay, Sir. Thank you for that advice. I'll see what I can do. And, if you're interested, I'll stay in touch with you. I don't believe she knows you and I are talking."

"That's a good idea. And I wish you success, Roger. You sound like a terrific guy. She thinks so. So I hope you can rekindle your relationship with her. I want her to be happy, and she hasn't been truly happy for several months."

"Thank you, Sir. I'll succeed or die trying."

They rung off.

When Roger hit the office Tuesday morning, he was immediately consumed by his anticipated conversation with Hans Essen and the probability that he would be receptive to the acquisition proposal he, Brad and Josh had made to him the prior week. He pressed a button on his phone, asked Brad and Josh to join him in his office so they could make a conference call to Hans. Dana placed the overseas call at 9:00 Cleveland time, 2:00 in Amsterdam.

"Good afternoon, Hans. This is Roger Manning at AeroMarine International. Brad Lewis and Josh Steinberg are on the telephone with me."

"Good morning, Roger, Brad and Josh. How is everything on your side of the pond?"

"Excellent, Hans, and it will be even better if you give us the answer we're hoping for."

"Well, you fellas certainly gave me a lot to think about. There are pros and cons no matter which way I go, and I've thought them over very carefully. And, Yes! I would like to be part of the empire you're building."

"Ahhhh, that's fantastic, Hans. Brad and Josh are actually dancing on my desk!" Lots of laughter at both ends of the phone.

"I have three caveats, Roger. I would like the deal structured in such a way that I retain a sizable share of the ownership of my company. It's my baby, and I cannot bring myself to let go of her completely."

"That's understandable, Hans, and I'm absolutely certain we can make that happen. Brad's nodding his head 'Yes!'"

"That's good, fellas. Thank you. I'd also like to take you up on your offer to structure a profit sharing plan for my employees, not just my key managers."

"That's very doable, Hans. This is Brad. I'll make sure we have that built into the agreement, as well."

"Thank you, Brad. Also, Josh referenced the possibility of constructing a cockpit simulation facility here so we can train European flight crews in Amsterdam instead of Cleveland or London. I'd like to get that underway as soon as possible, because I'm convinced it will contribute substantially to our bottom line."

"Hans, this is Josh. Consider that a 'Go!"

"Hans, this is Brad. I know Roger will be preoccupied with a critical meeting and other business for the balance of this week. May I suggest you fly here on Monday of next week. I'll have an agreement drafted for your review, which will embrace all three of your caveats, no problem."

"Brad, that sounds fine."

"Hans, this is Roger, again. Please stay on the line and I'll have Dana McBride, my admin, pick up. She'll handle all of the flight and hotel arrangements for you. Will you be bringing anyone else with you?"

"Yes, Roger, I'd like to bring my Treasurer and my legal counsel."

"Awesome, my friend. Give Dana the names, and she'll Fed-X airline tickets to you. One of us will pick up the three of you at the airport here. Let's plan to have a relaxing dinner on Monday evening, and we can review the contract details on Tuesday."

"That sounds terrific, Roger. Many thanks, and I look forward to seeing you all on Monday."

"Now hang on for Dana." He pressed a couple of buttons to transfer the call to Dana, dropped his handset onto its cradle, and turned to Brad and Josh.

"Goddamn, fellas. We're close to hitting another home run!" He was smiling broadly, as were the others. "How do you want to structure the deal, Brad, given his caveats?"

"I've thought a lot about it. Frankly, his caveats are no surprise, Roger. Here's what I think we should propose."

Brad described several issues designed to make the acquisition of Electronique, N.V., an attractive fit and financial contributor to the overall plan he, Roger and Bill had been planning: retention of the firm's name to benefit from its European market equity; class B voting shares and non-voting common to be traded on the Amsterdam exchange as an additional source of revenue.

"And finally," Brad said, "let's structure a pension plan for Hans' company. He didn't ask for the pension plan, so that will be a *piece de resistance*! That and the profit sharing plan can come in a year, after we have a good fix on the company's cash flow."

"Hans may want the profit sharing plan to come earlier, Brad. And, Josh, let's make certain he *does* have the room for a cockpit simulator so we don't have to incur the expense of a second location."

"No problem, Roger."

"Brad, please get the agreement drafted this week so we can review it at the COC meeting next Monday. I'll review our plans with the Board, and we can review the actual agreement with Hans and his colleagues next Tuesday. I want to keep our dinner Monday evening social because those guys will be tired from traveling."

"Got it."

"Now listen. At some point in the coming months, I want you two to meet with Jose and Frank -- in their territories -- to scope out a similar acquisition opportunity in the Americas and the Far East or Australia. If we can pull that off within, say, the next twenty-four months, we can establish cockpit simulator facilities in every major corner of the world where we do business, dropping our training expenses considerably.

"And nothing would prevent us from using the same Class B ownership idea, or the non-voting listed common, so we're generating revenues from the businesses as well as the sale of stock. We'd be flying . . . pardon the pun!"

"I'm all for it," Brad said, "and we'll work our butts off to make it happen!"

They all stood, shook hands followed by a high fives.

Roger was flat out for the remainder of the day, spent a lot of time in the company of Bill preparing for the next Board of Directors meeting. He prepared a full agenda not too different from that used at the COC meeting yesterday. There was an abundance of positive activity internationally he knew the Directors would find of paramount interest and importance.

15

Wednesday evening Roger sat on his couch, his collar unbuttoned, shoes off, legs stretched out in front of him, relaxing for the first time since he had entered the office Monday morning.

Before long, Jennifer, climbed onto his lap, rested her head on his left shoulder, her right hand brushing his neck. She sat quiet in his lap for several minutes, snuggled tightly by her Dad, who kissed her forehead, whispered "I love you, Jen."

"Daddy, can I ask you a question

"Absolutely."

"What was Mommy like? I sorta remember sitting in her lap with her arms around me. She read me a book, and kissed my forehead like you just did. But I can't really remember her."

The question caught Roger's breath. He kissed her forehead again, then began to speak.

"Well, you and Tommy were just little squirts when Mommy was taken from us. She was beautiful, Jen, just like you. You have her eyes, her pretty smile, her lovely hair. And she loved you and Tommy with her whole heart."

"Then how did she love you?"

"Ahhhh, grownups have a special kind of love, Jen. Mommy and I loved each other very, very much, and we were thrilled when we had you and Tommy."

"Why did she die, Daddy?"

"Well, as I've said before, she was crossing a street downtown. She waited for the crossing signal, like I've told you and Tommy to do, but a car shot through the intersection and hit Mommy as she was crossing the street. I don't think she felt any pain, Jen. She was killed instantly."

"What happened to that driver?"

"He's in jail, Jen, for a long time."

"Do you think he feels sorry for killing our Mommy?"

"I'm sure he does, Honey."

Jen lay her head quietly against his shoulder for some time.

"You know, Jen, you can talk to Mommy any time you want to. You won't hear her reply, but you'll feel it in your heart. It will feel very warm, and beat real hard, and that will be Mommy speaking to you."

"Do you talk to her like that?"

"Yes, Honey, I do. I spoke to her just a few nights ago."

"You called me 'Honey' like you used to call Cecily. Have you seen her lately?"

"Yes, in fact I met with her a few weeks ago and we had a long conversation. That was in Boston. She lives there now."

"Are we ever going to see her again?"

"I'm not sure, Jen. I hope so, but it will depend upon how she and I feel about a situation which came between us. I think, I hope, we both are trying to put that behind us so we *can* get together again. Time will tell."

"Well, just so you know, Daddy, Tommy and I both like her a lot, and we would like to see more of her."

"Yes, I understand, Jen. But you and Tommy should stay calm and let Cecily and me see if we can work things out. It's really up to her and I, not you or Tommy. Okay."

"Okay." Jen cuddled quietly for a minute.

"Would you be upset if I phoned Cecily to say 'Hi'?"

"Oh, Jen! I think you should let her and I settle our differences without you intruding."

"I don't want to intrude, Daddy, I just want to hear her voice."

"I guess that would be alright, as long as you don't pry."

"Okay." She snuggled closer in his lap. "I love you, Daddy. And when I get into bed tonight I'm going to talk to Mommy. I'm excited to feel her answer in my heart!"

Roger kissed his daughter again, his eyes starting to well.

Cecily's phone rang that same evening about nine. She was preparing to go to bed with a book, got the phone on the third ring.

"Hello!"

"Cecily? This is Dick Martin. We met a couple of weeks ago in a loud sports bar where your girl friend played Wonder Woman with a drunk."

"Yes! I remember! How on earth did you find me?"

"Turns out we have a mutual acquaintance."

"Really! Who's that?"

"Wonder Woman!" He was laughing. "I bumped into Hannah in a sandwich shop a couple of days ago. She was reluctant at first to give me your number, but I finally convinced her my intentions are just social and platonic!" Cecily laughed.

"Yes! Hannah's a very good friend."

"The purpose of my call, Cecily, is to see if you will permit me to buy you dinner one night soon."

"Dick, you said you're married with two children."

"Actually, I'm recently separated with two children."

"Well, Dick I don't want to get caught in the crossfire between you and your family!"

"You won't, Cecily. I presently reside in a hotel in Cambridge, and I'm tired of dining alone and watching TV. I thought perhaps we could enjoy a social evening, no strings attached."

"Well . . . I'm . . . well, okay, if you promise our evening will be just social and platonic!"

He laughed. "Cross my heart."

They agreed to meet the following evening at seven in the steak house a short walk from Cecily's apartment. He was already seated when she entered, stood to shake her hand and hold her chair, no attempt to give her a hug or kiss on the cheek. She joined him in a cocktail, he also ordered an expensive bottle of red wine to accompany their steak dinners.

Their conversation over ninety minutes was light, easy and enjoyable, rambling over a variety subjects including their jobs, where they grew up and went to college, travel, favorite activities in their free time. Toward the end of dinner, Cecily popped *the* question.

"It's really none of my business, Dick, but what's happened to your marriage?"

"Oh, it's a long story, Cecily. The short version is I had a brief fling with another woman, Charlotte found out, and we've separated. I'm a complete ass. She's a lovely woman, and we have two terrific sons, five and seven. I pray that this separation is temporary. We're both in counseling, and I hope that will help us reunite. I really don't want a divorce. I want to stay close to her and to our sons."

"Has the counseling helped?"

"Yes, I think it has. We've only been at it for two months, but I do think it's helping us get over my screw-up."

"I'm asking because I've had a very traumatic situation in my life, and I wonder if counseling would help."

"Well, you have nothing to lose by giving it a shot, Cecily. Sitting alone in your apartment and moping, wondering what the hell your next step should be . . . gawd, I've been all through that and it's a terrible waste of time. You and I don't *really* know each other well, but I'd advise you to look into counseling."

"Thank you, Dick, and thank you for this dinner and an evening of relaxing conversation."

"You're very welcome, Cecily. My pleasure. Now I know I said this evening would be social and platonic, but if by some chance my marriage explodes, may I call you again?"

"Dick, please. Let's part the way we started. New friends, but nothing more." She stood, shook his hand, quickly left the restaurant for home.

The following Monday afternoon Brad Lewis met Hans, his Treasurer (Ton Wolfe) and his lawyer (Ron Storqe) at the Cleveland airport, checked them into a hotel to shower and rest after a long day of traveling. They would meet at 7:30 that evening for a relaxing dinner with Bill, Roger, Brad and Josh. The evening was entirely social, no business discussion of any kind.

Brad collected the three Dutch executives again Tuesday morning at 9:30, gave them a thorough tour of the AeroMarine International headquarters facilities, including a hands-on experience operating the high tech cockpit simulator featuring much of the company's newly designed avionics. The three European executives were suitably impressed.

The four then filed into the conference room adjacent to Roger's office and were soon joined by Josh. Bill and Roger were in a meeting, but soon entered, handshakes all around. Dana was the last in, introduced by Roger who also clarified her presence as a recording secretary, not part of the discussion group.

The meeting was opened by Roger, mostly courtesy comments about their pleasure in hosting Hans and his colleagues, with some elaboration of the effort Brad and his people had put into drafting the agreement they were about to review. He also added that AMI's Board of Directors had read and approved an early draft of the agreement, so it was a done deal pending an okay by Hans, Ton and Ron.

Brad passed out copies of the draft agreement to all participants and gave them time to read it and/or ask questions of any paragraph or clause they found disturbing.

There weren't many pauses, questions or comments. Hans did question the proposed 70/30 split of the Class B voting shares, pressed for a 60/40 split, which was granted by Roger, et al. Hans also wanted shares of the non-voting common stock which would be traded publicly and potentially increase in value. It was agreed he and his key managers would each receive 10,000 shares.

"Listen!" This was Hans. "I'm particularly happy that you've chosen to keep my company name, Electronique, with a sub-line identifying it as a subsidiary of AMI. I was worried you might want to change that."

"No way, Hans. You've built considerable brand equity as an innovative and reliable company. We all felt we should retain that and let it work for us. Brad and I were especially firm on that, as was Josh, and I made that clear to the Board members when Bill and I met with them."

"Thank you, Roger. And thank you, also, for the pension plan. That's a very pleasant surprise."

"Thank Brad, Hans. That was completely his idea."

"Well, thank you, Brad." Hans turned to Ton and Ron. "Are you fellas comfortable with everything you've seen and heard?"

"Wait a second, Hans!" This was Josh. "When we met in Amsterdam we spoke about establishing a cockpit simulator in your facilities so we could train airline crews in Amsterdam. We've kind of skipped over that clause in this draft agreement."

"Oh, I'm sorry, Josh! You're right. Yes! We are very eager to do that. Brad allowed us to play on your simulator here this morning, and I know we have ample space in our plant to accommodate the installation of a similar facility in our place. When can you start that?"

"Give us a couple of weeks to compile equipment and I'll have a team of my people on your doorstep. I assume you'll delegate a team of locals to work with my guys."

"Ya, absolutely, Josh."

"Good. That's all I have, Roger."

Hans turned to Ton and Ron. "Are you fells okay with the agreement as we've amended it this morning?"

"Ya, Hans, I am comfortable. It is a good agreement."

"Thanks, Ton. Ron, how about you?"

"I am comfortable, but the buyer does not have legal counsel present. Are we clear that you fellas will not make any changes if Hans signs this agreement today?"

"Let me address this, Roger," said Bill. "Ron, we have three corporate attorneys on our Board. They are independent, not AMI employees. They have reviewed and approved this document, as Roger has said. The ownership and stock changes Hans has requested are not major adjustments, in our opinion, and I speak as Chairman of the Board. You can execute today knowing that the agreement is final." He turned to Dana.

"Dana, is there a possibility you could incorporate those changes into a clean draft so we can execute this agreement this afternoon?"

"Yes, Bill. I can do that right away, just as soon as this meeting breaks."

"Okay, then we're going to break and have lunch at Chez Francois while you bang your keyboard. I'm sure Roger will make it up to you. Can we plan a signing here for about 2:30, Dana?"

"Yes, Sir. I'll have everything ready for you."

"Gentlemen, let's retire and leave our future in the hands of this very capable woman." They all laughed, stood, shook hands around the table, and exited for lunch.

The agreement was executed that afternoon as planned. There were more handshakes and expressions of goodwill, Brad took the three executives to the airport so they could make a connection in Chicago that would deliver them to Schiphol Airport in Amsterdam. Electronique, NV, was officially a member of the AeroMarine International family of companies.

It was Thursday, very late afternoon. Roger was bushed from a day of meetings. He sat staring at the scattered paperwork on his desk, spun around to face the large window behind him, eyes closed, he thought of Cecily, her smile, her voice, her body bundled close to his.

He grabbed his phone and dialed her number.

"Hi, Cecily. It's Roger."

There was a slight pause.

"Oh my gosh, Hi! How are you?"

"Lonely. It's been almost four weeks and I haven't heard word one from you following my proposal of marriage. How should I read that?"

Cecily caught her breath, didn't answer for several seconds.

"Oh, Roger. I'm so confused, upset and scared. I do still have feelings for you . . . I think you know that . . . but . . . but I'm having a hard time . . . ."

"Really! Well, I'm not the only one who caused a problem, Cecily. We probably wouldn't even have this so-called problem if I didn't learn of your past from a drunk in a bar . . . ."

"I regret that so much, Roger. I'm truly very sorry."

Roger let a few seconds pass, thought about what to say next.

"Cecily, I can't continue wondering if we're on or off. I've told you I love you, I want to marry you, I want to spend the rest of my life with you. But, it's becoming clear to me that, while you may have feelings for me, they aren't strong enough for you to say 'Yes' to my proposal. When we met in Boston, your parting words to me were that perhaps we each should each go our separate way.

"That's not how I was hoping this would end, Honey, but I'm getting the message loud and clear that you're not interested in a life-long commitment with me. I'm very sorry to hear that, I really am. I still love you very much . . . but it's clear you don't share my feelings."

There was no response.

"I wish you well, Cecily, but I . . . I'm moving on. I do love you with all my heart. I hope you will remember that always. I'm sorry, Cecily, truly sorry. Good night!"

"Roger! Wait! Please!"

"For what?"

There was long pause, no response.

"Good bye, Cecily."

"No! No! Roger, please! Will you give me until Monday? I promise to call you Monday!"

"What will you tell me Monday that you can't tell me now?"

"I just want to be sure . . . ."

"Sure of what?"

"I want to see if I can stop being scared that things between us won't work out long term."

Roger paused, collected his thoughts. This was not going the way he had hoped.

"Cecily, no two people in love know if things will work out long term. They certainly believe they will, they hope they will, but who can be sure. So, No! I won't give you until Monday. It's been a month since I proposed to you, and you haven't said 'Yes' or 'No'! Your silence is your answer to my marriage proposal. It's 'No!'"

He could hear her draw a deep breath, and when she tried to talk he could sense she was beginning to cry. He held onto the phone for almost twenty seconds; she never did speak, so he ended the call.

"I love you, Cecily, and always will. But this dance is done."

No response.

"Good bye, Cecily." He hung up.

Roger sat with his elbows on his desk, his head buried in his hands, for a solid ten minutes. Did he just cut his throat? He almost called her back, resisted the urge. The ball had been in her court for weeks, but she never played it. How would he break the news to his kids? They'll be crushed.

He again swung around in his chair, stared out the large window into the darkness, nothing visible. Had trouble believing he would never see her again, never hold her, never hear her laugh or whisper "I love you, Roger." What the hell had he just done!

His hand dropped onto the telephone, he'd call her back, give her until Monday. *("For what purpose. Wake up. It's over. Screw it!")*

He began to clear his desk, pack up his briefcase to head for home and his children.

In Boston, Cecily, too, dropped her phone back onto its cradle, sat next to it cross-legged on the floor, tears streaming down her face, her torso rocking back and forth. Had she just lost him? She could sense his frustration, his anger at having been strung along for weeks while she struggled to make up her mind.

("Maybe he's right! If I can't make up my mind, maybe that means I've really made it up, and I should just forget about him! But I can't! I don't want to! I do love him! Oh, god! I'm going nuts!")

She picked up her phone, dialed her friend Margi in New York.

"Margi, it's Cecily."

"You're crying! What the hell have you done now?"

"I may have lost him . . . for good!"

"What happened?"

Cecily gave Margi a summary of her conversation with Roger, including his statement that all was over because he was tired of waiting for her answer to his marriage proposal. She admitted not replying to Roger for almost a month. He had sounded frustrated and angry that she continued to waver on a decision to renew her relationship with him or call it quits.

"Are you telling me it's been a month since he proposed to you and you've not had the courtesy to tell him 'Yes' or 'No'?"

"Yes!"

"What the hell is wrong with you? Don't you think he has feelings, just like you? If someone did that to me, I'd tell him to stick it where the sun don't shine! Consider yourself lucky he even called you, let alone gave you an opportunity to give him an answer! And you still waffled.

"You're crazy, is what you are. If you love him, say 'Yes'. If you don't, at least tell him 'No'! I can sure as hell sympathize with him. You've left him hanging. You deserve to lose him! I'm damned disappointed in you, Cecily, that you would treat a guy who loves you so much like he's a . . . a what? A nothing? Who the hell do you think you are?

"You should have solved this problem months ago! You created it by not telling him yourself about your goddamn past. You didn't deal with it. Leave me out of it! You either trust him or you don't. I can't help you. Good night, Cecily."

"Wait, Margi, please wait. I'm thinking of getting counseling. What do you think?"

"I think you should have done that months ago, Cecily. I'm sorry I didn't think to suggest that. Do it, but do it *now!* And call me again once you've started. I want to hear you say 'I'm in counseling!'"

The line went dead.

It was 7:30 Friday morning. Roger was dressed for work, scheduled to drop Jennifer and Tommy at school on his way to the office. The kids had been crushed last evening when he told them they would never see Cecily again, that he and she were not coming back together, their relationship was kaput! Both kids had sobbed, could not understand why, what was so important, more important than their desire to have Cecily in their young lives after so many years without a mother.

Roger had tried to be reassuring, but failed miserably. Both youngsters were still crying when he tucked them into bed. He's not sure when they stopped crying, but assumed they did not have a full night's sleep. That was confirmed when he saw their drawn, sad faces at breakfast, no conversation, no laughter, no joy.

He held is cell phone, dialed, his call answered on the second ring.

"Mr. Sommers, this is Roger Manning."

"Good morning, Roger. How are you?"

"Not good, Sir. I phoned Cecily late yesterday afternoon. It's been almost a month since I proposed to her and expressed my love for her in plain English.

"I see."

"But she wouldn't have it . . . didn't say 'No!' to my proposal, but didn't say 'Yes!' either. She asked for more time. I told her I can't keep wondering if we have a future, and her constant hesitation is all the answer I need. I regret to say it's all over, Sir."

"Roger, I'm terribly sorry to hear that. I know she still has strong feelings for you. I also know she is scared stiff you may walk out on her again . . . can't seem to shed that concern, that fear."

"Well, I've got to move on, Sir. And my children, who also like your daughter, can't continue to live with false hope. It's not fair to them, or me. When I broke the news to them last night, they were devastated. Still are. This is not a happy home this morning."

"No, that certainly isn't fair to the little ones, nor to you, for that matter. I'm sure it was a very tough decision for you, Roger, and I admire your courage."

"Courage isn't the word I'd use, Sir. I'm very sorry we won't have an opportunity to know one another better. I suspect your daughter may welcome a little fatherly comforting about now. Good luck."

They both hung up.

Cecily thought of Roger all that evening, all night, and again Friday morning. She re-lived their love-making in Rome, New York, Cleveland, the warmth of his breath on her cheek, his lips pressed against hers, the flick of his tongue against hers, his lips and tongue caressing her breasts, her stomach, even lower.

She thought of their laughter, holding hands, his invitation to help him think of something -- some*one* -- other than his work, and her success, his arms cradling her body, his whispered endearments, his expressions of love, his proposal of marriage.

She thought of his children, their acceptance of her in their motherless young lives, Jennifer's phone call because she was lonely, her and Tommy's desire to see more of her, "when are you coming to Cleveland again?" Their hugs, their excitement when they opened their apartment door and saw her standing there, Tommy's tears at the airport when she flew back to New York.

But mostly, she thought of Roger, his love for her, her love for him . . . the agony of loss . . . the shock . . . the terror . . . the horrible knot that gripped her stomach when he said "This dance is done!" followed by "Goodbye."

("Oh my god! Oh my god! Roger! Margi said I don't trust him; don't trust his proposal, his love! Is that my problem? Really? I don't trust him! If I do, why can't I say 'Yes' . . . 'Yes' and make us all happy again? What the hell is wrong with me?")

Roger's Friday was dominated by a day-long discussion with Bill regarding the priorities, domestic and international, which Roger would face, or was likely to face, over the next ninety days. Bill knew Roger was a strong advocate of advanced planning; did not like business surprises, good or bad.

It was this management discipline which Bill had observed and admired during their ten years together: the discipline which prompted him to select Roger as his successor, to consider him for the position as Chairman of the Board.

Late that afternoon Roger sauntered back to his own office, his arms loaded with file folders, his face drawn, exhausted. Dana had already left for home, as had most of the administrative staff. The office was eerily quiet, semi-dark with most overhead lights in the open secretarial and reception areas extinguished.

Roger slumped into his desk chair, stacked the folders in front of him, kicked off his shoes, opened a folder. Didn't really see what was in it, didn't care, his mind lost on Cecily. Why? For god's sake, Why? What more could he do? What more could he say?

After several minutes he vowed not to stay in the office, to go home, spend time with his kids. He really needed time with them. They were unbelievably upset last night when he told them he and Cecily would not be getting back together. They could not understand adults and their "crazy" decisions.

He was eager to give them a fun weekend: feed the ducks in the park, maybe take in a matinee movie, Chinese food or pizza and ice cream, a long bike ride: anything to keep their minds, and his, from thinking of the woman they wouldn't see again.

He stretched, stood to slip on his shoes.

His office phone rang. He gave it a tired look, debated whether to answer it, reluctantly reached for the receiver.

"Roger Manning."

"Roger. It's Cecily."

Silence for several seconds.

"Cess! What's up?"

"Roger, I want to meet with you and have a conversation, a serious conversation, on where we stand."

"We don't stand any more, Cecily. I thought I made that clear yesterday. It's been well over a month since I proposed to you and you still haven't given me an answer, at least vocally. Frankly, I'm now having doubts just like you."

"Please, let's not end like this. Let's at least sit with each other and have a calm, rational conversation."

"Okay, I'm open to that. But I can't get out of Cleveland, Cecily. I have an awful lot percolating here and I probably won't be able to get away for a couple of weeks. I'm sorry."

"No problem. I'll fly to Cleveland tomorrow so we have the weekend to chat."

"No! Cecily! No! You can't stay at my place, and I don't want my children to see you or even know you're in Cleveland. They'll get all excited, then whip-sawed again if you don't stay. I won't permit that to happen to them. It's just not fair, and they've already been through hell."

There was a long silence.

"Cecily?"

"Yes, I'm still here. I'd love to see Jen and Tommy."

"I'm sure you would, but try to understand what my kids have already been through. No more! I don't want you calling them, I don't want Jen calling you: nothing, unless you and I agree that we're prepared to start over."

"You sound like you've already decided."

"I had, until you called me just now. I'll agree to talk, I'll be happy to do that, as long as it's just you and me and nobody else."

Silence for several seconds.

"Okay, Roger, okay. I'll fly out tomorrow. I can get a flight that lands about two."

"Sounds good. I'll email you a place to meet, say about 3:30."

"You won't pick me up at the airport?"

"I'll meet you at a spot I pick, and I'll email you. That's best for everyone at this end."

Silence again.

"Alright, Roger, I'll see you tomorrow."

They met Saturday afternoon in a barely furnished office Roger had secured from a temp outfit that rented offices by the hour, day or week. It was private, but somewhat less than comfortable: functional furniture, no flowers, no art on the walls, no carpeting, no hard-wired phone.

Roger was seated behind the desk when Cecily entered, his briefcase open in front of him, cell phone pressed against his ear, open collared shirt, short sleeves. He motioned her into the guest chair opposite him, quickly completed his business call, stood to walk over to her, greeted her with a hug. It felt good.

"You look terrific, Cecily. A little tired, but terrific nonetheless."

"Thank you, but I don't feel terrific."

"I know what you mean." He returned to his seat behind the desk.

"Roger, I . . . ."

"What seems to be your problem, Cess? I think I've made it abundantly clear that I love you and want to marry you. I've said I'm very sorry for reacting so quickly the night that drunk spoke about your past, but I think I've made it clear that no longer interests me nor bothers me. All I want to hear from you today is 'Yes' or 'No'. Will you marry me? Do you still love me? Do you trust me when I say I love you and want to spend the rest of my life with you?"

"Roger, please. I can't find the words . . . oh, god, I don't know how to help you understand how terrible it was when you walked out. I know I had changed your life . . . got you to think of something besides work. But you also changed mine, helped me understand I could be loved, that I was capable of happiness with a man that meant the world to me."

"So! What's your hang up?"

"I'm terrified, Roger. If that were to happen again . . . if somewhere down the line what happened in the restaurant that night . . . if that were to happen again, in front of your client . . . I'm terrified you'd walk out on me again."

"Well, it wouldn't, because I no longer give a damn and it's just not going to happen anyway. What are the chances? I have the impression that behavior was not your full-time occupation, you've moved to a different city, and time has flown by. Any old fart who paid you for a tumble is probably dead, or wishes he was!"

Roger smiled. Cecily didn't. She sat hunched over, a handkerchief in her hand, dabbing at the moisture in her eyes. The silence dragged on, and dragged on.

"Tell me, Cecily. 'Yes' or 'No'. Are you staying here or flying back to Boston? If you're staying, we can have dinner and continue to talk. But if you can't bring yourself to say 'Yes' then this is it. We're done!"

She looked up at him, tears welling in her eyes. The silence was erie, seconds ticked by, became minutes. Neither spoke, he kept looking at her, she stared at her lap. More minutes passed, she continued to softly cry, the handkerchief crumpled in her hand. She looked at him staring at her, looked away again.

He realized she was not the same woman he fell in love with. She was detached, stressed out, lack of self worth. She was more than scared; she was depressed, seriously depressed, incapable of making a decision that would bring her happiness.

"Honey!" She looked at Roger. "Honey, I don't know what else I can say to you. What can I say or do to convince you that I want to marry you, to spend the rest of my life with you. My kids like you. But I'm lost, Cecily. I don't know what to do or say, that I haven't already said." He was pleading.

She looked away, wiped her eyes, didn't say anything. Minutes passed.

Roger's anger had dissipated, replaced by sorrow, sorrow for the basket case sitting opposite him. She was not the same Cecily. She needed counseling, serious psychological counseling, and even then she might not be ready for marriage. She could not let go of her past; a past that continued to haunt her; a past which made it impossible for her to make a decision which maybe, perhaps, would lead to another break, shatter her emotionally a second time. She was subconsciously condemned to never forgive *herself* for behavior which was a permanent scar, an indelible part of her life.

And he had seriously aggravated her condition by calling her a "whore!" Goddam he was stupid, downright fucking stupid!

Roger sat silently observing her for several more minutes. His sorrow deepened, clear in the understanding she was a prisoner of her memory, her depression. And clear that despite his proposal, it would be a mistake to marry her until she underwent extensive counseling. Even then . . . .

He finally stood, walked slowly around the desk, gently took her hand to help her stand. He gave her another warm hug.

"Goodbye, Cecily. I wish you well." He kissed her cheek, led her to the office door, watched her walk out of his life. She didn't say a word.

Cecily checked into a "rep's roost", a small nondescript hotel/motel on a side street in downtown Cleveland. Like similar spots in other big cities, it earned its nickname and reputation because it was cheap and catered to traveling sales people: independent reps for distributors in a variety of industries, pharmaceutical agents who called on doctors with free pens and prescription pads to hype branded drugs, food brokers selling to grocery buyers, any number of other sales people armed with overstuffed sample cases and a line of bullshit a mile long.

Her room was comfortable and clean, but not at all homey. It included a double bed, a desk and ladder back chair, A/C, a small TV and a bathroom the size of a refrigerator. The hotel had no dining room: it offered morning coffee from a large thermos-type dispenser and directions to a cafe around the corner. It did have a bar.

That's where Cecily headed after leaving her overnight bag in her room. The bar was heavily populated, mostly men, a few women. The chatter was loud, everyone talking in groups about travel schedules, easy or detested buyers, expense accounts, dining spots in cities across the U.S., mileage allowances, and so on. Rock music pulsed from speakers imbedded in the ceiling.

Cecily slipped onto a bar stool between two men, both with their backs toward her as they engaged in animated conversation with compatriots. The fella on her left ultimately turned to rest his beer bottle on the bar, caught sight of her next to him: a magnificent blond bombshell.

"My goodness! Where did you come from?"

"I just slipped into this seat to enjoy a cocktail." She smiled.

"Welcome! Do you get here often? I don't recall seeing you before."

"No, I don't. This is my first time here. Not my first time in Cleveland, but my first time here."

"My good fortune." He smiled, fifty-ish, fairly good looking, cheap suit, white shirt, open collar with an ugly plaid tie pulled down an inch or two. "What's your name?"

"Cecily. How about you?"

"Harvey. Harvey Slimsty."

"Well, Harvey Slimsty, what do you do for a living?"

"I'm a distributor's rep selling automobile hoses and belts, the after market stuff. I spend a lot of my day working with spiders in the overheated lofts where gas stations store their inventories. Crappy job, but it pays the bills."

She smiled. "Sounds gruesome."

"Not as bad as my old job. I sold backless suit jackets to undertakers so they could dress dead bodies to look good in caskets. Also sold backless white shirts and elastic black ties, trousers and underwear weren't needed."

"My gawd, that *is* gruesome!" They both laughed.

"It's gruesome to know the undertakers strip the body before they close the casket, and reuse the garments on another body. It's a damned good thing we're dead or we'd vomit!" He laughed.

"Gawd, that's disgusting. Wish you hadn't told me!" She was smiling.

"How about you, Cecily? Your name is as pretty as you are!"

"Thank you, Harvey."

"What business pays your bills?"

"I'm in the entertainment field." She sipped her drink.

"Really! Well I don't doubt it, you're very good looking." He smiled again. "What part of the entertainment business is your specialty, Cecily?"

"I help guys like you relax before you have to climb back onto overheated gas station lofts full of spiders." She winked, he looked stunned.

"Really!" He was smiling. "So you're a relaxation specialist, of sorts."

"Yes! Of sorts. Would you like to relax tonight?"

He chuckled.

"What's your specialty?"

"Ahhhh, that's my surprise!"

"And if I want to be surprised?"

"That'll costs you two hundred dollars."

Printed in the United States
By Bookmasters